THE
GOOD
PRIEST

GILLIAN GALBRAITH

THE GOOD PRIEST

A FATHER VINCENT ROSS MYSTERY

Polygon

First published in 2014 by Polygon,
an imprint of Birlinn Ltd
West Newington House
10 Newington Road
Edinburgh
EH9 1QS

www.polygonbooks.co.uk

ISBN 978 1 84697 279 9
eBook ISBN 978 0 85790 785 1

British Library Cataloguing-in-Publication Data
A catalogue record for this book is available from the British
Library.

Design by Studio Monachino
www.studiomonachino.co.uk

Set in Sabon at Birlinn Ltd

Printed and bound in Great Britain by
TJ International Ltd, Padstow, Cornwall

ACKNOWLEDGEMENTS

Maureen Allison
Colin Browning
Douglas Edington
Lesmoir Edington
Robert Galbraith
Daisy Galbraith
Diana Griffiths
Roger Orr
Aidan O'Neill
Dr David Sadler
An old friend from my childhood

DEDICATION

To my beloved mother
with all my love

PROLOGUE

It did not look like the Book of Judgement. All three men were listed on its faded, blue-lined pages, their names written in an identical hand. Scratched out below each name was a litany of obsolete addresses, multi-coloured biro entries, and with only the current one left intact. Their crimes were described too. Someone had taken the trouble to track their movements for years and years, to follow their progress from county to county, country to country.

The one at the top of page 20 was a retired casino owner with a liking for Cuban cigars. In February 2013 he was murdered in his home, a tree-lined avenue in the prosperous Edinburgh suburb of Colinton. Page 26 recorded an impoverished widower, then living by the foam-flecked shores of the Forth with only his Bichon Frise for company. He met a similar end less than a month later. The third man, described on page 30, a habitué of his local bowling club, bled to death on his bathroom floor to the lush sound of Ella Fitzgerald's 'That Old Black Magic'. All of the victims were pensioners, died from knife wounds, and their last words, which sounded like a prayer, incensed their killer. None of them knew each other, or their attacker. Despite their deaths, no one amended their entries, deleted their names from the book.

CHAPTER ONE

This one he would not spit out either. If the man then attempting to focus his blue eyes on the bottle's label had ever been asked what his passion in life was, he would have replied 'fine wines'. He might have been tempted to say, 'fighting injustice', 'feeding the starving' or even 'wind-surfing'. Any one of those would have sounded, he considered, seemlier, worthier and less sybaritic. But, unfortunately, also untrue. Beekeeping was, genuinely, close to his heart, but hardly deserved to be described as a passion, in his estimation at least.

That evening, he was indulging himself by carrying out a little research into the wines of the Bordeaux region. His cat, Satan, lay on his lap. He sniffed the contents of the next glass, tipped it towards his lips and took a deep draught. What flavours were now swirling upon his tongue? Blackcurrant with a hint of saddle leather, or was it aniseed, perhaps, or liquorice or celery even? Rolling the last drops purposefully around his mouth, he savoured them and held them there for a few seconds, saturating his taste-buds.

Once, he mused, he really had possessed a nose for fine wines, could truthfully have called himself a connoisseur. But the gaining of such erudition was an expensive business, ill-fitted to those, like him, with shallow pockets. Nowadays, he had to make do. In his twenties, in the brief period when he had been a sharp-suited criminal defence lawyer, only the best had passed his tonsils. Of course, in those far-off days his own nose was little more than a button, not the crooked protuberance which now dominated his face and made him blink every time he accidentally caught his own reflection in the mirror. And all thanks to the unexpected rebound of a hammer held in his own careless hand. Worse, of late, the misshapen thing seemed to have found its mission in life, betraying him by periodically flushing fiery-red like a beacon, as if to warn the world of his weakness for drink. But was weakness the right word? Fondness would be more accurate. Less Calvinistic, certainly, and that had to be a good thing. Whichever it was, he need not worry yet, he reassured himself, he had a long way to go before reaching the bottom. After all, neither Blue Nun nor Buckfast Tonic Wine had passed his lips so far.

Catching sight of the TV remote on the floor, he leaned forwards in his armchair to get it, forgetting about the cat and making it mew in surprise as, for a second, it was crushed between his chest and his lap. Stroking it by way of apology, he leaned back again, catching, out of the corner of his eye, sight of his desk. A pile of unanswered correspondence, bills and catalogues lay on top of his computer. They seemed like a rebuke. Deliberately averting his eyes, he pressed the 'on' button and the TV sprang to life. At this late hour, *QI* would probably be showing.

But it was not Stephen Fry's horse-like face that greeted him. On the screen two scantily clad black women were rotating their hips, shimmying together with their heads thrown back, dancing in unison to some silent beat.

Gazing at them, enchanted, he marvelled at their extraordinary beauty. They seemed like fit young panthers, sleek and lithe, each synchronised to the other as perfectly as a shadow. Once their routine had finished and they were taking their bows, he increased the volume and caught the audience's riotous applause, an occasional wolf-whistle cutting through the excited clapping.

Forgetting all about the quiz, still spellbound by the sight of the pair, he watched as the next contestant trooped shyly onto the stage. Liking the look of her, and to get the best possible view, he put the cat on the sofa beside him, perched on the edge of his seat and hastily clapped on his spectacles. She too appeared to manage without any unnecessary clothing, necessary clothing even, and must, from the look of her, surely be a professional dancer? No shop assistant could move like that. No one behind any of the counters in Kinross or Milnathort, more's the pity. But, if she truly was an amateur, then this time his vote might genuinely make a difference. It could 'change her life' as the commentator observed. No doubt it would cheer up her fiancé, allegedly bedbound at the moment – make him pick up his bed and walk, quite possibly.

Hurriedly, he looked on the nearby table for a pen, determined to note the number for her as soon as it appeared on the screen. As he was busily scribbling it down, his mobile rang, but he continued writing, trying to ignore it. After the first few rings each subsequent one seemed to penetrate his skull like a drill, maddening him and distracting him from his task. Finally, having missed the last two digits, he tossed his pen onto the table in frustration.

Ten calls in one evening? Surely to God, everyone, every single person without exception, was entitled to some time off, some time to themselves, to eat their food and digest it, if nothing else? Mobiles were a curse. No one should be perpetually on duty, and he had been on his feet for over fifteen hours already. Feeling drained, exhausted by the efforts of the day and his own anger, he looked back at the screen again, and, at that precise moment, the phone rang once more. This time he snatched it up, clamped it to his good ear and said through gritted teeth: 'Father Vincent Ross.'

Unable to make out the faint-voiced reply above the thump-thumping beat of the dance music, he added, 'One second, please.' So saying, he turned the volume on the set down and started to speak again, already feeling calmer and more collected in the silence.

'Now, what can I help you with?'

'It's me, Father, Mamie.'

He rolled his clear blue eyes heavenwards. She had already called twice earlier, that very evening. But he made an effort to keep the impatience he could feel rising within him from his voice and replied: 'Good evening, Mamie. What seems to be the trouble now?'

His enquiry was met by an extended silence so, smiling, telling himself to put more warmth into his tone, he repeated the question. After a few further seconds of silence his effort was rewarded and his caller deigned to reply, 'It's John, Father.'

'Yes?'

'I'm having a problem. He's pressing for Nevaeh again.'

'Nevaeh?'

'Heaven backwards. I ask you, what kind of name is that?'

'Was it you calling a second ago, Mamie?'

'Yes.'

'I see. Well, we've spoken about this before, haven't we? This very evening. About John, I mean.'

'We have, Father . . .' She hesitated, not completely impervious to the suggestion of annoyance that had leaked into his tone despite his best efforts. 'We have. Yes. But he'll still not come round.'

'Well, it could be worse. He could be pushing for Lleh – Hell backwards – or Beyoncé or something. You've some weeks to the birth. He might yet settle for Bridget – or Uncumber, which is a saint's name, as you are wanting . . .'

'I know, I know.' She hesitated. 'Uncumber? But if you were to speak to him about it, Father?'

'But I have, Mamie, too many times . . .' For a second his attention lapsed, catching his breath at the sight of another dancer. Her boneless body was as sinuous as a snake's, and she appeared to be simulating some kind of limbo dance. When, finally, the camera panned onto the grinning faces of the judges, the spell was broken and he managed to finish his sentence: '. . . and I've failed, I'm afraid. How do you know it's a girl?'

'A woman knows these things, Father.'

'Was there anything else tonight, Mamie?'

This was her cue, and a torrent of words came tumbling out, disclosing the real reason for her call.

'About the brass candlesticks, I don't see why I should

do them again this Friday, or the big chandelier. I only done them on Tuesday last and then only because Ann-Marie . . .'

'I'll stop you right there,' said Vincent. 'The candlesticks have nothing to do with me. You know that, Mamie. Speak to Veronica, she's in charge of the Light Brigade. Now, if that's all I'll say goodnight to you . . .'

He paused for a split second, murmured 'Goodnight', waited for her echo and switched off his mobile. With her on their side the rebel angels would have triumphed, he thought, because she never gave up. He smiled, a vision of the pregnant woman in breastplate and armour brandishing an aerosol, flitting into his mind from nowhere. She would have to change her name though; Mamie did not really inspire awe in the same way as Lucifer, Azazel, Lilith, Moloch and the like did.

Switching channels, he saw the credits for *QI* scrolling upwards. Muttering to himself in his disappointment, he scooped the Siamese cat up from its nest on the sofa, climbed the stairs to his bedroom and plumped it down on the blue-and-white striped duvet which covered his bed.

There was little other furniture in the room. The only piece in it which actually belonged to him, as opposed to the parish, was the wardrobe. It was a heavy Victorian artefact, made of mahogany. Once it had belonged to his grandparents and, as a child, he had played hide and seek inside it. Now it housed his beekeeping suit with its integral veil, looking, he often thought, like the husk of a dead Cyberman. Every time he opened the heavy double doors the scent of honey billowed deliciously from it. Beside the wardrobe was a chest of drawers, left by a predecessor, which he had painted navy blue. Catching sight of the framed photograph of his mother resting on it, his eyes were drawn to hers. He picked the frame up, murmuring to himself in a tone that he might have used to reassure an anxious spouse: 'I know, I know. Don't worry. I haven't forgotten.'

Then, his eyes heavy with exhaustion, he knelt down by the bed and began to read the night prayers from his black, leather-bound copy of *The Divine Office* regretting, as he was doing so, that he had not said the whole lot first thing in the morning in a oner. His batteries would not have been so flat before breakfast. Once he had finished, he glanced up from his kneeling posture and saw the ivory figure hanging on the cross, pinned halfway up the wall.

The crucifix was no longer perfectly perpendicular. He could not resist getting up to straighten it, shaking his head as he did so, as if Jesus had swung himself squint again, deliberately to annoy him. Dust from the pierced feet coated his fingertips.

Starting to undress, he placed his folded jacket on the back of his little armchair and made a mental note to take it to the cleaners the next morning. Black might not show up the dirt but his nose warned him that he could economise no longer. As he was unbuttoning his clerical shirt, his cigarette packet already extracted from the side pocket, the sound of hymn-singing drifted up through the floorboards of his bedroom and made him pause. He had forgotten all about the collection of ecumenical dafties below. Monday bloody Monday. There would be no sleep for him now with them loose in the hall, with their tambourines, recorders and guitars, all fizzing with evangelical fervour like damp sherbet. Satan had destroyed his earplugs, and he would have to lock up the presbytery once they had vacated it. As he listened an unaccompanied off-key treble started up: 'Amazing Grace, how sweet the sound . . .'

Not tonight, he thought, a sour sound tonight. Telling himself to be more charitable and relax, he climbed onto his bed and stretched out his full length, his small, square-toed feet nowhere near the end of it. Sighing loudly, he lit a cigarette and inhaled, watching the smoke curl upwards in the air as he breathed out, trying to force himself to calm down and enjoy their service.

Gradually, as the nicotine worked its way through his system, he began to feel less tense, less agitated. Head wedged in his pillow, he lay still while two further hymns were sung by the group. By the third, he was mouthing the words himself, joining in with the concert below. They were harmless enough, and would go soon. Listening to 'The Lord of the Dance' he closed his eyes and his breathing became deeper and more regular. Sleep did not feel too far away.

Suddenly, hearing a distinctive, nasal voice, he sat bolt upright. It was her! That *soi-disant* actress was up to her tricks again. Performing here! Ignoring his repeated plea that she refrain from such practices in his hall, in his home. And in front of him, to his very face and less than a fortnight ago, the petite charlatan had given him her word. She had had no charism, no special gift from God. She was in complete control of all her faculties, which was more than could now be said of him. How dare she gabble away in tongues, like a thing possessed, and on diocesan premises to boot! In the quiet of his bedroom, he listened intently, concentrating on her voice and making out one or two French words in amongst her babbling. Finally, catching the words 'Veni, Vidi, Vici', and laughing out loud at her audacity, he determined to end the charade, tipped Satan off his lap, snatched his trousers from the chair and began to zip up his fly. Came and saw, maybe, conquered, never!

Striding through her rapt audience, he reached the podium where she stood and tapped her lightly on the shoulder. Her eyes remained closed; she brushed her cardigan as if to dislodge a fly that had landed and murmured with renewed intensity something that sounded to his ears suspiciously like 'Vorsprung durch Technik . . .'

'It's very late, Rhona. So, we'd better close up for the night,' he said, patting her shoulder again and whispering in her ear, 'unless you want a full-blown exorcism performed on you.'

Like someone coming to from a trance, she blinked rapidly, shook her head and favoured her followers with a weak but radiant smile which, eventually, she turned on him. Then, apparently drained by her communings with the spirit, she sank into the nearest red plastic seat, clutching her tambourine tight against her breast. While the rest of the chairs were being stacked by the faithful, she remained there, head down and motionless.

'Well?' he said, squatting on his haunches down to her level.

'Well?' she replied, favouring him with a slightly sheepish, sidelong glance.

'We'd agreed, hadn't we? There was to be no more of your phoney glossolalia in this hall,' he began, but a whisper cut him short.

'Don't worry, Father, my work is done. I'm off to Loughborough in two days' time. I've got a job in telesales.'

'Good luck to you, then,' he said, unable to resist adding, '. . . and I hope they're fluent in double-Dutch there.'

Locking the hall door behind them, he returned to his room. Now wide awake, he leaned on one elbow and gazed out of his bedroom window, over the road and across the bowling green. Beyond it, through the bare trees flanking its eastern boundary, moonlight shimmered on Loch Leven and, in the far distance, a dusting of late snow lay on the Lomond hills, highlighting the deep creases etched into them. In the still air, the joyous sounds of a ceilidh drifted from the nearby Green Hotel, clapping interspersed periodically by a whoop as the reels speeded up. Everything about the scene in front of him pleased him. He lit another cigarette, inhaled deeply, and looked down the High Street towards the town centre, tapping the window sill with his fingers in time to the music.

Along it, a couple of giggling pedestrians were returning home from the pub, The Salutation, their arms linked companionably at the elbow, just managing to dodge the lamp posts that punctuated their route and remain, mostly, on the pavement. He knew and liked them both. High above his head, the full, white moon looked down from the sky, illuminating their path, and everything around, including the parklands of Kinross House, the ancient clock tower of the town hall and the glassy waters of the loch. Magically, it had turned the War memorial opposite the county buildings to silver. Some of the names inscribed on it were those of businesses still flourishing in the town: Anderson, Beveridge, Drysdale, Stark and Wilson. Beyond the black-and-white nineteenth-century frontage of the Green Hotel, in The Muirs, the descendants of a few of them lived in substantial stone villas behind high privet or lonicera hedges, as far from the only industry left in the town as they could make it. At the Bottom End, quarter of a mile away, the woollen mill's high chimneys puffed away, steam from them sometimes drifting lazily across the waters of the loch like an early morning mist.

From his second floor eyrie, Father Vincent was conscious that he could see, at a glance, much of his domain. The prosperous county town of Kinross stretched out in front of him, and its smallness did not trouble him. On the contrary, it comforted him, reassured him, because in the sparsely populated little place, he felt he was someone. No better respected than the local bank manager, doctor or lawyer, perhaps, but a recognisable face nonetheless, a well-kent one even.

Thinking about it, nowadays 'respect' might not be the word that first came to mind at the mention of those professions. Bankers and priests were routinely reviled, pariahs both, and any respect for those practising the law, in his experience, bordered too often on fear. There were other differences too. Dr Hume, the only untainted one of the quartet, genuinely did cater for all ages, cradle to grave and everything in between, whereas most of his own flock had lost their teeth. At least three-quarters of them were old enough to remember the words of the Latin Mass and were uneasy eating anything but fish on Fridays. They still thought of him as young, despite his four-plus decades on the earth. His roots in the place went deep, had mingled, become inextricably linked to all those Andersons, Beveridges, Drysdales and the rest of them. Having no close family left apart from a rarely seen brother, they were the nearest thing he had to one.

Hearing the town clock striking eleven, he tossed his cigarette butt out of the window and shut his thick blue curtains. The cat lay occupying the very centre of the duvet, its long, creamy body stretched to its full length as he basked in the warmth of the electric blanket. Its master, now in a T-shirt and striped pyjama trousers, climbed onto the bed, snuggled under the cover and, careful not to disturb the drowsy animal, spooned his body around its tiny form. Taking one hand out from beneath the cover, he stroked its burnt umber-coloured ears, listening to the low rumble of its purr in the silence of the room. As he did so he smiled in the dark, imagining the sneer on his own youthful lips at such a picture, at the thought that any human being could be so reliant on the company of a clawed, whiskered creature. Still less that he should one day turn into such a one.

Yawning, he settled himself more cosily round the cat, adjusting the pillow beneath his head to make himself more comfortable. Tonight, for some reason or none, he felt oddly anxious, ill at ease. Maybe it was the weather, or something he had eaten, like Barbara Duncan's Stilton and broccoli soup. Or that second black coffee. Or the antics of the fork-tongued actress? She had brought his blood to boiling point. Whatever it was, it had robbed him of his equilibrium and left him instead with some vague feeling of dread. A premonition that some unwelcome change was in the offing, was in the air. Something that he would be powerless to resist, and would be malign in its effect. The feeling reminded him of how he had felt as a young trainee lawyer, waiting to appear before a crusty sheriff, knowing little about the case he had been allocated and praying that decree would be granted with no more than a nod. Yes, dread was not too strong a word to describe it.

As sleep begins to overtake the priest, a young man, quiet as a cat, pushes open the door of a familiar sitting-room and looks inside. The place is lit only by candles. Lying on the sofa, unaware of his presence, is the person he has come to meet. He has his eyes closed, headphones on, and is smiling, not at the Chopin nocturne which is working its usual calming magic, but at the thought of this very visitor. Seeing him, the young man advances on tiptoes across the brown carpet until he is standing inches away from the man's head, which, as he studies it, suddenly seems fragile as an eggshell. He looks back towards the doorway and signals for his companion to join him. But the only response is an emphatic shake of the head. Unmoved, he shrugs his shoulders and turns his attention back to the figure on the bed. In the silence, he can hear the man breathe: in and out, in and out. As he stands there, transfixed by the steady rise and fall of the man's chest, he becomes aware, with a strange, unexpected intensity, of his own physicality, his own flesh; his heart seems to have abandoned its customary rhythm, now forcing the blood into his arteries as if to burst them, making his temples throb and his hands tremble. This excitement is better, more energising, than any drug he has ever taken and, in the half-light, he exults in himself, in his power. He could do anything; needs no help from anybody. Clutching the claw-hammer in both hands, he raises it above his head and then smashes it down onto the man's upright, flexed kneecap.

CHAPTER TWO

The next day at the five o'clock Mass in St John's, Father Vincent stood facing the congregation in the church, took the host and broke it over the paten, whispering the words of the prayer. As he watched the stream of his own breath in the cold air, he was glad of the warmth provided by his alb and the long red chasuble that reached almost to his feet.

At that moment, a loud wail emanated from the only baby in the building and his attention was caught by the sight of its mother bending over it, trying to coax it to be quiet by donning a monkey glove puppet and playing with it. Unfortunately, the woman's ploy failed, and for the next few minutes, until it was finally bundled out of the building, the air was filled by the baby's high-pitched, frightened cries. Smiling broadly at the departing woman, determined to signal to her that he was not upset by the noise, he advanced towards the line of people waiting to be given Communion.

At the head of the queue, tongue extended in readiness, stood Lady Lindsay, the old guard made flesh. She was as well-dressed as ever, with a silk Hermès scarf partially covering her blue-grey helmet of permed hair. Tanned and broken-veined, she looked every inch the countrywoman with her muscled calves and padded waistcoat, dog hairs trapped in the seams. Most, including her husband, were accustomed to obeying her orders, and she only attended

St John's Church as there was nothing grander nearby. On first being introduced to Father Vincent she had explained that she came from an 'Old Catholic' family, looked him beadily in the eye as if to subordinate him too and when that had failed, she had flashed her ace. Her uncle, she explained, had been the Provost of the Brompton Oratory in London. 'Really?' he had replied evenly, trumping her with his joker: 'Mine was the Provost of Musselburgh.' St George killed his dragon; he had tamed his with a combination of charm and steel.

Now, open-mouthed before him, she fixed him in the eye, frowned, and unsubtly inclined her head towards the empty pew from which the child's crying had emanated. She had let him know many times before that she did not approve of babies in God's house. 'Something,' she had said in her loud, martial voice at their last meeting, 'must be done.' Meeting her eyes with his own ones of forget-me-not blue, he ignored her mime and, adopting a beatific expression, shut her up by laying the host on her tongue.

As she moved away, head bowed modestly and unable to berate him, he found himself faced with Elizabeth Templeton and, seeing her, he had to make a conscious effort to stop himself from smiling. It would not be proper to do so here and now, and it would likely disconcert her. But the sight of the librarian invariably made him feel happy, and that feeling was difficult to hide. She usually came only to Sunday Mass. Today, he had not expected to see her.

Over the years he had considered the effect that she had upon him and puzzled over it, but he still could not work out exactly why he was so susceptible to her. It was not as if she was a conventional beauty; on the contrary, she was as big-boned as an ox, big-bosomed too, and stood a good six inches taller than him. Her clothes reflected her personality; large, generous and free-flowing.

But her appearance did have a part to play in the attraction; he recognised that. Whenever he looked at her face he knew that whatever expression it showed would be entirely genuine. Like a young child, she appeared to be incapable of dissembling. Nothing was produced for effect. And while such a trait could, at times, be slightly alarming, it also meant that when she did smile, the warmth of it set the world alight and him with it. Sometimes he would borrow books from the library just to see her.

As she was still unaware of his scrutiny, eyes downcast, he allowed himself the luxury of gazing at her for a moment longer. She had such a generous, upturned mouth and fine, high cheekbones. He knew, with an unshakeable conviction, that his high regard for her was fully reciprocated. Alone in his house, when he was unable to get to sleep, he sometimes amused himself by wondering how his life might have panned out if he had taken a different path. If, instead, he had married her, and become a partner, a Writer of the Signet in some dusty Edinburgh firm. In his mind's eye he had created a whole life together for the pair of them. It was all too ordinary, too dull for most people, but to him it was exotic beyond compare.

As she opened her hazel eyes in surprise, seconds having passed and finding that nothing was placed in her hands, he said quickly, 'The body of Christ', as if by gabbling the words the delay could be made up.

While he was speaking to one of his parishioners after the service, Mamie Bryce edged the startled pensioner out of the way, accosted him and tried to revisit the telephone conversation of the night before.

'Mamie,' he said reproachfully, looking at her and at the retreating back of Mr Munro.

'Veronica's not answering her phone, Father,' she said, ignoring his implied rebuke, 'but it's not right that I do the brass lamps myself week in week out. Either you or Veronica will have to sort this out, for once and for all.'

Faced with all the woman's pent-up annoyance he found himself, momentarily, at a loss for words. How could those blessed brasses be so important? Elizabeth must be somewhere nearby, and he did not want to miss her. Maybe he should just give in to Mamie, tell her to leave the matter with him to sort out? No, she would still refuse to move and her demands would multiply, become more strident.

'I told you last night, Veronica's in charge,' he said implacably.

'And she's over there, Mamie, talking to Lady Lindsay,' a low voice interjected. Elizabeth Templeton helpfully pointed at a group near the gate, the square body of the rota-organiser obscuring many of the slimmer frames of her companions.

'Right. I'll catch her the now,' Mamie Bryce exclaimed, moving off and determined to corner her quarry before anyone else did. Past experience suggested that she would be a much softer target than the priest. She had crumbled instantly over the hoovering.

'Thanks, Elizabeth,' Father Vincent said, smiling broadly and showing his even white teeth, 'but she'll be back, you'll see.'

Elizabeth simply nodded by way of reply, and he added as an afterthought: 'How's Michael doing?'

Michael, her only child, suffered from attention deficit disorder and Tourette's syndrome, and these had ensured that she had not had a good night's sleep for many years. The last two decades of her life had been spent explaining the world to him and him to the world. The boy's father could not cope and had left them both, seeking solace for his loss in other arms.

'Not as well as I'd like,' she said. 'As you know, after that silly incident with the motorbike, his card's been marked. He still hasn't found a job. Whenever anything happens here that community policewoman comes straight to my door, determined he'll be involved.'

'You mean Effie?'

'Is that what she's called? So far it's been nothing to do with him, and he's infuriated at the injustice of it, so he argues with her and things go from bad to worse.'

'Where's he now?'

'He's spending the night with his dad; they're going together to the rugby at Murrayfield tomorrow afternoon. So I've no worries for the moment. I know exactly where he is for the next forty-eight hours. He'll love it. He needed a man's hand in his life, but he's had precious little of it. And you, how's life with you?'

'Fine,' he said, sounding suddenly and uncharacteristically guarded. Mamie was approaching them, and once in range, she slipped in front of Elizabeth and exclaimed loudly, 'Ronnie says that you're to sort it out. It's favouritism. I told her that I'm not putting up with it. She said I'd a brass neck. You're to decide who's to do the big vase this week. So, is it to be me or Ann-Marie?'

'You,' he shot back, annoyed at the interruption.

Re-entering the empty and echoing church, the squeaking noises made by his new rubber-soled shoes on the parquet flooring sounded shrill, like a gathering of angry mice. So, for the fun of it, he started to take exaggeratedly large strides, placing his feet gingerly on the floor as if it was made of thin ice. Filling the ensuing silence, his tummy let out a loud rumble. With only five minutes to go before the confession hour, there had been no time for the cup of tea and slice of fruit cake that had filled his imagination so recently. Mamie's furious rant had seen to that. Still, in the face of her barrage he had not relented, and if she resigned from the rota so be it. Catherine Forbes might volunteer, others too; plenty of them had been put off by Mamie's involvement. No doubt it would prove an empty threat like the last time.

Now seated in the confessional, he leaned back against the wooden panelling, luxuriating in the silence after the woman's tirade. How wonderfully peaceful it seemed. He tried to stretch out his short legs but was unable to do so, due to a collection of broken vases, brushes and hoovers that had appeared from nowhere. The place now seemed to be being used as an overflow broom cupboard. Perhaps it was part of the vendetta between the various cleaning factions? Some point or other was probably being made by someone about something. Was he simply being caught in the crossfire? Tomorrow, he would convene a summit and, if necessary, knock some heads together.

Without thinking, he nudged one of the vases to one side with his foot, appalled when it toppled over with a loud crash. The noise was quickly replaced by complete silence once more. Sitting back, relishing the quiet, he basked in it until something told him that it was wrong. All wrong. Hell's bells! Where was the music? Without it, the making of confession became a public act rather than a private one, the penitent's words easily audible to those in the nearby pews. Others, further away too, if they strained to hear hard enough. The whole thing became more like *The Jeremy Kyle Show* than one of the blessed sacraments. Peering out of his door, he saw that the church was still empty, and hurried into the sacristy in his squeaking shoes. In seconds the building resonated to a Latin chant intoned by an all-woman Bulgarian choir.

'You just try and do your homework when your mum tells you, eh?' he said to the child, yawning silently. The tediousness and predictability of the sins on parade were acting as a soporific on him. So far there had been three mumbled accounts of using swear words, a brace of 'entertaining' bad thoughts, their content remaining unspecified despite a little prurient prodding by him, and one young woman's confession of lying to her spouse about her use of birth control. It was like being pecked to death by ducks. The sharper stab of some more inventive sinner would be almost welcome, wake him up at the very least.

The girl left and was replaced, quickly, by the next penitent. The newcomer was breathing heavily, every inhalation and exhalation audible until, suddenly, he wheezed, gasping for air and making a strange hollow, crackling sound. Instantly, the priest knew who was sitting behind the grille. He sighed wearily, having been expecting just such a visit. His friend, Barbara Duncan, had tipped him the wink that there had been a spate of thefts from washing lines in Sandport. Apparently the thief had been very selective, pilfering only ladies' pants, bras and tights. Inevitably, given the man's record, George Lumsden's name had been on her lips, on most people's lips. If only, Vincent thought, George had a little more grey matter encased in that strange, bullet-shaped skull of his, he would realise that such a haul could only be taken from the same place once, if he valued his liberty. Everyone in the town knew of his weakness; gossip was, after all, the lifeblood of the place. One missing Wonderbra and he would be the prime suspect. But, unless he was apprehended, that is all there could be, suspicion. But, after this latest confession, Vincent would know. If anyone had their finger on the pulse of the place it was him.

Later that same evening, he looked along the packed supermarket shelf, yearning to pick up a couple of bottles of the Saint-Émilion Grand Cru. But on seeing the price of them, he turned to the Lussac-Saint-Émilion, a poor substitute but drinkable. With over half the month gone, woefully little of his salary remained and there were only a couple more anniversary Masses still to be said. Worse, the McKinnons were notoriously late payers and, unfortunately, the Cockburns had not a bean between them. A baptismal fee was a possibility, but that could not be relied upon nowadays. Half the infants practically walked to the font, and a few could have made their own responses. The Argentinian Cabernet Franc might be a good compromise – it was both on offer and well-rated.

To his disquiet the woman at the till, a Baptist married to one of his flock, gave him a wink as he began stowing the bottles into their carrier bag. Disconcerted, he resolved to avoid her in future. He could feel his cheeks reddening, blushing from the neck upwards. But, he reminded himself, the only vow he had given was one of celibacy, not abstinence from *all* the other good things of life. So he was not some sort of rogue as no doubt she fondly imagined. Alcohol was not forbidden to him. Trying to get across that he had nothing to hide, he looked her straight in the eye as he opened his wallet. She winked at him again, three times, and he relaxed, realising that she had a facial tic.

'Will that be all, Father? Of the drink, I mean,' she said in a whisper, wrong-footing him again, and grinning conspiratorially at him.

'Well . . . for tonight at least,' he replied, joining in with her, smiling too, amused at the thinness of his own skin.

As he was walking up Station Road, humming under his breath, he saw a pack of youths ahead of him in the Sands car park. They were noisy, drinking. Feeling the biting cold for the first time, he zipped up his navy anorak and quickened his step. Some of the group were seated on the low stone perimeter wall that ran along the pavement. A couple more stood immediately below the street light kicking a glass bottle between them, and one sat astride a green plastic rubbish bin, drumming his legs against it. In order to avoid them he would have to cross the road, which had suddenly become unusually busy. Briefly, he closed his eyes It had been a long, tiring day. He was not in the mood to return their quips, deflect their rude, adolescent banter. But somehow he had to get past them.

As he continued onwards, putting one foot resolutely in front of the other, a cider can bounced into the gutter beside him and a girl, an unlit cigarette in her pouting mouth, marched straight up to him. The sound of glass breaking filled the air, followed by a stream of angry swearing. He could feel himself tensing. Just as he was about to collide with her, she jinked to one side, laughing at the near-miss that she had engineered. She had been so close he could smell the alcohol fumes on her breath. Determined to get away and avoid any more of their attention, he hurried on. A missile hit his back. Someone had hurled a full can of Tennent's lager at him. On impact, he staggered slightly and the carrier bag that he was carrying hit his lower leg. The bottles inside it clinked loudly as if to raise the alarm. Instantly, the boy on the rubbish bin sprang off it and stood in front of him, blocking his path.

'Aye, aye. Bit of an alky are we, Father?'

'No,' he replied, stunned by the blow, rubbing his back with his hand, feeling the bruised muscle below his ribcage through his shirt. He recognised the boy, became aware that he knew his parents. He had buried his great-grandfather less than two months earlier.

'No. No, Thomas, I'm not,' he repeated crossly, side-stepping the youth, trying to continue on his way but finding his path blocked by another of the group. This boy, dressed in a hoodie, skinny jeans and trainers, towered over him. His face was unnaturally pale, peering from his hood like a sickly monk. Every time the priest moved to the side he mirrored his movement, making progress impossible.

''Cause it's a sin, eh, Father?' the boy said, his eyes fixed on the plastic bag and then, as if an idea had struck him, he added: 'We could help you there, Father. Take your sins off you. Gie us what's in the bag . . . they bottles, for the good of your soul, like.'

'No. I'm on my way home – if you'd just get out of my way.'

'I said gie us what's in the bag!' the boy shouted, shoving him in the chest and trying to snatch the swinging carrier. The rest of the gang clustered around him.

Alarm washed over the small priest. There were at least seven of them, and although he knew some of their families, and had baptised two of them, in their drunken state he knew that would mean nothing. Creatures possessed by the Devil would be more amenable to reason. Here and now, he was simply their sport, their prey. He knew one, at least, already had multiple convictions for assault.

'Kyle, is he one too?' the girl, Erin, asked, staring blearily at the priest's face and then fixing a tall, thickset youth standing beside her with her slightly glazed eyes. He had fair, curly hair and the smooth, apple-cheeked looks of a farm boy.

'What? An arse?' Kyle replied, giggling at his own reply.

'No. A paedo.'

'A paedo? Like Father Bell you mean?'

'Father Bell's not a paedo – a paedophile. I'm not a paedophile!' the priest said hotly, furious at the suggestion and inadvertently drawing their attention back to himself.

'She wasn't talking to you. Anyway, he is,' Kyle said, advancing aggressively towards him. One hand was hidden inside his jacket.

'No, that's not true . . .'

'No, that's not true . . .' the boy said, mimicking the priest's accent. 'Aye, he is!' he added, shouting in his rage, his head suddenly rammed so close to Father Vincent that he felt a spray of saliva on his cheek. 'The bastard tried it on with me in that wee red room of his. The one wi' the ship picture. He started putting his hand on my thigh – that's what paedos do, eh? But you'll know that, won't you, "Father"? 'Cause, like my brother says, you're all the same until you're stopped . . . dirty scum!'

He whipped his hand from under his jacket. In it he clasped a broken bottle by the neck, its glinting, jagged end now millimetres from the priest's face.

'Leave him be.'

Hearing the voice, Father Vincent did not move. He did not dare, the glass now touching his skin. His heart was hammering against his ribs and he could feel sweat trickling down his aching spine. Another youth had emerged from the darkness and was now walking along the top of the car park wall, his arms extended on either side of him like the wings of an aeroplane.

'No, Burns,' Kyle said, his back still to the newcomer. 'He's mine.'

'I said, leave him be.'

It was, unmistakably, an order, and as he issued it the boy jumped off the wall and walked up to the group.

'But he's got drink!' Kyle expostulated, his voice now higher, waving his weapon excitedly at the full carrier bag in the priest's hand, then moving it back to his face, resting it on his cheekbone.

'Leave him.'

The girl, Erin, giggled tipsily and, after openly eyeing up the newcomer's physique, sashayed towards him. Reaching him, she circled round him like a cat on heat before planting herself by his side and saying loudly, 'You heard what Burns said, Kyle. Put it away. You're to leave the paedo alone.'

'Can I go?' Father Vincent asked, looking up anxiously first at the youth holding the broken bottle against his skin and then across at Burns. An almost imperceptible nod of Burns' head signalled that permission had been granted, and taking his chance, the priest moved forwards, desperate to get out of range of the bottle. Whether his blood was spilt, his eye gouged, depended on no more than the whim of a drunk adolescent.

After about three minutes' walking, turning left along the High Street, he came to a halt opposite the black-

and-white frontage of the Kirklands Hotel. He slumped against it, closed his eyes and let out an audible sigh. The pounding was still going on in his chest and he felt short of air, unable to breathe, as if someone had placed a plastic bag over his head. Trying to calm himself, he slowly inhaled, then exhaled, several times, telling himself to relax, flexing and extending his fingers in rhythm with his breathing.

His mind was buzzing, a mass of unwelcome thoughts rushing in, forcing their way into his head like gate-crashers to a party. Seeing the jagged glass, an inch from his eyeball, his mind had turned to mush, ceased functioning at all. He had not had the wit to try and talk them down, reason with them. Here he was, a grown man, reduced to silence, powerless. But there had been seven of them, all young and fit. Crazed, out of their skulls with drink, or whatever it was. Reason would have been wasted on them.

But to be called a paedophile, of all things! Of course, Father Bell was no more one than he was! It was just a sick insult proceeding from a sick mind.

Or was it? The man's sitting-room was red, wasn't it? How on earth did the boy know that? And about the ship picture too? It was obvious: he must have been there on an ordinary, innocent occasion, a youth group meeting or something. But why had he lied, and chosen that particular term of abuse? Thrown it at him!

A stupid, stupid question; the clergy were all tarred by the same brush nowadays. The pedestal had been replaced by the pit. A bright light had been shone into the church, his church, and it had not revealed the exquisite beauty of the monstrance, the contours of Christ's ravaged body or a marble floor worn uneven by the passage of the faithful. No, it had illuminated corners in which curled snakes lay, loosely coiled, hissing together, the shadow of nearby rats flitting over their cold bodies. The fall into the pit was well deserved.

But if the accusation was untrue, if it was some kind of nasty joke dreamt up by the boy, why was he so angry? Could anyone be roused to such fury from nothing?

Thank God that Burns, or whatever he was called, had appeared and ordered the attack dogs off. Who was he? Erin's parents would be so ashamed if they had seen her. Thomas's too. They were respectable people, the Wallaces.

But how did the boy know about Father Bell's house, and *why* was he so furious? They had probably been on the white cider for hours. Taken ecstasy with it, quite possibly. Tomorrow, he would have an informal word with Effie, see if she would go around in her uniform, knock on their doors and put the fear of the law, if not God, into them. He would go with her, if need be. A tap on his shoulder brought him out of his thoughts and, the knife-edged glass still vivid in his mind, he spun round.

'You all right, Father?'

His heart again pounding like a steam-hammer against his ribs, he looked into the concerned eyes of Maggie Stark, one of his parishioners. She had come through the hotel door, her shift at the bar completed. He answered her, attempting to sound normal, 'Fine, thanks, Maggie. I just stopped . . .' he racked his brain for a reason. 'Because

I thought I'd forgotten something from the shops. But I've checked, and it's all here – in my bag.'

'You're awfully pale!'

'It's late. Is that you finished work? Shall we walk home together, eh? Give me that bag, I'll carry it for you. It looks heavy. To be honest, the company would do me good tonight.'

'Can you manage mine? You've your own bag.'

'Easy. It'll balance mine nicely.'

CHAPTER THREE

The next day, as he was standing by his kitchen window, holding a can of soup at arm's length in an attempt to read the label, the doorbell rang. Discarding the tin and putting his spectacles back on, he went to the door. Let it be the delivery man, he said to himself. An Amazon parcel was overdue, and he was impatient for his secondhand copy of Michener's *The Social Behaviour of Bees*, his chosen bedtime reading. The Moir Library had demanded their copy back.

Facing him, a tray held in her outstretched hands, was Laura Houston. The sight of her made him immediately uneasy. Although she was married, he suspected she harboured some kind of designs on him. Twice in the last fortnight she had posted a flowery notelet through his letterbox, each one ostensibly seeking his advice, but her writing style had seemed oddly personal, intimate even. Whatever it was, couldn't it have waited for their next counselling session? But, perhaps, he was imagining things. No doubt he was deluded, puffed up with the sort of overblown vanity to which clerical bachelors were prone. After all, he was forty-plus, on the stocky side and, most crucially of all, unavailable.

On the other hand, a man sworn to celibacy, whatever he looked like, might be challenge enough. That had, certainly, been his old Scotch College friend's thesis. In a dog-collar, Hugh had assured him, the elephant man would have been in demand. The observation had been offered as if it might be of some consolation to him. Cheek! Hugh, of course, had had no cause for complaint. He was like catnip for women, whether in a dog-collar or collarless. And the big peacock knew it. Satan, loyal cat that he was, pleasingly fled at the sight of him.

For a second, he was tempted to simplify things, step briskly over the threshold and declare that, sadly, he was just on his way out. Then she would not be hurt. He need not even lie, could genuinely change his plans and go to the local café for lunch. An all-day breakfast was probably on offer. But, looking at her tray, he saw on it a plate of rare roast beef with Yorkshire pudding and gravy, and was smitten. The apple pie and cream in the blue-and-white striped bowl beside it looked heavenly too. And, not to be overlooked, she had gone to the trouble of cooking the food and transporting it to him, somehow managing to keep it hot at all times. The gravy had not congealed and the cream seemed to be melting against the pie crust. There was even a white napkin. Breakfast, no more than a hurried half croissant with his own honey, had left him feeling hungry.

He knew his Bible. Had he remembered Eve's role in the Garden of Eden, he might have been more circumspect, but thoughts of a two-course home-cooked lunch drove all caution from him. When, months later, he was in the depths of despair and looking for a narrative to make sense of everything, his next words always came back to haunt him.

'Laura,' he said, his mouth watering slightly, 'come in.'

As he sat, knife and fork busy in his hands, she talked. With her warm brown eyes sparkling with pleasure, she chattered on about a recent holiday in Croatia. Dubrovnik had entirely lived up to expectations, despite the hordes from the cruise ships; the highlights being St Saviour's and the tour of the city walls. The views from the cable-car had been to die for. Split, naturally, had been as advertised, mind-blowing, and Diocletian's Palace beyond description. But the burek was not worth sampling, whatever the guidebooks might say.

'The burek?' he murmured, wondering what on earth it might be.

'And the heat – we had wall-to-wall sunshine! See my tan?' she said proudly, displaying her bare, shapely, brown arms to him.

She continued in the same vein while he ate, expressing marked enthusiasm for all things Croatian until, the tone of her voice changing subtly, she confided that the trip had also been an oddly lonely experience. Now, sounding subdued, she said that Mark, her husband, had been with her in body alone.

'I'm sorry,' the priest said, mouth half-full of beef.

As ever, Mark's mind, his spirit, his heart, for all she knew, had been elsewhere. She could not, even on holiday, compete with the attractions of his kitchen-fitting business. Hewas never off his iPhone and half the time it felt as if she was visiting those breathtaking sites on her own. A romantic supper together, when she'd worn the red blouse she had bought on Hvar, had been wasted, with scarcely a word exchanged between them. She might have been made of wood for all the attention he had paid her. It had even crossed her mind that he might be gay.

Cheeks distended with another mouthful, Father Vincent nodded a few times, regretting that he had ever succumbed to temptation. Alarm-bells were ringing in his head. Somehow they had drifted into very deep water.

Encouraged by his apparent sympathy, Laura Houston continued voicing her reservations about her husband, detailing the vacuum in her life, in her heart. It was hard, she explained, gazing into his eyes, to go through life without a soulmate. Sometimes she had to stop herself from sobbing out loud, expressing the desperation, the desolation that she felt.

And then, with a tinkling laugh and as if the thought had just crossed her mind, she apologised to him for her thoughtlessness, her self-absorption. Who would know better than him where she was coming from? With his mouth now full of apple pie he nodded, swallowing as fast as he was able, determined to end this unwanted tête-à-tête as soon as possible.

'I suppose,' she said, flashing him a brave little smile, 'it's the lack of closeness that I miss the most. That I crave.'

He put the tray aside, poised to respond in a suitably brusque and businesslike manner when, to his amazement, she pressed an index finger to his mouth as if to quieten a small child. Paralysed by the unexpected and intimate gesture, he said nothing. Reading his momentary silence as encouragement, she leaned her body towards his and said in a low tone, 'You know. I know. We both know, don't we? Closeness is what we both seek, isn't it, lovey? To be close together at last . . . just you and me.'

So saying, she laid one of her soft, perfectly manicured hands on top of his and stretched up to bring her face, her lips, within kissing range. Then she closed her eyes.

After his initial surprise had subsided, Father Vincent found himself gazing at the face now so close to his own. Her long dark eyelashes contrasted with her honeyed complexion, and her lips, slightly parted, seemed to be inviting him to kiss them. *Him*! A beautiful woman was offering herself to him, wanted him. He was so close to her that he could smell her scent, feel her warm breath on his cheek; see the peach down on her flawless skin. But, just as he was about to place his lips on hers he paused, imagining the kiss, longing to feel her touch but delaying the moment to prolong it. Wanting to savour everything, he allowed his gaze to drift slowly down her neck, taking in the whole of its slender length and then settling on her breasts. They would be so smooth to the touch, so warm.

As he was admiring the deep cleft between them, he noticed, glinting in the shadow, a golden ornament suspended on a thin gold chain. Looking harder, he saw that it was a crucifix. The sight of the crucified Christ hanging there jolted him out of his trance, appalled him, immediately robbing him of all desire.

What on earth had he been thinking about? What was he doing? How had this happened? Christ! Had he allowed it to happen, led her on? As good as encouraged it? All those months ago, when she first began to confide in him about her depression, hinting about her unsatisfactory marriage, he should have stopped her dead. *Dead.* Then this situation could have been avoided. Why hadn't he referred her to a marriage counsellor, instead of attempting to deal with her himself? What an idiot! As if he knew anything about marriage! About relationships at all, come to that. He was rusty from disuse. Nowadays, he was better acquainted with bees than women.

But he knew why. Because she was so pretty, so easy to talk to, and she needed his help. And she was married, for heaven's sake. She should have been safe. She wore a ring, had three children, one of them soon to take first communion from his hands. Wasn't friendship, pure and simple, enough any more? How had he so misjudged things?

Suddenly her eyes opened.

'You've had your chance, Father!' she exclaimed, humiliated, looking at him angrily and drawing back into her chair.

'Laura, I'm a priest . . .'

'Don't bother apologising,' she replied, cutting him short, standing up and walking towards the door, the tray of plates and cutlery forgotten. Turning back to face him, she added: 'And don't fool yourself that I fancy you – that you're attractive or anything. Others might think so. Not me. I was lonely, bored. Anyone would have done. You were available, that's all.'

Sitting in his favourite armchair that evening, with the lights out and the cat on his knee, he stroked the beast's warm, creamy back. His affection for Satan was straightforward, could not be misunderstood by woman or cat.

He was still feeling bruised from his lunchtime encounter. Taking a swig of his Rioja, he allowed it to travel all around his mouth, until, satisfied with its notes of vanilla and toast, he let it trickle down his throat. What *was* going on? In the last few days more unpleasant things seemed to have happened to him than in the whole of the preceding fifteen years. It was as if someone had taken a great paintbrush and splattered black and red paint onto the beige canvas which, up until then, had been his life. And in retrospect, beige had been pretty good. His old life, even if he had been in a rut, had a lot to recommend it. That rut had provided shelter from the storm; a degree of invisibility from the unwanted attentions of half-cut youngsters and lonely women.

Thoughts of Laura Houston invaded his mind again, making him cover his face in embarrassment at the debacle and curse himself for his folly. 'Unworldly' was how he had recently described a particularly clueless colleague, but the word fitted him. Better. Worst of all, he had wanted her. But, thank God, *thank God*, he had not actually touched her. At least he had not done that.

Needing someone to talk to, he picked up his phone.

'Hugh?'

'Vincent? What on earth . . . it's the middle of the night over here, you know.'

'I know – but I need to speak to you. You know the rules.'

'OK. OK. What is it?'

Leaving nothing out, except his weakness for rare roast beef, he described the events of the last few days.

'I warned you about dog-collars . . .'

'Thanks. But I think it was a little bit more personal than that. It's never happened before, you know. And I've been a priest for nearly fifteen years.'

'It doesn't affect them all in that way, obviously. Anyway, it's not so bad. You've done nothing – been a bit naïve, stupid or whatever. But you never touched her, there was no affair or anything like that, was there? All it amounts to is a few meetings, nothing more. No harm done. She'll recover. You'll recover and you won't set yourself up as a marriage counsellor again in a hurry.'

'Ever.'

'What are you doing about the youths?'

'I got the local community policewoman to look in on them.'

'No, about Father Bell.'

'What d'you mean?'

'Well, you said that they said, one of them said, that he was a paedophile, didn't you?'

'Yes. They called me one too, I told you.'

'What do you know about him?'

'Very little.'

'In that case, you'll have to find out . . .'

'Hugh? Hugh?'

The phone was dead. The problem lay not in the telephone line from Kinross, despite the gale blowing in the darkness outside, but in the one leading to the mountain town of Trongsa in the kingdom of Bhutan. It had happened before, many times, and still Hugh refused to use a mobile. 'Pointless,' he'd say. 'None of my parishioners have one.'

Father Vincent let out a sigh. He could not answer for somebody else, particularly somebody he hardly knew, but, thinking about it, he had no reason to suspect his fellow priest. At their only meeting, when Bell had first moved into the adjoining parish, he had seemed an amiable man, ordinary enough. With his luxuriant black beard, he had resembled Hergé's Captain Haddock, but his manner was mild, no danger of shouts of 'Blistering barnacles!' from him. He appeared gentle, ineffectual even. On first impression, he came across as a shy, reserved sort of person. Such a man could not be a paedophile surely? They were hard, ruthless creatures, capable of a high degree of cunning and manipulation. Certainly, the few he had come across in his previous career as a solicitor had been like that.

In his head he could hear Hugh's dismissive response to such an argument. Knowing him, he could guess the very expression he would likely use: 'You know next to nothing about those men.' Then, adopting his usual tactic he would probably go on, try to goad him into action, taunting him: 'But it's easier just to hide your head in the sand, and not bother, isn't it? The boy was lying about you, Vincent, so he must have been lying about Father Bell, mustn't he? You know it doesn't follow. Still, you just ignore his fury, ignore the boy's knowledge of Father Bell's house. If you want a quiet life, best turn a blind eye. But face up to what you're doing.'

He could write the script himself. Unsettled, consumed suddenly by the need to do something, Vincent stood up, dumped an annoyed, meowing Satan onto the floor and began striding up and down his small sitting-room.

A moment later, the cat, dodging to avoid being mown down by the pacing figure, knocked over the full glass of Rioja. A large, blood-coloured pool spread out on the green carpet. Hastily, the priest rushed into his kitchen to find the salt. Returning, he sprinkled it all over the wet patch, watching with relief as the layer of white grains gradually became stained by the red wine. The parish could not afford to replace anything nowadays, and even rugs were expensive.

Suppose Father Bell was a paedophile? What then? What exactly was he supposed to do about it? Expose him, obviously, and stop him from hurting and abusing any more children. But how, how did one find out if he was one? How could it be done without alerting the world to what might be, most probably was, a truly hideous and false allegation. It was all preposterous. He was no private investigator, had no experience in such matters, no feel. Blundering about blindly might well make things worse, cause monstrous offence.

Looking down on the stained salt, he shook his head. But, as Serena Lindsay would say, 'Something must be done,' and this time she would be quite right. Just as Hugh had been. Otherwise he would be, effectively, complicit. If only he had gone to the Markinch Wine Gallery instead of Sainsbury's, then he would not have encountered the drunken youths, never heard them make that frightful accusation. But he had heard them, and could not pretend otherwise. He must do something, because there was no one else.

Tomorrow he would go to the man's parish and find out all that he could about him. His old friend Barbara Duncan was the person to see. She was a one-woman listening station; GCHQ could learn from her. None of her seventy-plus years in the field had been wasted. But skill would be required of him too, in such a delicate exercise; otherwise intelligence might travel in quite the wrong direction.

CHAPTER FOUR

Hunched in his car on the Leslie Road with the heater blasting hot air into his face, he looked, for the third time, at his wristwatch. Three minutes still to go before their appointment, plenty of time in which to finish his fag before entering yet another no-smoking zone. He needed the nicotine, felt ambivalent about the whole exercise. Barbara was invariably fun to see, but she was also formidable, and quite capable of working out what he was really up to. Then the slander would be loose, run free. Outside, the rain streamed down the windscreen, sliding off the curved bonnet and splashing onto the pavement below. The gutter had been transformed into a foaming brown river with litter, like little boats, swept along in its current. The few pedestrians unlucky enough to be caught in the deluge scurried along with their heads tucked into their chests, zigzagging from side to side to avoid the puddles, finding themselves splashed instead by passing cars. Thick white condensation misted the windows of the car and, together with the blue haze of cigarette smoke, obscured his view of Barbara Duncan's home.

Her house, one of the grandest in the old 'fermtoun' of Scotlandwell, sat back from the road, screened from it by a high stone wall. Above the wall, only the upper storeys of the Victorian building were visible, with their carved barge boards and barley sugar chimneys, the tops of the apple trees in her orchard in the foreground. In more devout times, the minister of the nearby Portmoak Parish Church had lived there. The current minister, a woman, was quartered in a bungalow in one of the nearby dormitory estates in Kinross, Sutherland Place, or, as it was fondly known by the locals, 'Spam Valley'.

'Island View', as the former manse had been rechristened, currently functioned as a Wolsey Lodge offering bed and breakfast to the rich and discerning, word of mouth amongst its middle-class clientele producing most of its custom. Barbara Duncan, recently widowed, enjoyed the company of her guests and had developed a small guided tour for those who wanted such a thing, showing off the best of the family portraits (which included a Wilkie), her collection of samplers and her late husband's stuffed birds.

Forcing himself to step out of the car and into the pelting rain, dropping his glowing dog-end into the overflowing gutter, Father Vincent yanked up the collar of his anorak and strode towards Barbara Duncan's door. As he waited, rain dripped down his forehead and into his eyes, a few drops trickling down his neck and onto his chest. A minute passed and still nothing stirred behind the closed door, until his hopes began to rise. Maybe she was not in and he would simply have to return home, having tried but failed. Shivering, he turned to leave, when a voice close behind him said: 'Father Vincent, how lovely, and exactly on time as always.'

'Tribute for the Queen,' he said, placing a jar of honey in her hand.

'Your own?' she asked delightedly, holding it against

the light as if to marvel at its amber colour. A couple of black particles were discernible, suspended in the viscous fluid.

'No, I'm a drone – but my workers, yes.'

Shown into her spacious kitchen, he found a tea laid before him that was worthy of the Green Hotel. There was a plate of egg sandwiches, garnished with cress, another of cucumber and a third of ham. A container of warm potted shrimps and pre-buttered toast appeared from the oven. Two cakes were on a cake stand, one a shiny black gingerbread, the other a Victoria sponge with strawberry jam glistening between its layers. The silver teapot was warming on the Aga, and she had even gone to the trouble of making butterballs for him to spread on the ginger-bread. He looked at her, smiled and sighed.

'What a wonderful sight!'

'You sound like Mole in *The Wind in the Willows*,' she said, delighted by his reaction.

'And you,' he replied, 'are like Ratty and Nigella all rolled into one. Perhaps with a twist of Gordon Rams–'

'Don't go there. Tea?'

'I will, thank you.'

They talked easily, each enjoying the company of the other, moving from the dangers to swimmers of the toxic algae blooms in Loch Leven, onto the latest McCall Smith novel and thence to the antics of a cabinet minister's wife, seamlessly, and without effort on either side. The old woman took satisfaction from feeding a man, particularly one not spoilt or blasé from a constant diet of home-baking. And he was, she thought, always so charmingly appreciative. Nowadays, in this uncivilised, housekeeperless age it was the least the women of the parish could do. Not that, from the look of him, he was wasting away.

'I've made flapjacks, if you could manage one?'

'I've room for no more,' he said, patting his tummy contentedly.

'Not even a small one? I made them especially for you. Go on!'

'Just one then.'

The time had come, he decided, to start trying to find out what he needed to know.

'Father Bell,' he began. 'He was in Lanarkshire before, wasn't he?'

In fact, he had no idea where the man had come from, but he suspected that she would.

'No, he was in Helensburgh,' she replied, busy struggling with the lid of the flapjack tin. 'He left in a bit of a hurry, I gather. Woman trouble, I understand. You may know, I suppose?' Hers was a casual enquiry, light as a fly dapped on a loch, made as if no answer was expected.

He ignored it.

'He's been here now . . . what, a year? Could it be so long already?'

'Over a year. I'd say a year and a half. He came in June and I started up my B&B a couple of months before,' she answered, preoccupied, still battling with the lid.

'Let me do that.'

Smiling, she handed it over. In seconds, he had opened it, passed her a flapjack and taken one for himself.

'He'll have fully settled in now – Father Bell. It takes a little while, of course,' he continued, mouth now half-full.

'Mmm.'

'Now he's settled in, he'll have started up all the normal groups, I dare say?'

'Yes,' she replied sounding a little puzzled, as if unsure where the conversation was going.

'A ladies' prayer group?' he persisted.

'He has. We've thirteen members presently. Two new ones joined us just last week. It's thriving. We meet on a Tuesday evening.'

'Football?' Father Vincent enquired.

'A ladies' football group?' she sounded amused. 'Yes, I'm on the right wing.'

'No, no,' he laughed. 'Sorry, I should have made myself clear. A boys' football group . . . team, you know, games for the lads. Has he set one up? Is he good with the children, the youths and so on?'

'Why?'

He would have liked to tell her, to confide in her. But the allegation was too scandalous, too dreadful to share; and doing so he might even give it some kind of spurious credence. Instead he sipped his tea, took another bite from his flapjack and began chewing, trying to give himself time to formulate a convincing answer.

'Because . . .' he began, now chewing on air but needing a few more seconds, 'because it's an important part of parish work, helps keep the kids off the street. Out of trouble.'

'Football? In this day of computers, Game boys and Xboxes?' she replied, eyebrows cocked, a sceptical smile on her lips. 'I don't recall you starting up anything like that, Vincent. Did you?'

'No,' he conceded, 'it's not my sport. But it could be Father Bell's, for all I know, and a very useful one to have. You need something to keep their interest, the youths, I mean. I suppose the youth group, if he has one, meets in his own house, eh?'

'They could well do,' she replied, not trying to hide her bemusement at his line of questioning. 'I've no idea where they meet. Not exactly being a youth myself. You should ask Father Bell about that when he gets back. He'll tell you all about the football, boys' groups and so on. If you need to know . . .'

'When he gets back? Is he on holiday at the moment?'

'No, he's not. He's in Ward 10 of the Infirmary. I sent him a get well soon card only today. He was in his car, and was involved in a road traffic accident somewhere near Blairingone, I gather. Another car went smack into him, stoved in the driver's side, and carried straight on. Dreadful! But do tell me, Vincent, why exactly are you so curious about him?'

'Well, he's a neighbouring priest and,' he replied, adding quickly, and as if as an afterthought, 'incidentally, how did your hives do over the summer? Mine were *very* productive.'

Beekeeping, often thought of as a solitary hobby, is, in fact, a competitive sport featuring the beekeeper as manager, coach, sports doctor and groundsman all rolled into one veiled figure. Gold medals for the clarity of the honey (his had already failed her inspection), the perfection of the comb and the purity of the wax, amongst other things, were all at stake. Barbara Duncan knew fighting talk when she heard it.

'One hundred and thirty pounds from the two. You?'

'Double my body weight.'

Momentarily, her jaw dropped, and then she said, 'Rubbish!'

By way of reply, he simply widened his eyes at her. Looking hard at him, letting him know his ploy had not worked, she drained her teacup in a leisurely fashion and continued: 'As I was saying, Vincent, why are you so curious about him?'

As her question hung in the air, the telephone rang and she answered it immediately, showing by her excited expression that she knew her caller well.

'It's Joan,' she mouthed. Joan was her only and much-loved daughter. She worked for an NGO in Mozambique and did not contact her nearly often enough to satisfy her limitless maternal interest.

The priest stood up, whispered 'Thank you,' in return, waved and left the room.

Afterwards, he went over his encounter with Barbara Duncan several times. It had not been by any means a waste of time, he decided, but he could have handled it better. Sherlock Holmes or Father Brown would have left with the information they had come for. Still, he was a beginner, new to this game. By now word would have spread about his visit to her; she would have regaled others with it, describing his uncharacteristic discretion, remarked on the fact that he had been less forthcoming than usual. It was a tactic he had witnessed her using, deployed to see what her audience already knew. He should be grateful, really, having participated in many a master-class with her. One valuable lesson he had learned. Without that phone call, he might have cracked and inadvertently disclosed something of his purpose. He would not get himself in that situation again, for sure. But, all in all, and to his surprise, he had found the whole episode oddly exhilarating – enjoyable, even.

Opening the double doors of the cupboard in the sacristy, he moved the Tupperware box containing the unconsecrated hosts to one side and reached for the bottles of communion wine. Holding them up to the light, he saw that one was full and the other half-full. More would have to be ordered from Hayes and Finch, and soon, or else the faithful would have to imbibe one of his bottles of Cabernet Sauvignon again. Surely someone would notice the difference, and comment on it? Hayes' stuff was sweet as fermented Irn-Bru.

He must, must, *must* attend to his desk, otherwise chaos would prevail. Red bills were already flying through the letterbox. There were no Mass cards left and he was behind with the registers too. If only administration was not so dull.

An old picture of Pope Benedict XVI, his dark eyes glittering in their deep sockets, caught his eye and he looked away. Ratzinger seemed so unsympathetic, resembling

Fester from the Addams Family, and too far removed from his image of the Good Shepherd for his taste. John XXIII was The Man. Or maybe Francis; they had chosen a good one this time.

Hearing the sound of footsteps on the floor of the church he removed the Wild Myrtles CD from its sleeve, wiped it on his cassock and put it into the player. A few of their tracks were religious and the rest were in Finnish, so no one would be any the wiser. And they had lovely voices, those women, particularly the contraltos.

Trade in the confessional was slow. With luck, the allotted time might be up, and if so he could finish for the night. He looked at his wrist, and was dismayed to see that he had left his watch by the sink in the kitchen. Surely it must be eight o'clock by now, he thought. If, as he suspected, it was after eight, on any other night he would, by now, be sitting down to eat supper in his kitchen. But that evening, to be on the safe side, he decided to stay another few minutes in case anyone else showed up. Latecomers were not unknown.

As he waited, he amused himself by planning his own funeral. One thing was certain; he would not be taken out in his box to that frightful dirge 'Be Still My Soul'. No wonder the mourners today, despite their sly drams, had shuffled out, sniffing and red-eyed to a man, after that so-called 'Service of Celebration'. He would have something rousing, something reviving, like 'Shine, Jesus, Shine' or 'Go Tell It on the Mountain'. Either would add a spring to people's step, and there were enough of those sorts of joyous hymns even if a few of them were infantile. The coffin would be willow-woven, perhaps, or cheap oak? Whatever he chose, there would be no brass fittings for some poor furnace-man to have to fish out from the ash, wondering whether he had got a charred humerus or a coffin-handle instead.

Who could be trusted to do the eulogy, to strike the right note? If Hugh did not go first then he would be the obvious choice. But would Hugh choose him? What the hell, there could be no reciprocation in these matters anyway. Hugh had a feel for these things, was able to extol the deceased's virtues while touching as lightly as a butterfly on their vices, and thus making them recognisable. He would even raise a quiet laugh. Would Hugh advert to his fondness for drink, he wondered. But it was not a vice, not a failing, simply a fondness. A fondness for golf or making things out of matchsticks would not be described as a vice. Wine writers like Hugh Johnson, Jancis Robinson and Robert Parker were held in high esteem, and they had sunk gallons of the stuff in the name of research. Tonight he would try out the Chilean Merlot with its lovely smooth tannins; it should go well with the lamb.

All thoughts of his evening meal fled when a bolt of pain shot through the heel of his left foot. Cramp! Drawing in his breath, he bent down and stroked it, and finding no relief, decided to remove his shoe. As he stretched out his toes, he decided to liberate his other foot from its slightly tight brogue as well.

With his right shoe still in his hand, a strange, unfamiliar smell suddenly reached the priest's nostrils. It was not the scent of his freshly laundered socks but an unusual odour, one more like raspberries, with a touch of Dettol and paraffin running through it. Unconsciously, he breathed in more of the aroma, trying to analyse it into its constituent parts, when a loud baritone voice startled him, booming out from the other side of the confessional box: 'Bless me, Father, for I have sinned.'

Between lengthy pauses, the man began to list his misdemeanours, giving an incoherent description of each one. As he spoke, the scent of raw whisky began to drift through the mix and, smiling to himself, the priest inhaled the heady fumes, trying to guess the brand. Bruichladdich or another of the Islay malts, at a guess.

Every so often, as if he had lost his place, the man would return to an earlier trivial sin, repeating himself before alighting on a new, equally slight one. It was as if he had something momentous to confess, something huge, crushingly heavy, but lacked the courage to put it into words and, instead, was skirting round it. Twice, he banged on the wooden partition with the heel of his hand, looking for a speedier reaction, and then he shouted, 'Wakey, wakey, over there!'

Though he'd given the man some leeway in recognition of his drunken state, Father Vincent finally told him to keep his voice down, warning him that the CD had come to an end and others might be listening in.

'Listening to me?'

'Yes, to you. Who else?'

'You not want to hear my confession or something?' the man bawled, sounding outraged at the idea.

'No, and there's no danger of that. I'm simply concerned about privacy. Your privacy,' Vincent explained, trying not to lose patience. 'Others may hear what you are saying to me. If you shout . . .'

'The earwigging bastards! Right!' the man said, slurring his words even more and sounding angrier. 'I'll give them something to make it worth their while, eh?'

'No, don't!'

'Here's the one you've all been waiting for . . .'

His words were followed by a theatrical drumroll, made by the man's knuckles rapping on the partition of the confessional and his feet drumming on the wooden floor.

'For Heaven's sake, be quiet!' the priest ordered, infuriated by the man's lack of respect for him, for the church and the sacrament. For everything that mattered. Was he insane? He sounded deranged, as if it was more than just the drink talking or, more accurately, shouting.

'Listen up, people! Listen up, the lot of you!' the man bellowed. 'Tonight – tonight I killed Jim Mann. Did you all get that? Tonight I *killed* somebody. But it's all right – I got it, all right. I got it, and that's what really counts!'

Laughing, the drunkard stumbled out of the confessional, smashing the small wooden door back on its hinges in his haste to leave. On the other side of the grille, the astonished priest bent down, groping amongst the lumber on the floor for one of his missing shoes.

CHAPTER FIVE

In the pitch-black of his bedroom, Father Vincent screwed up his eyes and turned onto his side once more, rolling his duvet with him as he did so to make a snug cocoon. A few seconds later, he turned over again to lie on his back. After hours of tossing and turning, his bedding was in total disarray; one pillow had gravitated towards his feet, the other had fallen to the floor and the bottom sheet had worked itself loose from the mattress. Sleep would not come to him, had eluded him since he had been woken by the National Anthem blasting from the radio by his bed. At two o'clock he had made himself a cup of cocoa and, holding his nose, forced himself to drink it. Two hours later he had searched in his medicine cabinet for a particular cough mixture, remembering, from a previous cold, the warning on the label. It had advised against driving and the use of machinery after taking it, due to its drowsiness-inducing qualities. But four swigs of the mixture, a double dose, had failed to knock him out, despite the two glasses of Norton Privada Malbec which had preceded it down his throat.

The man had confessed to murder! In his fifteen-plus years as a priest Vincent had heard it all; every one of the seven deadly sins, from youthful, rosebud lips, moustachioed mouths and toothless, puckered maws. An alphabet of sins, venial and mortal, and the Ms had gone from masturbation to moodiness, but never as far as that one. Never murder, bloody murder. If only, he thought, I could turn the clock back! I would listen in contentment to an unending stream of dull, drab and petty sins and never utter a word of complaint. Welcome the very sound of them, be happily pecked to death by ducks, offer up thanks for it.

Someone had been killed and canon law decreed he could not tell a soul about it. The killer's gory handprints might be all over the confessional box, their fingerprints, too, and minuscule traces of their DNA. Tomorrow, Mrs Thorburn or Mrs McMullen or, God help us all, Mamie, would flick their feather-dusters over those very surfaces and, if they did the job properly, would remove all traces of the killer's presence. Unless, of course, it had all been made up, the bizarre fantasy of some inadequate attention-seeker?

But it had not sounded like that. Usually, those types restricted themselves to sexual sins, the more deviant and flamboyant the better, hoping to shock him, or titillate themselves and him too, for all he knew. Alcohol made them bold. And it had not been absent this time either; you could have set light to the fumes from the man's mouth. In Salmond's fiefdom, money was not the root of all evil, that title went to drink. He should know.

But what had that other distinctive smell been, mingling with that of the whisky? Nothing he had ever come across before and, God willing, would ever encounter again; the perfume of a murderer.

'I've killed somebody,' the man had said, and then he had laughed out loud! It had been less like a confession, more of a boast. No doubt he knew what he was doing, knew he would be quite safe, with excommunication awaiting any confessor who betrayed a penitent. He had, at least, supplied his victim's name. Jim Mann. And it was a common enough surname in Kinross-shire – why, his own bishop shared it. James Reginald Mann . . . Jimmy Mann.

At that thought, Vincent sat bolt upright in his tangled bedsheets. Suppose it was his bishop? Suppose he was the actual victim? But, even if he was, there was nothing to be done about it. He could not raise the dead.

At that moment another thought struck him, making his mind race. What if the man had not killed his victim, as he had crowed, but only injured him, leaving him for dead? While he had been agonising over the crime, over what to do, the victim's life blood might have been draining away, might *be* draining away. By his inaction he might be letting it happen.

It was a split-second decision. He threw his bedclothes onto the carpet and stamped across the floor to the chair where his clothes were. Grabbing his jacket off the back of it, he felt for the familiar bulge in the pocket made by his mobile phone. Locating it, he dialled 999. The second he heard the operator's voice he blurted out: 'Bishop James Mann may have been murdered. Try his house at 54 Oster Street, Dundee.'

Without waiting for a reply, he ended the call.

The next day's edition of the *Courier*, which he raced through from front to back, concerned itself with its usual diet of pensioners' flooded bedrooms, missing organists, unexplained seabird deaths and the like. No mention was made of any reported assaults on humans, far less murders. Even the diocesan grapevine, usually speedy, sometimes accurate, proved unfruitful, and he did not have the nerve to call the Bishop himself, although as each minute passed the urge to do so intensified. Every time the phone rang, he answered it breathlessly, expecting news of his superior from the mouth of some excited gossip or other. Each time he was disappointed, quickly becoming uncharacteristically terse, desperate to get the caller off the line.

By 8 am the following morning he was back in the super-market, intent on checking the latest issue of the paper. Despite the early hour, the place was crowded, buzzing with women, wire-baskets thrown over an arm, some jostling to get at the milk or peering inside the freezer cabinets. Others stood gossiping, nodding at him as he passed them by, holding their trolleys tight as if they might try to escape. An apologetic-looking man tapped him on the shoulder, offering a cube of cheese on a cocktail stick, determined to tempt someone with his plateful of sam-ples. It was quicker to take one.

Easing his way through the melee, returning smiles but unable to reply to the cacophony of cheery greetings with his mouth full, Father Vincent reached the news-stand. A single copy of the *Courier* was left. Desperate to get it, he snatched the paper up and began to examine the front page. The main headline was 'Fife Man Charged with Horror Blaze', but, immediately below it, he found what he was looking for. Pushing his glasses up until they rested on his unruly, sandy hair, he glanced at an old photograph of the Bishop in his mitre and then, holding the paper out at arm's length, he read the accompanying report.

Early yesterday morning Police were called to the house in Dundee's Oster Street of James Mann, Bishop of Inchkeld, following an anonymous tip-off from a member of the public. On arrival, the Bishop, 59, was discovered lying unconscious on the floor of his office with bruising to his face and head. Following treatment by paramedics at the scene, he was taken by ambulance to Ninewells Hospital. A spokesman for the hospital confirmed that the Bishop was expected to make a full recovery from his injuries.

Closing his eyes, the priest let out a long sigh. Thank goodness, Jimmy Mann had survived. He had done the right thing and betrayed nobody. The spirit of canon law remained intact, surely, if not the letter? And it had all been true; the confession had not been the fantasy of a lunatic. Putting his spectacles back on his nose, he rolled up the paper and, picking up a bag of fresh rolls, went to the till to pay for his purchases. Twice, as he stood, lost in thought, the assistant had to ask him for the money.

Trudging along the pitted pavement, rolls and paper under his arm, he kept his gaze down. He knew where he was going, could trust his feet to take him to Swansacre while his mind attended to other matters. What would happen now? In all likelihood, the police would come after him. Calls from mobiles were traceable, and emergency calls recorded. But whatever happened, surely, he had nothing to worry about? Thanks to his tip-off the Bishop had ended up in hospital hours earlier than he otherwise might have done. Those hours could have made a difference, saved his life, even. And no one need ever know how he had come by the information, so he had not betrayed that drunken brute in the confessional. But the feeling that he had become involved, enmeshed, tainted by the crime, did not diminish and the unpleasant fluttering sensation in the pit of his stomach remained.

The sick woman's daughter, Helen Compton, led him through a bright corridor into her mother's room. It was at the back of the spacious flat they shared. The walls were thick, the only window deeply recessed and covered by a pair of net curtains. The little daylight that found its way through the netting was too weak to illuminate the room and the elegant stainless-steel standard lamp did not make up the shortfall. Even with it on, the room was full of dark shadows. But it was as warm as an oven.

'Thanks for coming, Father,' Helen murmured. 'She'll be pleased to see you, I know.'

As he approached the high brass bed, Father Vincent breathed in and found his nostrils filled with the aroma of death. He had come across it many times before, in bungalows, cottages, terraced houses, hospitals, hospices and elsewhere, and he knew it well. If asked to describe it he would have found it difficult to do so, eventually settling on an amalgam of known smells. It was part the musty, foetid smell of the long-term invalid, part wood-smoke and part cold boiled egg. Once he had asked a colleague, a young curate, if he had ever noticed it, but the man had looked at him uncomprehendingly. Hugh, for his part, had flatly denied its existence, suggesting it was a product of his own malfunctioning sense of smell. 'Look to your own drink-damaged schnozzle,' he had laughed.

As he sat down on the woman's old-fashioned green silk eiderdown, he slipped his fingers inside his pocket, checking that he had brought with him the phial of oil in case she wanted to be anointed once more. Sensing a presence in the room, the old lady opened her dull eyes and looked with alarm at him, not recognising him with the light behind him.

'Who's that?'

'It's just me, Jean, Father Vincent. Helen thought you might like some company.'

'Father, good of you to drop by again,' she said, her voice faint, her words tailing off with her failing breath.

'I was passing,' he replied, 'and I wondered if you'd like a bit more of the holy oil. It might give you a bit of a lift? Like the last time?'

'I don't want it now. I'm not in need any more, thank you.'

'Of course, that's fine with me.'

The old woman nodded, she could talk no longer. She held out a cold hand for him to hold. The other remained on the eiderdown, the skeletal fingers splayed out, her wedding ring standing proud from the knuckle. The skin of her hands was dry as paper, heavily mottled, with rivers of indigo snaking their way through the islets of brown liver spots. The last time he had seen her, a month earlier, she had still been plump, heavy jowls concealing the two muscles that now stood out like strings from her scrawny neck. Beneath her nightie, her cleavage, once something she had been proud to display, had disappeared, leaving behind it only the bony sternum below.

'Did you hear about the Kinross Ladies' victory in the league?' he asked, continuing to speak without waiting for her to answer, sure in the knowledge that she would be interested in his tale. In her glory days, she had been the manageress of the rink at the Green Hotel. By way of answer, she squeezed his fingers.

'Joyce was cock-a-hoop. She was the skip for the match and it paid off. She's got a good brain – like a snooker player's. It was neck and neck right up to the very end. Three each, right by the button, and it's always a grudge match against Dunfermline. Well, Isla delivered her stone and whacked the lot of them out the way. Ginny fell over – she'd been sweeping that much, her legs had gone, but they won, against all the odds. They did it!'

'Aha. I heard that,' she whispered, smiling, her eyelids remaining closed.

'Of course you will have. Isla won't have been able to resist boasting about it to you, I bet.'

'Aha, Pam as well. She says, maybe, we'll get a bonspiel on the loch yet.'

'Did Isla tell you the other news?'

On the pillow, the invalid rolled her head slightly from side to side, letting him know that she had not heard it.

'That young woman in the hospice shop, the one you liked so much, Jill. She's had her baby. Guess its weight? That sounds a bit like a competition, eh? Guess the weight of the baby and win . . .' he hesitated, trying to think of an appropriate prize, 'the *baby*! Or maybe not. Anyway, it was thirteen pounds. Imagine that! Luckily, they're both fine.'

'My Helen was just a wee thing,' the old lady said, licking her cracked blue lips.

Her eyes remained shut, whether with weariness or sleep he could not tell, and so, expecting it to be the latter, he whispered her name several times to see if she would respond. Hearing nothing, he slipped his hand from hers, edged off the bed and knelt beside it, his head bowed, almost level with hers. But the second he murmured the words 'Hail Mary full of grace,' her eyes blinked open and she sat up, glaring at him indignantly.

'I'm not that far gone! So you can get right up off your knees. You're vultures, the lot of you. Helen's every bit as bad.'

'Doves, maybe, Jean, but not vultures.'

'Well, you wait and see. I'll be leaping out this bed yet, like a phoenix, and surprise the lot of you!'

Content that the danger was now over, she lay back, closed her dark eyelids and let out a long, rasping sigh. For another ten minutes he sat on her eiderdown, holding her hand and trying to think of things to say, passing on snippets of local news but getting no response to his efforts. As he was trying to extract his hand from hers once more, without waking her, she said, 'You know something, Father . . .'

'What?'

'You've a lovely soothing voice. It's as good as a lullaby ... reminds me of my dad's.'

Sleep, when it overcame her, was accompanied by an oddly powerful snore. The second it started up, her daughter put her head around the door and signalled for him to leave.

'Thirteen pounds, eh? What a whopper,' she said as they walked towards the front door.

'How did you know?' He had thought he was passing on a scoop.

'Oh, I heard it all on the baby monitor. I always listen in. Calling you a vulture indeed! She may be dying, but there's no excuse for that!'

That evening he sat down at his desk, determined to apply himself to the mound of untouched mail and impose some sort of order on it. With luck a fair bit would be circulars, free papers or other junk that he could safely ignore. Priority must be given to the red electricity bill, before all the lights in the parish house and the church were extinguished.

Taking a last draw on his cigarette, he opened his cheque book, biro at the ready, to find that it contained nothing but stubs. In one of the drawers there would be a new one, but in which one? Pulling out the first on the left-hand side of the desk he rummaged about in it and found, to his delight, his long-lost copy of Beasley's *Wines of the Côtes du Rhône*. Why had he put it in there, he wondered?

Browsing through it, his attention caught by a column describing the involvement of seven successive Popes in the commune of Châteauneuf-du-Pape, the purpose of his search was quickly forgotten. Avignon, that would be a fine place to go on pilgrimage, to sample the wines of Bedarrides, Courthezon, Orange and Sorgues too. His euros from the last trip to France must be somewhere about in the house, or had he remembered to change them? The sound of the doorbell made him look up from his book and, unworried, but curious who it might be at this hour, he went to answer it.

The young man who he found facing him did not return his smile. A stubble of reddish bristles covered his broad skull, and his unblinking eyes were fringed with white lashes, giving him a pig-like appearance. His bomber jacket was unzipped to display a too-tight T-shirt and his jeans appeared to have been sprayed onto his fleshy thighs. Fixing his eyes on the priest, he looked boldly at him, letting him know that he was no humble parishioner seeking assistance.

At the stranger's first words 'Detective Sergeant Spearman', the priest nodded. It was no surprise. He knew a policeman the instant he saw one. But always before, in his previous life, the 'polis' had been interested in his client, not in him.

In his sitting room, he showed the man to his favourite armchair and sat, very upright, opposite his guest on the hard wooden desk chair.

The Sergeant looked around the room and then, in a tone which conveyed slight disdain, asked: 'The parish provide you with this stuff, eh, sir?'

'That's right, they do.'

'Have they not heard of IKEA then? No offence meant.'

'None taken. I don't need anything new'.

'Right,' the policeman said, ostentatiously surveying the room and then adding, ''spose not. 'Cause you lot take a vow of poverty, sir, don't you?'

'No,' Father Vincent said. 'Priests don't. But it's a common misconception.'

'No? You'll be telling me they can marry next, eh? Now, sir,' the man said, changing his tone to signal that he was getting down to business, and returning his gaze to Father Vincent's face, 'a call was made from a mobile to the emergency services. Early yesterday morning, like. Did you make that call?'

'I did make a call.' The priest held a match to his cigarette and took a deep draw.

'The caller we're interested in reported a murder – a possible murder. The victim was named as the Bishop, the Bishop of Inchkeld. Was it you that made that call?'

'I made a call, certainly.'

Smiling, but without any humour, the policeman leaned towards the priest as if about to confide in him.

'We know that. Actually, we know you made *that* call. I heard a tape of it this afternoon. What I'd really like to know is how you knew, before anyone else I mean, what had happened to the Bishop?'

Father Vincent slowly exhaled his smoke, determined to gather his thoughts before replying. He must not, on pain of excommunication, betray the sinner in any way, 'by word or in any other manner or for any reason'. To do so would be to break the seal of the confessional. But he would have to say something. Apart from anything else, for his own sake, he must be seen to be as co-operative as possible.

'I just heard about it . . .' He paused again, considering whether there was any more he could safely add.

'Aha. You just heard about it?' the policeman repeated, chivvying him on, prompting him to continue.

In response, Vincent said nothing, drawing on his cigarette again. As he pondered, the policeman, now sounding impatient, boomed at him, 'Well? I do need an answer to that one, sir!'

'*I heard about it*. That's all I can tell you, Sergeant,' he repeated, raising his eyes and meeting the fellow's stare.

'You heard about it? Yes, I've got that much. But what I need to know is where, who from, how? I need more than you just heard about it.'

For a few seconds, Vincent rubbed his face with both hands, blocking out the man and his insistent questions. Behind them, his mind was buzzing, trying to work out what he could say and what he could not. What was safe? What was allowed? Whatever happened to him, he must not betray the sinner. So what more could he say?

Another impatient-sounding 'Well?' was fired at him.

'Sergeant,' he began, looking into the man's unlined face, 'I'm a priest, a Catholic priest. There are certain things I can't tell you. Some of the things told to me in the course of my job, I can't tell anybody. They're confidential. That's just the way it is. I'm sorry. You know that I rang 999, you know what I said. I alerted you to what happened. I did all that I could, more than I should.'

'Look, sir, a man was assaulted in his own house, do you understand that?'

'Of course I do,' he shot back testily, irked by the predicament he found himself in and by the condescending tone of the question.

'Right, you've got that. The man was hit hard, he might have died. Do you appreciate that, sir?'

'Yes. That was why I phoned you, precisely to get help for him.'

'Fine. So out there – in the big bad world outside, as you might say, a violent criminal is loose. This time, he – she, whatever, did not manage to kill. But what about the next time, eh? Has that crossed your mind, Sir? So, I'll ask you one more time – how did you know about the assault?'

'I told you. I can't answer your question, officer.'

Once more he held the youthful policeman's sharp gaze, trying to get him to comprehend. Everyone knew about the seal of the confessional, didn't they? It was not difficult to grasp. Policemen too had duties, including ones of confidentiality where necessary. Sanctions would apply to them, if they breached them. Their immortal souls might not be put in jeopardy, but their pensions could be vulnerable. However, the man gave no indication of understanding. Instead, shaking his head in exasperation and with a new note of menace creeping into his voice, Sergeant Spearman said, 'I think you'll find that you can, sir. Maybe not here, but down at the station instead? I can arrange for that to happen. Shall I send for a marked car, blue lights flashing and everything, to pick you up? Of course, the neighbours will wonder what's going on, they'll talk, won't they? The whole town, I expect, because there's no smoke without fire, is there, in a wee place like this? I expect you'll be able to explain everything away, all right. A violent criminal running free . . . Dundee's not that far away. All because you won't help us. He might strike again. So, shall I arrange such a transfer for you, sir, or would you like to answer me here and now in the privacy of your own home?'

The Sergeant rubbed his hands together, revelling in the display of his power. Checkmate. He had, he was sure, struck the right note with this little man.

'Here or there?' he added chirpily, confident of his victory.

Father Vincent answered him by sitting back in his chair and folding his arms across his chest. The policeman had miscalculated.

'Are you attempting to threaten me, Sergeant?'

'Eh?'

'Because where it is makes no difference to me whatsoever. I can tell you nothing. Here or there.'

'There is,' the Sergeant responded, shaking his head as if disappointed, and with a final change of tack, 'such a thing, well, such an offence, such a crime, as obstructing the police in the course of their duty. You'll be aware of that, sir, eh? Breaking the law. That's what you're doing right now. Right now. See, you could help us, and you're refusing point-blank to do so. Tonight, tomorrow or the next day this man may strike again. He might kill this time. Do you want that, to be responsible for that?'

'Don't be ridiculous.'

'Well then, help me.'

'Believe me, I am doing all I can.'

'For all I know, you may have done it – assaulted the man. That's maybe how you knew. Because you done it.'

'Are you expecting an answer to that ludicrous suggestion?'

'Well, you know him, don't you?'

'So?'

'He's your boss, isn't he? Perhaps you'd a grudge against him? Perhaps he'd blocked a promotion?'

The priest shook his head, nettled.

'Sacked your . . . what shall we call her – housekeeper?'

'This is pitiful. I don't even have one. I never have had.'

'Threatened you with exile to a backwater? Oops, sorry, what am I saying? This is a backwater – of a backwater.'

By way of reply, Father Vincent stubbed out his cigarette and rose to his feet to signal that the interview was now over. The heavily-built policeman didn't move, settling deeper into his seat, glaring defiantly up at the priest. Consciously raising the stakes, Father Vincent crossed his sitting-room and held open the door for his visitor.

'I've not finished yet,' the Sergeant said, leaning back in his chair as if to suggest that he would have to be extracted from it by force, adding sarcastically, 'sir.'

'No. But I have – unless you have a warrant to arrest me, or intend to detain me under section 14 of the Criminal Procedure Act, 1995,' Father Vincent said angrily.

'Eh?' the policeman sounded startled.

'I wasn't always a priest, Sergeant. There was a time when Gordon's *Criminal Law* and Renton and Brown were my bedtime reading. I know about your right to question, but also about mine not to answer.'

'Detective Chief Inspector Keegan is not going to like this, sir.'

'In that case, he will, no doubt, have an opportunity to tell me so himself, at the station. Now, if you don't mind, I have things to do.'

CHAPTER SIX

Less than a week later the priest stood queuing in the Clydesdale Bank, waiting his turn to be served. The Kinross branch was housed in a cream-coloured Georgian building on the High Street. The bank was set apart from its neighbouring shops; what was once a large garden tarmacked to transform it into a car park. From the outside it remained untouched, retaining its classical proportions Roman Doric doorpiece and astragalled windows, but its original architect would not have recognised its modernised interior. The entire ground floor had been turned into a banking hall, and a lowered ceiling hid the cornices and ceiling-roses that had once ornamented three separate rooms. Elegance had been sacrificed to utility and the deity now worshipped within was Pecunia.

The sole bank-teller's attention was focused on a difficult customer. A squat woman, she was wearing a short leather jacket, tight black skirt with red fishnet tights and patent leather boots ornamented by gold spurs. Both her elbows rested on the counter, supporting her heavily made-up face, and one wide hip jutted out, as if she had settled in for a good chinwag. She was talking and laughing noisily, oblivious to the six people behind her. As soon as her latest anecdote had come to an end, she would straighten up as if she was about to leave, and the rest of the queue would relax, getting ready to move forwards. Then another query would occur to her and she would settle down on her elbows once more. After this had happened a couple of times, glances began to be exchanged between those behind her, and the boldest amongst them, the local undertaker, cleared his throat theatrically, attempting to draw her attention to the other customers who were waiting. It had no effect. An elderly woman, catching Father Vincent's eye, made a few loud tutting sounds for her benefit. This too had no effect. However, as if in response to these signs of impatience, the anxious, bespectacled face of the manageress appeared at a vacant teller's position. She smiled at the restive throat-clearer to let him know that she would attend to him now.

When Father Vincent reached the head of the queue, the lady in the high-heeled boots turned to depart, still talking, apparently blithely unaware of the hostility that she had engendered amongst a group of strangers. As she passed by one of them, a lanky youth with his hair tied back in a ponytail, cheeks flushed with anger, he said, in a loud whisper, 'Rich bitch!'

'Is my little pony in a hurry? Guilty as charged, Rick, I'm delighted to admit.' She cackled throatily, adding in a louder voice as she slipped out of the door, 'Loser!'

Further incensed, the youth abandoned his place in the queue and strode after her.

As the priest handed over his faded money bag to the assistant, she beamed broadly at him as if to acknowledge his long wait, and thank him for his good-mannered patience. She was a member of his parish, and sometimes stood in for the regular organist.

'Sorry about that,' she said. 'Is this the collection money?'

'That lad looked as if he'd explode. Who is he?'

'Don't know. His dad's got the new antique shop in Milnathort. The woman used to be his dad's bidie-in for a wee while, I think.'

'Really? Yes, it's the collection money,' he replied. 'Would you put it in the usual account for me, please, Patricia?'

'Certainly will.'

Her fair-haired head was bowed as she counted the coins, her hands moving skilfully from pile to pile. Looking up at him for a second, she said: 'Good that they caught that fellow, eh, Father?'

'Caught who? That boy?' he answered, preoccupied, his eyes resting on an advertisement for a loan. Most of it was taken up by a large photograph which showed a small, palm-fringed island surrounded by pale sands and an aquamarine sea. Across a cloudless blue sky flew a single, fork-tailed white bird. It looked like the sort of place where white rum would be served in a half-coconut, he mused.

'No, no, not him. You know, Raymond Meehan. The police have caught him.'

'I didn't know they were looking. What has he done?' Father Vincent asked, now giving her his full attention.

'The Bishop . . . he's the one who attacked the Bishop. Did you not see the article in the *Courier*? It was on the front page.'

'No. I must have missed it. Raymond? Are you sure? They've got him in custody, have they?'

Father Vincent was familiar with the man. Five years earlier he had lived in the Montgomery Road council estate and was well known within the town. He was the youngest of a family of ten and would once have been described as 'soft'. An albino, he lived for country and western music, had been teased at school for not being able to remember his brothers and sisters' names and was rumoured to live on a diet consisting solely of fish fingers. Like the rest of his clan he had a strong Glasgow accent, but unlike the rest of them, when talking, he honked adenoidally through his nose, sounding permanently surprised. Father Vincent had been instrumental in finding him a job as a cleaner in the Bishop's office, and over time he had acquired two further cleaning posts in Dundee, both early morning shifts, one in a shop and one in an old folks' home.

'No,' Patricia said, stacking a column of ten-pence pieces 'that's what I'm saying. He's dead. He hung himself, but he left a note. That's how the police know he did it. He confessed.'

'Raymond!' Father Vincent exclaimed, distraught, staring at the woman in disbelief.

Startled at his reaction, she said, 'It was in the papers. That's all I'm saying – it was in the papers.'

'It wasn't him,' the priest said firmly, as if speaking to himself, 'not him.'

Holding out a receipt, she said, 'You've two hundred and seventy-nine pounds and forty-five pence, Father. Look in the *Courier*. It was on the front page. I'm sorry, I thought you knew.'

As he crossed the bank's car park, his mind buzzing with the news that he'd just received, he failed to notice a car reversing and walked right behind it. He did not hear the driver's angry hooting, or feel the light drizzle that had begun to fall. One thought dominated his mind. It had not been Raymond Meehan's voice that he had heard in the confessional. The accent had sounded English, Geordie if he had to guess, and there had been no speech impediment of any kind, no honking sounds. In his head he replayed Raymond's strange, goose-like voice with its odd emphases and breathless endings. It was as unique to him as his own fingerprints, a sound characteristic of him and him alone. And one that would be heard no more, with the poor boy dead.

Still deep in thought he moved on, walking downhill past Sands, the grocers, and John & J.H. Sands, the ironmongers, oblivious to a lady in a headscarf hovering between the two, who held out a copy of *The Big Issue* to him, beseeching him with her coal-black eyes to buy it. Only her startling gold incisors registered, and then for no more than a second. Dodging a pedestrian, he strode onwards, head down, apparently hurrying to get somewhere.

Things were spinning out of control, moving too fast. He needed help, needed advice. The Bishop's office was, obviously, the place to get it. Where better to find out the part, if any, that Raymond Meehan was supposed to have played in the assault on the Bishop? But why would Raymond confess, in a note or anywhere else? It had not been Raymond's confession that he had listened to, Raymond's triumphant boast that he had killed a man. Maybe the papers had got their facts wrong, that was commonplace enough, and it was only a local rag after all. While he was there, he could tell them about the boy's allegations about Father Bell, gauge their reaction to all of that too. Find out whether anything should be done in response to it. Alert them to his visit from the police as well.

Finally resolved on his course of action, Vincent sighed to himself, and for the first time since he had left the bank, took in his surroundings. Finding himself in Parliament Square, standing by the red sandstone steeple of the town hall, he moved towards the octagonal gothic fountain, almost tripping over a board advertising 'Eye Lash Tints – While You Wait.' Beyond the beauty salon, he saw the red-and-white awning of Hunter's, the butcher's shop. He peered into their window. A family-sized steak pie caught his eye, and already visualising its filling and smelling the sweet scent of warm pastry, he fetched his wallet from his pocket and took out a five-pound note. It would be the perfect accompaniment to his left-over red.

Slightly ill at ease, he sat on his own in the overheated side-room, listening to the low hum of conversation from the two middle-aged typists who guarded the reception area. He could make out scraps of their talk, their doubts over the authenticity of Father Theo's explanation for a black eye mingling with their concern for his liver. Vincent had cleared his diary for the morning, determined to resolve matters as soon as possible. When asked the nature of his business earlier by one of the women, he had swithered for a moment or two, trying to think what best to say. He knew both of them well, and didn't want to offend them, but wanted to keep his business to himself.

'Yes, Father?' Alison had prompted, trying to hurry him up. Chatter had eaten away the morning, and she had an important call to make before one-thirty.

'It's about the Bishop. Well, not just him but . . .'

'Shall we just say personal?' her colleague interjected, looking up from her computer and beaming at him, sure she had solved the problem.

'That's right, Alison. Personal.'

'Urgent?' Maureen enquired.

'Yes. Urgent too.'

'OK. Monsignor Drew will see you shortly. You just wait over there, please, Father.'

As seemed so often to be the case nowadays, Vincent was not feeling his best. He had suffered another disturbed night and now had an ache behind his eyes and the beginnings of a headache. Earlier that morning, at 3 a.m., he had turned on the World Service only to hear yet another programme about the global financial crisis. It all seemed rather remote from Kinross, he thought. Money could only be lost if it had been there in the first place. Few of his parishioners had much in the way of savings, most living from week to week on their wages, or month to month on their salaries, if they were lucky.

The call made, Alison was eating her sandwich and gazing at him through the open door. He, lost in his own thoughts, was quite oblivious to her scrutiny.

'He's oddly attractive – nicely put together,' she murmured, wiping a bit of tuna from the side of her mouth.

'Who? Ol' Blue Eyes in there?' Maureen replied, taking the lid off her plastic salad box and looking in his direction.

'Yeah.'

'But they're not blue, they're brown,' Monsignor Drew said, catching the women unawares and pointing to his own eyes as he passed by them, embarrassing the secretaries and making Maureen, despite her years, blush.

With his usual hurried little steps, he continued into the side-room, closing the door noisily behind him. He was a busy man, small-featured and with quick squirrel-like movements. He assumed that everyone knew just how busy he was, and could not understand, or accommodate, those used to a more leisurely tempo. Sitting down opposite Father Vincent, and linking his chubby hands across his rounded belly, he came immediately to the point.

'Vincent, I understand that you have a problem – a personal problem?'

Sensing the man's impatience both from his manner and his tone, Father Vincent determined to be equally business-like and replied: 'I have, Dominic. As you may know, I was the one to alert the police to the assault on the Bishop.'

'Did you now? I had no idea,' the Monsignor replied, drawing his chair closer to his visitor and, after only a few seconds of silence, signalling impatiently for him to continue speaking.

'Yes. I heard about the Bishop's predicament and dialled 999.'

'You heard?' The man sounded surprised. 'How could you have done? You weren't here then. How could you have heard? Did someone contact you about it or something?'

'All I can say, is that I *heard*,' Father Vincent said, fixing his inquisitor in the eye.

'Heard?'

'*Heard* whilst attending to my duties.'

'Aaah . . .' The Monsignor hesitated for a moment, and then, nodding, he said, 'I see.'

'Do you? Thank goodness for that.'

'I do. How can I help, Vincent?'

'I heard, and having heard I don't believe that Raymond Meehan was responsible for the attack. I know him. I know him well, including his voice.'

The Monsignor nodded again, as if taking in this new information, paused, and then said, 'The police, the professionals in these matters, however, are sure that he was responsible, they're entirely confident of that. He confessed to as much in his note. The matter's closed as far as they're concerned.'

'I read about the note – but surely that isn't all there is? There must be more than just that. Didn't the Bishop see his attacker?'

'No, that is not all,' the Monsignor said, correcting him and sounding vaguely affronted, as if the version of events known by him to be true was being challenged,. 'Everything points towards Meehan. The attack happened late at night and there was no break-in. He had a key to the place. In his note he apologised for "doing it". What else could he have meant? Q.E.D., I say. And, yes, James, the Bishop, probably did see what happened but, unfortunately, he cannot remember. As a result of the concussion he suffered, he's got both pre-trauma and post-trauma amnesia. He'll be off recuperating for months and months. Furthermore, and this is, as far as I'm concerned, the clincher, the police are entirely satisfied that Raymond Meehan was responsible.'

'But what possible motive would Raymond have?'

'Vincent,' the Monsignor said, the edge in his voice warning that he had little patience for any more of this time-consuming question-and-answer session, 'It is no concern of yours, but a couple of days before the attack, Raymond was sacked. He was working out a week's notice.'

'What on earth for?'

'I'm not sure that that concerns you either . . .'

'In these circumstances, it does.'

'Since you ask, then, for theft.'

'Of what?' Father Vincent said in disbelief. 'Raymond might be all sorts of things – backward, learning-impaired or whatever it's called. But he's not a thief. I don't believe that.'

'You seem to be forgetting that I know Raymond every bit as well as you. Quite possibly better, since he's worked here for over two years. Anyway,' the Monsignor said, his severe expression indicating that further argument would not be tolerated, 'I'm not sure that your belief has anything to do with it. I believe it, the Bishop believes it, the police believe it. That is belief enough. Now I'm due at a school prize-giving in Scone at three o'clock. Was there anything else?'

'One other matter, Dominic,' Father Vincent said, looking into the man's deep-set eyes, 'it's about Father Bell. You know, Connor Bell. He's at Scotlandwell.'

'What about him?' The man sounded impatient, eager to get on with his packed schedule. Making no attempt to hide it, he glanced at his watch.

'He's been accused – not by me, obviously – by others, he's been accused of paedophilia.'

Hearing the word, the Monsignor's expression changed instantly, his brow furrowed and he covered his mouth with his hand.

'No! Who exactly accused him of such a thing?'

'A boy. Well, a couple of boys actually. I met them by accident one evening and they . . .' Vincent breathed out loudly, hesitating as if summoning the strength to carry on, 'They . . . in fact they called me a paedophile too. I was on my own. He wasn't with me. They said he was one and that I would be one too.'

'And are you?'

'What?'

'A paedophile?'

'No. I am not! Of course I'm not!'

'So,' the Monsignor said, sounding slightly less tense and leaning back again in his chair, 'just so that I understand you properly, Vincent, boys in the street called you and Father Bell, both of you, paedophiles?'

'Yes. But he wasn't there.'

'That's all? That's all there was to it? They were name-calling, in a word?'

'Yes, but it went further than that. The boy, Father

Bell's accuser, seemed to know things about Father Bell's house – the colour of his sitting-room walls, the sort of pictures in it . . .'

'How many people in Kinross know the colour of your walls – the pictures on your sitting-room wall? Hundreds, I imagine, maybe thousands, over time.'

'Yes, but . . .'

'Should I take that as evidence that you are a paedophile?'

'No, of course not.'

'Vincent,' the Monsignor said patronisingly, 'we live in the twenty-first century now, don't we? As priests we have to accept insults in whatever form they may be thrown at us. The current favourite, in Kinross evidently, and elsewhere, is paedophile, isn't it? It's almost an occupational hazard to be so slandered nowadays. That horrid Greek word is the slur of choice for every malcontent. If Connor really was a paedophile, don't you think, in this day and age, that complaints about him would have been made by the boy's parents to this very office? Such complaints are being made up and down the country, without compunction – although not here, to date, thankfully.'

'I know all of that. I'm not completely naïve. Probably, the parents would, yes, but . . .'

'Where are they then? No such complaints have been made. If they had been made, then, naturally, we would take them very seriously indeed. We would investigate them. We have protocols, procedures in place, even an appointed safe-guarder nowadays. It's not like the bad old days before Cumberlidge, I can assure you. But, on the basis of a few catcalls, a few street insults – I don't think so, do you? That would be the equivalent of a Salem witch-hunt, wouldn't it? I'm not sure, in these circumstances, what precisely you expect me to do? Are you suggesting that I investigate you? You were accused too, after all?'

'No, that's ridiculous,' Vincent said, running out of steam, aware of the man's impatience to leave and unable to find fault with his logic.

'I thought not. And do try to develop a thicker skin, eh? I'm all for vigilance, of course I am. But there has to be *some* evidence, doesn't there? A proper complaint, even. More than simply name-calling from a few drunken – and I bet they were drunken – youths.'

Three weeks later, peeling a potato in his kitchen, Father Vincent was pondering obsessively over a small and apparently inconsequential event. He had been standing behind Jimmy McCrae in the queue at the Milnathort post office and had, in an idle fashion, tried to start a conversation with him. The queue was moving slowly, and along its length people were gossiping with each other, to pass the time. Suddenly, and saying nothing in response, the man had abandoned his place in the queue. At the time Vincent thought little of it, assuming that he had remembered some errand or other. Before long he found himself looking into Elaine's dark features at the counter. Her manner, he thought, had been a little peremptory, almost unfriendly, but she was very busy and her superior was drinking a cup of coffee within sight. Perhaps he was monitoring her performance?

On his way out of the post office he had noticed Jimmy standing at the tail-end of the queue and had gone to commiserate with him for losing his place. But Jimmy had stared straight ahead as if he was invisible, ignoring him. Baffled by the man's behaviour, he had lightly patted him on the arm to get his attention and try to find out what was going on. As if incensed at being touched, Jimmy had whirled round to face him and shouted angrily, 'Do that again, you . . . you . . . Just don't do that, OK?'

Vincent's startled apologies met silence and no further explanation was offered.

Thinking about things, some kind of pattern seemed to be emerging. On Thursday the prayer group had, without explanation, failed to turn up, and the attendance at Mass on Sunday had been derisory. Twice, when he had rung to check on the health of a parishioner, the phone had gone dead and when he tried again his calls received no answer. Although Jean Fleming must, by now, be on the very edge of death, or dead, the messages he had left on Helen's answerphone had elicited no response. Even Satan seemed a bit remote.

Gouging an eye out of one of the potatoes with the point of his peeler, he muttered out loud, 'If only Hugh would get a mobile!'

Out of desperation, having got a continuous tone every time he tried to contact Hugh, he had eventually spoken to another friend, Damian Malloy, a priest ministering to a parish in Dunfermline. But Malloy had had little to say and most of his replies were monosyllabic. In the course of their brief discussion, Father Vincent had conceded that an innocent explanation could be provided for each apparent rebuff. It was undeniable that people lived hectic lives, had bad days, failed to answer their phones and overlooked messages. He knew that, had always known that; but, he explained, he was also aware of a definite change, something he could feel in his bones. His greetings in the street were no longer being returned, people avoided catching his eye. It was not, as Father Damian would have it, 'just a bad day' – in other words, all in his head.

'Sorry, Vincent, must dash,' his colleague had said, ending the discussion after less than a couple of minutes. 'I've a first Holy Communion class to take. Can't be late or they'll pull the place apart. I'm rushing. I'll have to go now.'

He poured boiling water from the kettle over the potatoes, put the lid on the pan and then gave the beef casserole a stir. It looked dry and unappetising. A little red wine would perk it up, give it a better colour too.

As he was extracting the cork, he heard a loud rapping on his front door. Hurriedly putting the bottle down he went to answer it. Two large men were standing on the doorstep.

'Come in, come in,' he said in a welcoming tone, waving them inside. He was delighted, despite the hour and his imminent meal, to have the company. One of them, he was sure, looked vaguely familiar. It would not be anything to do with marriage or baptism, as there was no woman with them. A funeral, possibly. With luck, once they'd got all the practicalities out of the way, they would accept a consoling glass of wine, perhaps finish off the bottle with him. No doubt Father Damian had been right after all; the cold-shouldering had all been in his head.

With the two bulky men in it, his sitting-room seemed to have shrunk. Although he gestured for them to sit down they remained standing side by side, shoulders touching, looking awkward and uncomfortable.

'Can I help?'

As he spoke, he suddenly realised that both men were glaring at him aggressively. The bigger of the two, a man whose pendulous beer-belly overflowed his belt, moved towards him, coming so close that Vincent stopped breathing momentarily to avoid the fumes of garlic on the stranger's breath. On the man's head was a coal-black wig, tilted at a slight angle, and minute beads of sweat were visible on his brow.

'Know who I am, Father?' he demanded.

'No, I can't say I do,' Vincent replied, shaking his head, 'but please take a seat.' He gestured once more towards the chairs, trying to set the men at their ease and lighten the atmosphere in the room.

'I'm Mark Houston and this is my pal, Norman.'

'Right,' the priest said, feeling the blood rushing instantly to his neck and cheeks. His face felt hot and he knew he had gone red. He held out a hand as if to shake Houston's, but the man ignored his gesture.

'Laura told me what you done to her,' Houston said.

'I don't know what you mean. I haven't done anything to her.'

'No? Don't give me that . . . shit! She's my wife. I love her, I believe her!'

'Honestly, I don't know what you mean,' Vincent repeated, looking from one man to the other as if for an explanation.

'Some fucking priest you are,' Norman said, shaking his head in disgust, 'like a wolf in fucking sheep's clothing. Never understood why she went to your church in the first place. It's all mumbo-jumbo – and now you've been laying your hands all over her.'

'I never touched her!'

'She was unhappy, depressed. She just needed a friend, someone to talk to,' Houston added, suddenly raising his hands as if about to strike, 'and you, you a priest, took advantage of her.'

'No,' Father Vincent said, 'that's not what happened at all. I have been counselling her, but, honestly, that's all.'

'Counselling – that's a new word for it!' Norman guffawed.

'You calling my wife a liar?' Houston demanded, his voice louder than before. 'She's my wife, you understand? She's been lying to me, has she?'

His mouth unpleasantly dry, Father Vincent said: 'No, not lying. I'm sure she's not lying, but I can assure you that I have never touched her . . . never taken advantage of her.'

'Run out of nuns, eh?' Norman chipped in.

'You don't belong here any more,' Houston said. 'Do you understand me?'

'How do you mean? This is my home, this is where I live,' Father Vincent replied, momentarily unable to think, puzzled by the man's remark.

As if enraged by his seeming defiance the two men advanced towards him and Norman poked him in the chest with a stubby forefinger.

'Leave!' he commanded.

Shocked at this treatment in his own house, the priest did not immediately reply.

'Leave!'

This time it was Houston's finger which prodded him, and as he did so the man growled in his ear, 'Get the fuck out of here, Father, or we'll be back and make you. Understand? Force you to go. Everybody knows about you and your ways now. We've made sure of that. Kinross doesn't want you any more – not after what you done to Laura. You're not a proper priest . . .'

As Father Vincent remained silent, Norman slapped him hard across his cheek and, simultaneously, kicked him on the shin. Losing his balance, he fell to the ground, clutching his injured leg. Instantly, he felt a boot on his spine and then another kick, this time to his jaw. His mouth filled with blood and he almost choked on it, spluttering, finding himself spitting out one of his own teeth.

'We mean it, Father,' said Houston, bending over and delivering his message directly into the priest's ear. 'There's no place for you here. Do you understand?'

Vincent did not answer.

A kick to his nose followed. 'Do you understand?'

'I heard you,' the priest whispered, and the words were accompanied by the sharp whistling noise of his breath through the gap made by his lost tooth.

CHAPTER SEVEN

'Is that you, Dominic?' Father Vincent asked, conscious once more of his new sibilance. In his mind's eye he could picture the irritation on the Monsignor's face as he realised the lateness of the hour.

'It is, yes. To whom am I speaking?' The voice at the other end sounded blurry with sleep.

'Vincent Ross.'

'Very good, Vincent. What do you want with me?'

'I'm sorry to bother you, particularly so late, but . . .' He hesitated, momentarily unable to find the words to describe his ordeal, knowing how sordid it would sound. 'I know it's late but . . . I'm in trouble. In my parish. I'm in trouble . . .' The right words would not come.

'Yes?'

'I've been accused of . . . well, actually I'm not sure exactly what I am accused of. Having an affair – no, having sex with – one of my married female parishioners. I think that's it . . . something like that.'

'It is late, yes. Very late, and I was away at a conference in Birmingham all day. I didn't get back until after nine. Forgive me, but could this not wait until the morning? It doesn't, to be frank, sound like an emergency.'

A pulsating pain was building up in his lower jaw. Vincent closed his eyes, forcing himself to continue talking. 'I'm sorry, Dominic, but it is. I don't think that it can wait. You see, the woman's husband, plus one of his pals, a heavy, have just been here, after me, threatening me. With the Bishop still in hospital I thought I ought to speak to someone. To you, as you . . .'

'Heavens above! Are you all right, Vincent? Did they hurt you?' the Monsignor interjected, sounding startled and now fully awake.

'Yes. Well, no, I've lost a tooth . . . otherwise I'm fine. But they say I have to leave – here, I mean, leave here. And they left me in no doubt that they meant it. So I'll have to go . . . for the moment at least. Until everything settles down.'

'Mother of God! They hit you? When did all of this happen?'

Father Vincent glanced down at his watch. 'I'm not sure. Forty minutes ago. Half an hour, maybe? I don't know. I've just washed my mouth out, and then I contacted you. I wasn't sure who to speak to, with James still being off.'

'I'll contact the Dean right away and he'll be with you within the next hour. Somebody will be with you, to give you some support. Will you be all right on your own until he gets there?'

'Fine, thanks, Dominic. I'll be fine.'

The paper tissue that he had been pressing against his mouth to staunch the bleeding had become soggy with blood. Disgusted, he threw it into the nearby bin and picked up his tumbler. His second mouthful of malt whisky went down more easily than the first, although he still did not enjoy the taste. It was as peaty and smoky as advertised, and therefore disgusting. But it would knock him out, be a good antiseptic, a good anaesthetic too, quite possibly. The ache in his jaw was thumping away, moving up through his cheekbone and into his already tender left temple.

Satan, intuitively aware of his master's trauma, sat on his knee, providing comfort with his heavy, warm presence. In the silence, the sound of his purr was as loud as a chainsaw. The telephone rang and he picked it up.

'Vincent?'

'Hugh!' he replied, thrilled to hear his friend's voice.

'Good to . . .'

The line went dead.

'Hugh, for Christ's sake, get a sodding mobile!' he shouted down the receiver, before slamming it back onto its stand. The intense disappointment made him clench his teeth until he felt a fragment of his forcibly dislodged tooth crumble between them. Drink would wash it away.

Screwing up his face in anticipation of the unpleasant flavour, he forced himself to take another swig, quickly gulping the whisky down. Once it had gone, his tongue, with unerring accuracy, returned to explore the crater where his missing lower incisor had once been. It felt vast. As he probed its pulpy surface again, his mind involuntarily flashed back to the exact second when the man's boot made contact with his jaw. Feeling the kick afresh he instinctively put his hands in front of his face to ward off another blow. In his mind, the blows continued to land, with the shocking sound of the thud made by leather on flesh and bone. Unconsciously, he moved his lower jaw from left to right, right to left, checking that it had not been dislocated. Sickened by a sudden gush of salty blood into his mouth, he rose and began to walk up and down the room, trying to distract himself, jerk his brain out of its obsessive loop. Twice, and unaware that he was doing so, he poked himself in the chest as Mark Houston's meaty hand had done, as if by repeating the action he would disarm it, rob it of its obnoxious significance. His pacing stopped only when the sound of the doorbell roused him, returned him to the present. Having peered through the dusty spyhole, he unlocked the front door to allow Father Bernard, the Dean, into his house.

The Dean stood in the vestibule, twirling his black umbrella from side to side, allowing the rain to drain from its gilded point onto the wooden floor by his feet. A satisfactory pool having accumulated, he removed his black Homburg from his head and tossed it like a deck quoit onto the nearby hook.

'How are you, Vincent?' he said, shepherding him with a stick-thin arm round his back into his own sitting-room as if he was elderly and confused and in need of guidance. Seconds after his entry, and effortlessly, he had taken over the territory, his authority exercised so lightly as to be almost imperceptible. Obeying him seemed natural.

The disparity in size between the two men might, in other circumstances, have been comic. From his six-foot-six vantage point, the Dean literally looked down on the parish priest, as he did on most of humanity. It was difficult not to condescend from such a height and it, together with the way he carried himself, inspired confidence. A surprising number of people, reverting to some childhood pattern, found themselves deferring to Bernard Hume as to a benign parent. Steering the diminutive Father Vincent towards his own armchair, he gestured for him to sit down before planting himself by the fireplace and muttering, as if to himself, 'Awful. It all sounds quite awful.'

And then, looking into his colleague's eyes properly for the first time, he added in an almost exaggerated tone of concern, 'And your face – what on earth has happened to your face, Vincent?'

'Would you like a drink, a whisky?' Father Vincent asked, embarrassed by the whistle in his voice, pointing to the bottle by his chair.

'Mmm . . . what is it? An eighteen-year-old, eh? My, my, that's a generous offer,' the Dean replied, picking up the bottle and bringing it to within an inch of his nose, checking the label again as if he could not believe what he had just read.

'Dalwhinnie,' he murmured, 'I'll certainly take a glass of that.'

Father Bernard looked like the establishment man that he was. Central casting, had it been searching for someone to play a priest, would likely have rejected him because he was too close to type; he was overly handsome with a well-shaped head, clear brown eyes and fine cheekbones. He would have appeared clichéd, too unimaginative a choice to be true to life. Fortunately, his brethren, those who had elected him Dean, were unconcerned by considerations of dramatic plausibility. They knew him to be competent, 'a safe pair of hands' and, invariably, 'the man for the job'. To be fair to him, he did not thrust himself forward. He did not need to. People came to him, and thus his ambition remained concealed, hardly recognised even by himself. Wherever he went, whatever he did, he was always the chosen one: the head boy, the chairman, the spokesperson, and he did not have a subversive bone in his body. Any tendency to unorthodoxy in others both mystified and disturbed him. A desire for anarchy was incomprehensible, and he considered disaffection to be the affliction of the bitter, the unsuccessful or the disappointed. To date, life had run smoothly for him, and he was unaware of the large part that luck, including his looks, had played in it. Preferment, he believed, simply followed ability. Everywhere, although he did not examine the reasons, his face fitted.

Savouring the malt on his tongue, he glanced down at the battered figure opposite him, and, suddenly, felt a great rush of pity for him. He looked so small, so anxious, like a dormouse in shock having just escaped the blades of the combine-harvester. For a second, it crossed his mind to take the tartan rug from the wing of his chair and tuck him up, make sure he was warm and comfortable.

'Tell me all about it, Vincent,' he said, sitting down himself and pressing the sides of his tumbler with his long white fingers. As he listened, he nodded sagely, occasionally inserting a shocked 'Really?' or an outraged 'No!' Hearing about Laura Houston's request for help, her problems, the frequent meetings and Vincent's growing fondness for her, he knew already what was coming next. His own view, formed within less than five minutes, and which could be summed up as 'What an unbelievable mess!' remained unspoken. It would be unhelpful. And Father Vincent probably shared it by now. Loneliness, all too often, in his experience, led to a lack of judgement; and everyone knew that women, like tigers, were best admired from afar.

Seeing his colleague's empty glass, he gestured at the bottle as if to urge him to get a refill. The interruption, however, stopped Vincent's story in mid-flow, as the embarrassment of his predicament hit home. Seeing an opportunity to move to other less painful topics, the Dean began to speak. There were, he said, the practicalities to attend to. Masses still had to be said, baptisms and funerals conducted. In short, the life of the parish must continue. As Father Vincent returned, almost involuntarily, to the subject of Sarah Houston, wondering out loud whether she had known about the assault before it happened, Father Bernard was flicking through the card index of his memory in search of a suitable standby.

'I don't think she can have,' Father Vincent repeated, 'because we were close. Genuinely close. Good friends, I thought. Too close, I now appreciate. But I'm sure she wouldn't have let that happen.'

'Father Roderick . . .' the Dean interrupted, unaware of his non sequitur, pleased that the parish problem had been resolved. 'He's retired. But he's helped out often enough before. He's always willing.'

'Father Roderick?'

'He was at St Mungo's – a good standby. Now, have you anywhere to stay?'

'Yes,' Father Vincent answered, massaging his bruised jaw with his fingers. 'I think I'll see if I can stay, for the moment, with the Sisters at the Red Retreat. For a bit anyway.'

'The Red Retreat? Do I know it?'

'It's the rump of the old convent near Dunning. There are only seven sisters left now. They offer retreats, reiki, talking therapies . . . my pal Sister Monica's in charge.'

'Monica McDermott? Doctor McDermott – with the build of a sumo wrestler – learned scholar and all round tough egg? That's one powerful woman.'

'I like powerful women.'

'Each to his own, Vincent. But you're more than welcome to use my spare room for a while if you prefer.'

'Thanks, but I've already spoken to her.'

'You've no parents left, no relatives, no siblings even?' the Dean said, standing up and shaking his umbrella to get rid of the last remaining droplets.

'I've a brother but . . . we're not close. He's married, got a very busy job. Our lives have taken different paths.'

'Right. I'll ring Dominic tomorrow and he'll be in touch in the very near future, I'm sure. He'll let you know where we go from here. Now, the police . . .'

Seeing his pet slinking past the open door, and suddenly struck by the realisation that his household was likely to be split up, Vincent exclaimed, 'Satan! What shall I do with Satan?'

'Satan?' Father Bernard replied, baffled.

'My Siamese cat. No, it's obvious. Of course, he'll have to go into kennels or something.'

'Yes, kennels or a cattery, or something,' the Dean echoed, nodding, patting Vincent on the shoulder and looking around for his hat. 'But have you spoken to the police yet, Vincent?'

'No, I contacted Dominic. I thought I'd better speak to him first.'

'Quite right too. He and I discussed it. It's up to you, of course, but at the moment everything is still within the family, a Church matter. We don't want a scandal, do we, if we can avoid it? Our view, *quantum valeat*, is to let sleeping dogs lie, otherwise we up the ante, don't we – involving outside agencies. We don't want to lose control, if we can keep it. We certainly don't want the press involved. All it would do is damage the Church further.'

'No police. I don't want Sarah Houston's name involved, and a criminal conviction for her husband won't help her. There are children too. No doubt, the big brute will get his come-uppance from somewhere or other. Soon, I hope.'

The thin plasterboard walls of his room at the Red Retreat confined him. It was a guest room, blandly painted and blandly furnished. No one could be offended by it; or feel at home in it. The accommodation in a Holiday Inn had more character. In the fake fireplace, a bunch of fake flowers gathered dust, and a single reproduction watercolour in a gilt frame hung above it. The picture showed a vase of poppies, each bloom less red, more blurry and insipid than the last. Instead of the familiar scent of honey from his bee-suit, the air reeked of soap from the nearby laundry room.

Showing him round it with suitable proprietorial pride, Sister Monica had informed him that the lack of an ashtray was deliberate policy, thus letting him know, in her oblique way, that smoking was not permitted. Finding herself unable, because of her bulk, to manoeuvre between the bed and the armchair, she apologised for the smallness of the room. Its saving grace, in Father Vincent's opinion, was the view from it of the world outside. It was a wide vista of the distant hills, high and wild, clothed in a faded green, occasionally interspersed with the gunmetal grey of scree. Trees, dwarfed and windblown, hugged the lower slopes as if clinging onto them for their own dear lives. One peak in particular caught the eye. It loomed above the others, casting dark shadows on its neighbours, an exposed rock face on it recalling its ancient past as a quarry.

Within days of his arrival he had bought an OS map of the area from Waterstones, and amused himself by locating in the scenery the features named 'Hologrogin', 'Rossie Law' and 'Marcassie Bridge'. Sometimes, looking at the broad landscape in the warm tangerine light of dusk, he felt almost intimidated by it, unnaturally exposed within it. It was so large, so different from the enclosed townscape with which he was familiar and the mellow, fertile land surrounding it. The absence of a loch reflecting the ever-changing skies struck him every time he looked out, making the scene feel as abnormal as a face without a nose. But the nuns loved it, he reminded himself. They were drawn to its grandeur, even if to him it seemed cold, hard and unapologetically impersonal. There were no dwellings arranged higgledy-piggledy beside each other, no pavements, no shops, play-parks or people. No people.

If massacres came to mind in the windswept bleakness of Glencoe, they seemed not too far away here. Opening the window he could hear only the songs of moorland birds: the mournful cries of curlews, peewits and oystercatchers. In retrospect, the perpetual hum of traffic in his parish seemed soothing as a lullaby, and he missed it.

Many letters of support from his parishioners, plus a nightly glass or two of a good claret, warm as blood and consumed alone, comforted him and kept him sane. On day two, the cardboard box of bottles he kept under his bed was unearthed by the nozzle of Sister Clare's beloved Dyson. From then onwards, the nuns, largely teetotallers, teased him mercilessly. It became known as his 'Box of Delights'. Conviviality for most of them consisted of sitting together, breathless, spellbound by the latest Scandinavian murder series, arguing over who would do the sudoku in the newspaper and playing endless board games. Despite the lack of alcohol, their high-pitched laughter often penetrated his sanctuary, bringing home to him the otherness of his masculinity and, on bad days, making him feel as misanthropic as Scrooge. The only other male in the whole place was an African grey parrot called Bertie. He spent his days in a cage in the communal sitting-room, negotiating his perches, splitting and spitting seeds and squawking expletives. His fledgling years had been spent in a pub in Leith, fed on a diet of peanuts and absorbing the language of the patrons along with their cigarette smoke.

'One fuckin' IPA, eh – just the one fuckin' IPA, pal,' was his usual sing-song greeting. The nuns, to a woman, adored him.

The first time the priest listened to abuse hissed down his mobile phone, the venom warm in the caller's mouth, he became fearful, reluctant to pick up any more calls. Each time he heard the nerve-jangling ringtone he began to sweat, his pulse racing in anticipation of more verbal hatred dripping from a stranger's lips. At the very sound, the back of his skull began to tingle, as if a metal band was being tightened around it. But after the first call, it was simply Father Roderick with some practical query: where did he keep the keys to the prayer room? Was he aware that his dry cleaning was now ready? Had Hayes' last bill been attended to?

Consequently, he forced himself to answer the calls. Only one call in twenty would be malevolent, but it was enough to ensure that he remained tense, permanently living on adrenaline, expecting the worst. The name-calling he could bear, it was the silences that upset him the most. He sensed that his caller enjoyed his disquiet, hoped, sadistically, to hear his victim's racing heartbeat.

'You should be afraid of the dark, Father,' the man said, adding, in a voice suddenly laden with pent-up fury, 'we know what you are, we know where you are! You can't hide from us, you filthy . . .'

The priest ended the call before the speaker could finish. Mark Houston would not get that satisfaction.

In the Bishop's absence, Monsignor Drew had set in train an investigation. It would, he had explained on the phone to Father Vincent, be imprudent for him to return to his parish in the meanwhile. The diocesan lawyer, Fergus

McClaverty of Grant Borthwick WS, had been instructed to interview everyone involved in order that the Bishop, amongst others, could come to a view on the incident and the events leading up to it. He would, he was assured, get his chance to tell his side of the story but, in the meanwhile, he should bide his time at the Retreat. When he asked how long the investigation was likely to take, his question was answered with an extended sigh, followed by 'A fortnight? As long as it takes,' said in a tone that pre-empted further enquiries. Frustrated by his enforced idleness, he had, nevertheless, repeated the question the next week and the one after that, but no timescale was forthcoming. The third week that he asked the question, he was reprimanded by the Monsignor. In the circumstances it ill became him, he was told, to attempt to impose time-limits on anyone. Riled by the Monsignor's attitude, and frustrated by his loss of control over his own destiny, he replied, '"In the circumstances." What circumstances would they be, then, Dominic? I'm still a priest in good standing as far as I'm aware. No-one has yet asked me to give an account of what happened. Has a judgement been reached all the same?'

'Eh . . .' The man hesitated, clearly unprepared for any resistance. 'No. I simply meant that we have to let things take their course. The lawyers and so on. They operate in geological time, don't they? We're in their hands, I'm afraid.'

'He who pays the piper calls the tune,' Father Vincent said.

'The piper,' the Monsignor replied stubbornly, 'is only

103

required to blow a pipe. Thanks to you, a full-blown investigation is under way.'

'As long as it is under way.'

By way of reply, the Monsignor simply grunted. Imprudence would be unearthed by the solicitors, if nothing else, of that he had no doubt. And with that finding, Vincent's vessel would be holed below the waterline. And, all in all, that might be no bad thing.

Walking up along the metalled road that led to Gallows Knowe, that same day, Father Vincent bowed his head against the horizontal rain. Despite the high hawthorn hedges, the road was lashed by a gale, turning the drops into darts which stung his scarlet cheeks, lashed the right side of his head and made his ear ache. He pulled up his collar as far as possible, cursing himself for setting off without a scarf. His trousers were already soaked, and raindrops slid down his anorak and dripped off it into his boots. Turbid, muddy water had poured into the drainage ditches on either side of the road until both burst their banks, flooding the tarmac, streaming down it and forming a gargantuan puddle a few yards ahead of him. If he was to continue, he would have to wade through it.

As he was in the middle of the pool, a car came from behind and tore through it at high speed, making no allowance for his presence less than a foot away. A wall of water hit him, drenching his face and clothes. Momentarily his breath was whipped from him by the cold. Tempted to flourish a V-sign after the red brake lights disappeared round a bend, cursing the driver for his thoughtlessness, he decided to turn back home and accept that he'd been defeated by the weather. Now when he walked, his boots made an obscene squelching noise. As he was trudging back, the other side of his head exposed to the freezing rain, the car drew up beside him. Its window was rolled down and a cheery female voice said, 'Want a lift?'

'OK,' he replied, still aggrieved but opening the passenger door and getting in.

'Dreadful day,' the woman said, moving off in first gear, her windscreen wipers, despite their frenetic speed, hardly able to cope with the volume of rain. An air freshener in the shape of a miniature fir tree swung from the rear-view mirror, filling the interior of the Volkswagen with a sweet and sickly perfume. As he was still blowing life back into his numb fingers, about to give her a piece of his mind about the soaking she had given him, she added, 'Want a ciggie?'

Further mollified, he took one and lit up.

'You're not, by any chance, Father Vincent Ross, are you?'

'Yes,' he replied, taken aback by her question.

'Like the heater on? It's pretty parky today.'

'Thanks. How d'you know who I am?'

'That better, Vincent?' she said, turning the fan on full blast.

'Yes. Thanks. But could you please tell me how you know who I am?'

'You're the priest, aren't you? The one in Kinross who's been having it away with that married mother of twins, eh?'

'I have not!' He looked across at her indignantly, taking in her appearance for the first time. She had an unruly, plum-coloured thatch of hair and a fine, almost Grecian, profile. Placed beside her skin, ivory would have looked dark. A single silver stud glinted above an eyebrow. Her small eyes looked straight ahead, scanning the road, never meeting his. She was dressed entirely in black, and he noticed that her spade-shaped nails had been lacquered in the same colour. The contrast between her complexion and her clothing made her striking, as if she was at death's door, or drained of blood.

'That's not what I've heard, Vincent. Apparently, you and she have been having an affair for months. Meeting in the church, your home and God knows where else. You seduced her – took your chance when you were supposed to be counselling her about a recent miscarriage.'

'That's complete rubbish! I did no such thing. Who are you exactly?'

'But that's what they're all saying. If I were you, Vincent,' she added, glancing across at him for the first time, braking gently and flicking an indicator, 'I'd want to tell my side of the story. This is your chance, darling, to put the record straight. Best take it, eh? We've got enough, in fact more than enough, to go to press with, but I thought you'd like to put your side of things. Tell the world what really happened. We know you've had it away with her, she told us as much. But, perhaps, it was a love story, a real love story. You fell head over heels in love . . . you know the kind of thing.'

'Stop the car, please.'

'I was going to, so that we could speak. But maybe I should just carry on to the Red Retreat now, eh, Vincent? We're only minutes away and we could talk there. Better there than on the side of the road.'

'Stop the car, please – now!' he ordered her, his hand on the passenger door-handle.

'Here? Now? In the pissing rain? Are you mad? We're going to print the article, you do understand that, don't you? Know what your media people – the Catholic media office – said, this morning? No, I thought not. They said "No comment". Rather damning, I'm sure you'd agree. I think, probably, we'd better hear your side of things. This *is* your only chance, Vincent.'

'Stop the car!'

'You don't want to set the record straight?'

'STOP THE CAR!'

The Volkswagen having finally ground to a halt, he climbed out and slammed the passenger door with all his might. It made a satisfying bang. In response, the driver roared off, revving her engine like a rally driver, the spinning rear wheels splattering him in gobbets of mud. Walking onwards he could feel his heart palpitating. The cold now seemed even more intense, as if icy fingers were gripping his skull and pressing hard into his temples. What he had been dreading had happened. Now, everyone in the whole of Kinross-shire would read her nonsense, everyone in Scotland or beyond, for all he knew. He had become tabloid fodder, would join the ranks of 'Randy Reverends', 'Pants-down Priests' and 'Molesting Monks'. Maybe they would all believe it too. After all, he had left the parish – 'fled' might be a more accurate description – and no real explanation for his sudden departure had ever been given. Her garbage would plug that particular gap.

Increasing his pace in his haste to get back to the Retreat, he plunged his cold hands into his trouser pockets. In one he found the tooth that the Norman man had kicked from his jaw. Twirling its monstrous root between his fingers, he was struck how dissimilar it was to a milk tooth. He could picture the first one he had lost, a neat, compact little thing, with the tell-tale brown stain of caries on its chewing surface from sucking too many sweets, the hallmark of a Scottish childhood. While he slept, the tooth fairy had removed it from under his pillow, leaving a twenty-pence piece in its place. By the time the last obstinate tooth had come out the rate had increased to fifty pence. But the poor old tooth fairy was long since dead, and, today, that was a blessing. At least she would not have to read of his disgrace, catch gossips discussing him in the shops and feel the need to defend him. It would have broken her heart. No one had been more proud of him. In his mind's eye an image of her at the party after his ordination appeared, beaming, plump, clad in a red coat, darting about like a robin puffed out in its winter plumage. Graduating in law had been nothing, in comparison, in her eyes. He shook his head, determined to dislodge the picture from his thoughts. In disgust he threw the shattered tooth into the bushes.

As he entered the driveway to the Retreat, Sister Margaret came to greet him. Buffeted by the high wind her umbrella was swinging to and fro above her head, its sharp spokes ready to take an eye out. Her fine grey hair streamed behind her like smoke. She appeared to be dressed in some sort of cloak, which the wind periodically inflated, making her look like a puffball. Hobbling towards him, still wearing her furry bedroom slippers, she spoke as soon as she was within range. 'There's a lady to see you, Father. From the press, she says. She's told us that this really is your last chance, whatever that means. I've just come to warn you.'

Before he could answer, his phone went. Smiling at the nun to apologise to her for not responding immediately, he took it out and put it to his ear.

'Couldn't keep your grubby hands to yourself, eh, Father?' a voice sniggered at the other end. Instantly, he cut the line.

'She doesn't look well, does she?' Sister Margaret said linking an arm in his. 'Come to think of it, you're not looking so good yourself, Father.'

CHAPTER EIGHT

Dennis May's post dropped through the letterbox. Hearing it cascading onto the hall floor, he stopped what he was doing and wandered off to retrieve it. The first envelope that he looked at was brown and looked, he thought, dull and unattractive. Official. It had his name and address printed on it and advised, in large red letters, that it contained 'Important Information'. Thinking that he would be the judge of that, he stuffed it to the back of the pile and opened the uppermost white envelope instead. It appeared far more enticing, begging to be opened, with its looped writing in blue ink and an unfamiliar stamp. Taking out a greetings card from it he put on his spectacles to read it. 'Happy Birthday,' a grinning donkey proclaimed through tombstone teeth. Inside he found the message 'Many Happy Returns of the day on your 78th from Theresa and all the family.' Bemused, he looked at the date on his *Telegraph* and realised that it was Friday 25 February and, therefore, his own birthday. Without the card he would have missed it completely! He was, and would always be, a . . . a . . . The name of the star sign eluded him, but in his mind he could picture a woman holding a jug of water. Those born under the sign were all, as far as he could recall, due to meet a handsome stranger shortly. So Minette du Bois had predicted in some column or other. But who the hell was Theresa, never mind her family? As there was no mention of love or kisses beneath the message, they could not be his family, and that, at least, was a mercy.

Back in the kitchen he put the unopened envelopes on the oak table and picked up where he had left off in his hunt for the butter. It had not been in the fridge or the larder, of that he was fairly certain. For a second he wondered if Julia had got there first and eaten whatever was left. But close inspection of the dog's muzzle, twitching occasionally as she dreamt of a favourite rabbit burrow, revealed no evidence of theft. Sitting beside the old Alsatian on the white leather settee he fingered her ears, watching the rapid rise and fall of her chest as she slept on, unconscious of his presence. In the silver ashtray on the nearby Welsh dresser his half-smoked cigar glowed, dwindling away beside a dried out cigarette-stub stained with lipstick.

Catching sight of the empty butter-dish on the table opposite him, he was reminded of his task, patted the dog, and headed off to inspect the interior of the nearest wall cupboard. After five more minutes of intermittent searching he found the block of butter in the microwave and, laughing to himself, sat down to eat his lunch of olive bread and cheese.

The front page of the newspaper was devoted to another Taliban atrocity in Helmand. After glancing at a photograph of the latest casualty, he turned to his favourite part of the paper, the obituary columns. Perusal of them almost always cheered him up. While it was true that he would not be remembered in such a distinguished way, even though he had opened the largest casino in the New Town, it was also true that he was still alive.

And that was much, much more important. Alan Bridges might well have been 'A Daring Cold War Spy' and Arlene Summers, 'A Nightclub Chanteuse in a Class of Her Own' but they were both now either six feet under or stored in a dusty urn somewhere. He, good old Dennis, was sitting at his table, eating the very best Colston Basset Stilton and drinking tepid Hobgoblin. Simply remaining alive was his crowning achievement. Nowadays his best hope of being honoured with an obituary lay in winning the lottery and spending the dosh in record time. Perhaps he should buy a ticket this afternoon? Best not, maybe best that the obituarists don't delve too deep.

His reverie was shattered by the insistent ringing of the alarm clock in his pocket. He fished it out and silenced it. Attached to the back of it was a yellow Post-it note which read: 'App – 2 p.m. – HC on Colinton Mains Road.'

Sitting opposite the doctor, he wondered where his usual one had gone. This blonde doll looked younger, prettier, than any fully qualified MD ought to look. Perhaps she was a partly qualified locum or some such thing? She would have fitted in nicely at Jokers, spinning the roulette wheel in a low-cut frock. The punters would have liked her. Those blowsy types went down well with them.

'Has this been going on long – weeks, months or what?' she asked.

'Sorry?'

'The forgetfulness and so on, when did it start?'

'Well, Doctor Allan,' he began, watching her intently to see if she responded to the name of his real doctor. 'It's difficult to say. A while, a while . . . yes, that's how I'd describe it.'

Oddly, she did not attempt to correct the name. Perhaps she was indeed Doctor Allan, but if so she must be on some youth drug, some elixir of life. I'll take a prescription for a gallon of that, he thought, giggling uncontrollably and covering his mouth with his hand in order to hide his amusement.

'And you've no one you could bring with you? That I could talk to? It often helps, you see. They know you, know if you've changed.'

'I've changed, all right. I used to be beautiful!'

'In character – in your ability to recall things.'

'No one,' he said firmly, sure of that fact, if no longer of any other.

'Right,' she said, turning away from her computer screen and looking him in the eye, 'We'll get on with the little test I told you about, then, shall we?'

He nodded.

'I'm going to say three words. You say them back to me once I've stopped. Okay? Ready? Apple. Penny. Table.'

'Mmm . . .' He hesitated, running his finger along the bridge of his nose as he thought, 'Table?'

He smiled at her in what he hoped might be a winning way. In tests you always want the examiner on your side. That early lesson had not yet been forgotten.

'Right-ho,' she said, noting his answer down on her pad and picking up a yellow pencil.

'What's this?' she said brightly, pointing at it.

'Writing wood,' he shot back, uncertain as he spoke if that was right, trying to think if there was a more exact term for the object. Concluding from the fact that she was writing his answer down that he had given the correct one, he gave up trying to think of a better word.

Next, she held up a sign which said in large letters: 'CLOSE YOUR EYES'.

'If, Mr May, you could do what the sign tells you to do?'

Reading it out loud, he closed his eyes and then looked back at her, finding, oddly, that he was hoping for praise.

'Spot on, eh?' he said jauntily.

'Spot on.'

Purely to be on the safe side, she explained, she would arrange a scan and refer him to a consultant neurologist. He would have to have an MRI scan, probably. Feeling that he had got his money's worth, and how, the old man stood up and, to Doctor Allan's surprise, raised his arm in a flamboyant Nazi salute.

That evening, Dennis May was annoyed with himself. He was tired, and although it was past ten o'clock, he had not eaten his evening meal. Cooking it, once a pleasure, had become impossible. The recipe in the book stated that Chinese dried shrimps and peeled prawns were to be used. That was clear enough. But Nigel had then written, 'Add the seafood to the dried mushrooms.'

What was seafood? Food of the sea? Then shrimps and prawns presumably ate seafood? Plankton, krill or whatever. Nigel had made no mention of either of them in the list of ingredients and even Waitrose was unlikely to stock them. How could anyone hope to prepare Singapore Stir Fried Noodles unless precise and accurate instructions were given, involving obtainable foodstuffs?

Seeing a figure looking in the window Julia rushed at it, growling, showing her yellowing fangs below black lips.

'Sssh!' her master said, his back to the distraction, scrabbling in the cupboard for noodles amongst all the bags of pasta. 'Sssh, you bad, bad girl!'

The dog, which had not been fed all day, meekly obeyed and began prowling round the kitchen table. Seeing a plateful of shredded pork close to its edge, she raised herself on her hindlegs and managed to gulp down the lot in a matter of seconds.

Still fuming about the inadequacies of the recipe, and now wondering what 'soy sauce' might be in English, her master did not witness the theft. However, the smell of burning fat alerted him to a pan hissing and spitting on an electric ring. Grabbing its metal handle with bare hands, he screamed and dropped it onto the floor. Splashed by hot oil, the dog rushed with its tail between its legs towards the kitchen door. The old man, desperate to get to the cold tap and bathe his blistered hands, collided with the dog, falling over her and banging his head hard on the tiled floor.

After a couple of minutes he regained consciousness. Feeling cold and with aches in every part of his body, he dragged himself upstairs to bed. Once under the bedclothes he remembered that he had not undressed. Unwilling to get out of bed again, he wriggled out of his trousers and ejected them from under the sheets. As he was attempting to undo a cuff button with his teeth, he heard knocking on his front door. Forgetting that he was half-naked, he lumbered out of bed and went to answer it.

Stuck on the front door lintel was another yellow Post-it note. On it was printed, in blue ink, the following instructions:

1.Check through the eyehole who's there.
2. If you do not know them then, leaving the chain on, open the door and ask the stranger what he wants. He might be a BADDY.
3. If sure that it is safe to do so, undo the chain and open the door fully. Otherwise phone Theresa.

He had long ago given up reading these instructions. Unhooking the chain, he opened his front door wide.

The stranger before him, taking in his hunched posture, sunken cheeks and trouserless state, relaxed. You did not need a knife to kill a baby, and that was all this shrunken, wizened, toothless creature now was. Nothing but a husk. Everything would be his. Who was there to stop him?

'Do I know you?' Dennis May enquired, peering up into the cold brown eyes of the stranger as if for guidance.

'No, but I know all about you,' his visitor responded, slipping past him into the hallway. On his approach, Julia, her belly heavy with pork, gave a single token bark and then, after sniffing the intruder's outstretched hand, waddled off to her basket.

Everyone, including Dennis May himself, had expected him to die peacefully in his bed. After all, he was seventy-eight, tired and suffering from some kind of memory loss. But his end was like that of 'a pig in an abattoir', as the ashen-faced trainee photographer described the scene to her boss over the phone. As she talked, she was meticulously circling the pool of blood on the kitchen floor, carefully avoiding any contact with the dark spatterings on the bland white door of the fridge. Looking up at the ceiling, she snapped a galaxy of dark specks placed there by a last exuberant spray of blood.

Theresa, the old man's niece, reluctant carer and sender of the birthday card, watched her every move from the next room. No one had noticed her sitting there when the door had swung open. In response to the condolences offered in the ensuing days, she repeated over and over again, 'I told him . . . I told him.'

Two days later, a post mortem was carried out, but by then no one except Dr Allan was interested in the tell-tale tangles and plaques in the brain tissue of Alzheimer's disease. The severing of May's carotid artery by his murderer stole her thunder. She had diagnosed it instantly, she assured her sceptical colleagues, simply from May's failure to recognise her despite their meeting less than a month earlier about the itchy rash behind his knees. The cognitive tests merely confirmed her diagnosis.

'I don't know. You'd forsaken your raven locks in the meantime – and undergone the *procedure*,' one of them replied, with a mischievous grin.

'The procedure?'

'The . . . uplift?'

'Patient confidentiality, my arse!' she answered irritably, putting down her coffee cup and heading for the door.

CHAPTER NINE

Three days later, his mouth so dry that his tongue stuck to the roof of his mouth, Father Vincent contemplated the newspaper, trying to steel himself to open it. The newspaper itself seemed revolting; deadly as a snake, capable of inflicting harm on him, and his disgust with it was almost visceral. It would contain the reporter's distilled bile. Had he tongs to hand he would have been tempted to use them to pick it up, however preposterous he knew that would be. Since the journalist's ambush he had bought a copy every day and forced himself to read it. As a result he had now learned more about the misdeeds of celebrities than from all his previous newspaper reading, internet browsing and TV viewing put together.

A quick scan of the second and third pages revealed nothing of any interest to him but, turning to the fourth, his heart missed a beat. It was dominated by a single grainy colour photograph of a shambling vagrant, wild-eyed and scowling, his arm raised menacingly at the photographer. Instinctively and instantly, he recognised himself in the creature. The man he was staring at looked dirty, deranged and dangerous. He had been caught by the photographer standing on a lonely road, the wind and rain lashing him like a beast in the field. The impression created was of a damned soul raging against God and all of His works. But, he thought ruefully, it had all been as carefully staged by her as any shot taken by Diane Arbus or Mario Testino. First she had driven by and drenched him with water from the puddle. Then, when he reacted just as she had hoped, she had turned and caught him in all his sodden fury on her mobile. She had cast herself as the matador and him as the tormented bull.

The report accompanying the image was lengthy and scandalous, and its author's enthusiasm for her task could be heard in each breathy sentence. Vincent was described as 'small and scruffy, but not unattractive with piercing blue eyes and a mop of sandy-coloured hair'. The nuns, the writer observed, must enjoy having him 'livening up their convent'. An unnamed female parishioner had, apparently, volunteered that he had 'romped with countless of his female parishioners over the years,' adding that his career as 'a Casanova in a cassock' had come to an end when he was 'caught in the act in the sacristy by an enraged hus-band'. The reader was directed to further revelations on page seven. There below a photograph of 'Bab's baps' were two further columns about him. In them another unnamed parishioner listed his 'top ten trysting places', and his favourite chat-up line which, he learnt, was: 'Anything you'd like to confess to me, babe?' A 'broken-hearted' Laura Houston was then quoted as saying, 'Vincent Ross is insatiable. He won't be stopped until he's finally thrown out of the church. He's preyed on countless vulnerable women over the years. I'm simply the last in a long line.' The final sentence of the piece read: 'A spokesman for the Catholic Church said: "We have no comment to make."'

As he tried to light his cigarette, his fingers trembled and made it difficult to keep the flame still. Once it was lit, he took a deep draw and looked out of his window at the hills in the distance. The sun streamed through a break in the dark storm clouds, onto the highest summit, bathing it in a lemon-yellow light, creating deep shadows in the clefts of the cliffs and turning the old permanent pasture a startling lime-green colour. The sky had become a deep Prussian blue, darkening as if getting ready for nightfall. Gazing on the scene, he felt nothing, hardly took it in. Now it had happened; the waiting was over and the explosion had gone off. Smoke, dust and shrapnel dirtied the air, and body parts lay all around. She had pushed the detonator, but he had provided the dynamite.

Despite the wanton lies staring him in the face he found, to his surprise, that he was not angry. Anger had not, as he had expected and hoped, come to his aid, galvanising him into action, obliterating grief and shame. Instead, he felt numb, and as insubstantial as air, as if his entire innards had been pulverised by the blast. Overwhelmed suddenly by dizziness, he sat on the edge of his bed and took another deep draw on his cigarette. Everything, for the moment, seemed strangely remote and unimportant. After three days of anxiety, sweat running down his back as he scanned the newspaper daily, the story was now out. And it was a story: pure fiction. Reading it he had felt like a bystander, as if someone else was being pilloried, someone else was being vilified. But it was his name that was being invoked throughout. He had not 'romped' with women in his own church. Had he ever 'romped', he wondered? He glanced again at the open paper and saw once more the wild-eyed travesty of his photograph, read again his own name, but felt nothing. None of it seemed to matter any more. Nothing mattered. Nothing hurt. He exhaled, and smoke issued like steam from his mouth.

An insistent and ear-splitting beeping assaulted his ears and he looked round, trying to locate its source. As he stood up, Sister Monica bumped through his closed door, saw him with cigarette in hand, and, now shaking her head in annoyance, prodded the smoke alarm on the ceiling with the end of her wooden broom handle. Seconds later, Sister Margaret hobbled in, panting heavily, and, incongruously, holding a pink face flannel in her hand. She too looked askance at the stunned priest.

'Fuck!' he exclaimed, unaware until the word had left his mouth that he had said it out loud. Then, to the astonishment of the two nuns, he crushed his cigarette into his empty wine glass and marched straight out of the door. Sister Monica caught Sister Margaret's eye.

'Was that Bertie's foul-mouthed cry I heard?' she asked, cocking her head to one side as if to catch anything else the parrot might say.

With every footstep he took, the anger inside him rose, consuming him, making him blind to his surroundings. It was as if the shrieking noise emitted by the alarm had released his fury too, broken his trance. And he was glad to be awake at last. Yes. He had done wrong. He knew that. Foolishly, he had allowed himself to become too close to a woman. But that was all, all he had done. He had not so much as laid a finger on her, tempted as he had been, far less slept with her. Since his ordination, all of sixteen years ago, he had been celibate. As chaste as a statue and purer than holy water. And it had not been easy. He was not made of spirit alone, was no ascetic, did not share Ruskin's distaste for warm female flesh. Quite the reverse. He had longed to touch Laura, kiss every inch of her as she had offered herself to him. But he had not. Few, finding a bunch of ripe, black grapes hanging above their mouth would not taste it, caress the fruit with their tongue. But he had not. And here he was being trashed by the tabloids, sharing column inches with thrice-married love rats and disgraced porn stars. He had no home, no job, no income and, for all he could tell, no future. Something must be done, he said to himself, parroting unwittingly the war cry of Lady Lindsay. So saying, he turned on his heels and began the long walk back to the Red Retreat.

Catching himself at the mirror looking anew at his 'piercing blue eyes', he laughed out loud. Had the reporter not noticed the crooked nose then? 'Not unattractive', indeed! The impertinent bisom. Still, it was, he conceded, a more charitable verdict than the one he had reached on her.

Deciding to spend the evening with the nuns in their communal sitting-room, he finished his half bottle of Cabernet Franc in an attempt to make himself more convivial, less self-absorbed. Having flouted one of their few unspoken rules and sworn out loud in front of them he felt that an apology was overdue. How they would greet him, if they had read the paper, he did not know. The account in it bore little resemblance to what he had said to Sister Monica when he had first sought sanctuary in their home.

As he walked into the room, the entire community, all seven of them, were sitting in front of the TV, transfixed by Captain Mainwaring's antics in *Dads' Army*. Sister Susan, unaware of his arrival, was almost doubled up with hilarity, rocking back and forth in her chair. Choosing his moment, he tiptoed past the nuns and took the only vacant seat, an armchair opposite one of the picture windows. Every couple of minutes, a chorus of laughter would sweep the room, punctuated at intervals by solo chuckles and a descant of giggles. Looking at the TV he found himself unable even to smile at Croft and Perry's jokes, his fingers searching nervously in his pockets for his cigarettes as if they had a mind of their own. Staring at the backs of the women's heads, watching them as they exchanged glances at Pike's silliness or Private Godfrey's sweet smile, he felt, suddenly, lonelier than he had ever been in his own house. He wanted his life back. He wanted Satan back.

'A cup of tea, Father?'

It was Sister Ellen, and without waiting for an answer, she gave him one, murmuring softly to herself, 'Now, where's that sugar bowl got to?'

'Red card! Red card! Get the bugger off the park!' the parrot squawked.

'Shut it, bird – as that Mitchell man might say,' the old nun retorted, rattling a spoon along the bars of the cage and startling the bird into silence.

'We cleaned him out today,' she said, looking back at the priest, 'and put a copy of page four of the *Record* underneath his perch. That's where it belongs.'

'And when that reporter phones,' Sister Margaret giggled, 'we say, "What you wan'? Spare lib, Cantonese spare lib or prum sauce 'n' spare lib?" That gets rid of her!'

While the sisters argued over what to watch next, Father Vincent, heartened by their kindness and their resilience, cast his eyes over the *Scotsman*. A small piece caught his attention. It concerned the murder of someone called Dennis May. Late in life the man had, apparently, opened the largest casino in Edinburgh.

The name seemed familiar and he repeated it in his head trying to figure out where he had come across it before. Dennis May. Of course – a Dennis May had taught him for a couple of weeks at the Scotch College in Rome. Satisfied that he had identified the man he re-read the report and was interested to see that he had been a big wheel in the gambling industry in Scotland. That seemed perfectly likely. At the College, his Dennis May had been an ardent card player, relieving many a seminarian of his book allowance. In fact, it was all coming back to him. Hadn't the man been thrown out for some such misdemeanour? Some gambling swindle or, on reflection, had it been an affair with a woman? Somehow, a sticky end for him seemed unsurprising.

The next morning, the Monsignor, having told Maureen to emphasise on the phone that it was a favour, agreed to see Father Vincent. Already, he was regretting his generosity in cutting short his lunch to accommodate the meeting.

'I need to go back to Kinross,' Father Vincent repeated.

'No one's stopping you, Vincent.'

'Not as a visitor, as its priest. To do my job.'

Monsignor Drew, as before, was sitting opposite him, his arms hugging his plump little belly, his thumbs twirling in slow motion. His face was pale, but around his lips, like smudged orange lipstick, was a stain of tomato soup which made him look like a slightly cantankerous pantomime dame. Picking up on his subordinate's tone and considering it disrespectful, he leaned back in his chair and said, as if to a difficult child, 'And what, exactly, has brought this on?'

'You don't know? You haven't heard?' Vincent was incredulous.

'Haven't heard what?'

'About yesterday's article in the *Record*.'

'Should I have?'

'I would have thought so, yes,' Father Vincent said hotly. 'After all, it concerns the reputation of the Church too, albeit indirectly. In it I am portrayed – exposed might be a better word – as a "predatory" priest. You know the sort – the sort that has it away with half the female members of the congregation . . . no, of the town.'

'I'm so sorry, Vincent,' Monsignor Drew replied, shaking his head. 'Nobody told me. How horrible for you. How very distressing for you. I'm sorry that I haven't been a greater support to you in your time of trial. It's difficult with James still off – I'm often at sixes and sevens. Run off my feet. Surely the media office has been advising you, handling things for you? They certainly should have been. But, in any event, I fail to see, to be quite frank, why the publication of this sort of nonsense means that you should return to your job. Quite the reverse I would have thought. You've sprung this on me. Surely you're best away from it until all the smoke clears?'

'Dominic,' Vincent replied, trying to restrain the anger he could feel burning inside him, 'perhaps I should remind you that I have not broken my vow of celibacy. I did tell you that before – but, perhaps, its full import did not strike you then. Most of the people of Kinross know me, trust me, but my continued absence, unexplained to date, may be taken even by them as an admission of guilt. I'm prepared to face the Houstons and their thugs, I am prepared to face anyone, everyone. Currently I have nothing to do, no one to see, no tasks to accomplish, no services to take. Nothing! All I do, obsessively, is run over the events leading up to this . . . this debacle. I need my work.'

'Come, come, Vincent, you sound very sorry for yourself. It's not as bad as all that is it? Anyway, the inquiry is not yet complete . . .' The Monsignor sounded genuinely puzzled.

'Inquiry?' Father Vincent said, rising to his feet in his emotion. 'What inquiry? Four weeks have passed – a whole month! I am, obviously, central to any inquiry. My alleged misconduct lies at the very heart of it. So, a good starting-point for any inquiry, I would have thought, would be to speak to me. But nobody has. I remain, to the best of my knowledge, a priest in good standing. So why can't I return to my job?'

'Vincent,' the Monsignor replied, 'it is, as I've explained, out of my hands. You know what lawyers are like, they . . .'

'Yes,' Father Vincent replied, cutting him off mid-sentence, unwilling even to pretend to be conciliatory any longer, 'I do, only too well. I was one once, remember? What I know is that they are acting as your servants, on your instructions. A deadline, if it was imposed, would no doubt be met by any remotely competent member of the profession. The Church is, as we all know, big business. We are, to our shame, a plentiful source of litigation, aren't we? Our account is one that any prudent firm of lawyers would take trouble not to lose. I was foolish in my dealings with Laura Houston, I've acknowledged that and expressed my deep sorrow for it, but that is all. I shouldn't be deprived of . . . of everything, because of a false, I repeat, false accusation made against me.'

'Indeed, indeed,' the Monsignor replied, twiddling his thumbs faster now and looking uneasy. He did not entirely recognise the Father Vincent of old in the angry man confronting him. Nor, since he had assured the Church solicitors only that morning that 'time was not of the essence' in the inquiry, did he know what to do. However, he must take back control of the situation, otherwise the tail really would be wagging the dog.

'I would remind you, Vincent, that until the investigation is over, I . . . we, are unable to reach a conclusion in this matter. A *very* serious allegation has been made against you. I'm with you on the timing issue, of course I am, but . . . nonetheless, you must remember what caused all of this in the first place.'

Before Father Vincent could reply, his mobile rang, and without thinking he answered it.

'You are a disgrace, Father. Just couldn't keep your hands to yourself, could you? If I . . .'

'Shut up!' Father Vincent replied, looking the Monsignor directly in the eye as he did so, and ending the call.

'Vincent . . . Vincent, really! Have you been drinking?'

'No. Why? Have you?'

'For your sake, I'll ignore that remark. I can see you're overwrought. Now, don't you worry yourself. I'll be in touch with Borthwicks first thing in the morning. Fergus's been away. I'll tell them to treat the inquiry as top priority from now on, OK?'

'OK. Good. Thanks.'

'But are you all right, Vincent?' the Monsignor asked, coming across to slip a paternal arm round his shoulders and gazing at him with concern. 'Sleeping well and so on? Are you under the doctor?'

'The doctor, Dominic,' Vincent answered, aware from his superior's manner that he was now regarded as, at best, 'unstable', 'will not get me my job, my home, my cat, my life back. And that's what I need – not a doctor.'

CHAPTER TEN

Callum Taylor's lunch party for his elderly neighbours was not going as well as he had hoped. Setting the table had exhausted him and preparing the meal had seemed, to his septuagenarian, age-dimmed mind, of secondary importance. He had forgotten, yet again, that Marion was a vegetarian, and had had to offer false reassurance about the stock for the leek and potato soup. It could easily have been made with a vegetable base, after all. But could anyone tell the difference? Of course, not!

Now, a fork hovering above them, she was homing in again on the pork sausages. Her raised eyebrows queried their provenance. A half-eaten one lay in a scrape of French mustard on her plate.

'Oh, they're all right – tofu or Quorn,' Callum said blithely and then, unable to resist garnishing one untruth with another, he added, 'you know, made by that photographer woman, poor old John Lennon's wife.'

'Jolly good,' Marion replied, attempting to manoeuvre a couple more onto her plate and succeeding only in knocking one onto his candy-striped tablecloth.

'I'm so sorry, Callum,' she said, picking it up between finger and thumb and sounding genuinely penitent.

'It'll come off . . . the fat . . . the stain, I mean. With a detergent, I expect,' he said, looking mournfully at the greasy mark on the previously immaculate cloth. They were all actually using their decorative napkins too.

Shona, his dead wife, would have had more sense than to put them out. Paper, she used to say, was good enough for all bar royalty.

'Paul's wife, not John's, I think you'll find. And it's no use. I'll have to go again,' George said, throwing his napkin on to the floor and shuffling noisily out of the room, once more in search of the toilet.

'Eastman?' Bridget said.

'No, prostate,' Marion whispered.

'The sausage woman – Eastman?' Bridget repeated, pointing a trembling finger at a sausage on her plate.

'Eastman? The photo people?' Marion inquired, her head shaking slightly as she tried for the second time to spear her remaining half-potato with her fork.

'Linda Eastman was her name. You remember, the Wings woman? American.'

'Right,' Callum replied, 'I'm with you now. Marion, have you heard from Irene lately? Somebody said that her cataract had been unsuccessful. Usually they are a piece of cake, aren't they? Like getting a brand new eye, Shona said. She had both done, after her hip.'

'Nope,' Marion replied, still chasing a potato around her plate.

'You haven't heard from her?'

'Nope. Not since she turned into a Jew. I expect she has only Jewish friends nowadays like herself.'

'So long, farewell, adieu, Auf Wiedersehen, goodbye!' George sang, returning to the table and giving his wife an almost imperceptible shake of the head indicating that his attempt to urinate had been unsuccessful. He was certainly ready to say goodbye. But they would have to return home via the hospital.

'No. A Jew. A *Jew*. Not "adieu" – "a Jew",' Marion clarified. 'She has turned herself into a Jew. It's all something to do with Madonna and the Cabal. She's always been, as she puts it, "A seeker after truth", hasn't she?'

'More sausages anyone?' Callum asked, but nobody appeared to hear him.

'More sausages?' he repeated more loudly, trying to catch any of his guests' eyes. But they were all looking down, their attention focused exclusively on their plates.

'Paul McCartney's wife doesn't make sausages,' Nora said, mouth full of potato, 'she's involved in mine clearance. She's only got one leg left.'

'No,' Callum said, making a resolution that this would be his last party, 'she's got two legs now. Remember, she's called Nancy Cleaver . . . Nancy Lever, something like that.'

'Did he marry the *Strictly Come Dancing* woman then? The one that lived with the football manager, then Trevor . . . Trevor . . . that theatre man?' Marion asked.

'Frances isn't a Jew,' Bridget said brightly, as if at a sudden revelation. 'She's a Buddhist. She goes to a temple somewhere near the soap shop in Bo'ness.'

Once the party had broken up and he had stacked the plates in the dishwasher, Callum went to see the girls and take them some hay. The second he entered their shed, Heidi, the herd queen, came trotting over to greet him, nudging him and helping herself from the bundle to a few stalks before he had a chance to dump the armload into their communal manger. Watching her as she munched away noisily, he was struck by her resemblance to a small camel. With her caramel-coloured pelt, splayed feet and long eyelashes, she looked far more like a species of camel than a goat. The fact that she had won first prize at the Highland Show that year only proved that the three judges had known precisely nothing. Beano, on the other hand, would have been a worthy winner. She had classic Anglo-Nubian looks, with her long, heavily veined ears, Roman nose and fine antelope-like limbs. But there had only been a yellow rosette for her from the ignoramuses. And, as a past president of the British Goat Society, he should know.

The sweet smell and the warmth of the goat shed soothed him. He kicked the straw on the floor about the place, trying to even it out and make sure that they all had a comfortable place to lie for the night. He was relieved to see that the water bucket was still half full, and that none of the girls had deposited their cherries in it. That was one less task to do tomorrow. Minstrel, Shona's favourite and the only Alpine in his herd, sidled up to him and as usual he fished a carrot from his pocket and gave her it to chew on. By all rights she should have died, one of three kids and trodden on by her own mother before she was even free of the afterbirth. That one was a miracle goat.

Unexpectedly, he caught the smell of the Billy in the nearby enclosure and, at that moment, and as if to attract his attention, it let out a brutish, whinnying bellow. Sniffing his own sleeve, the old man wondered whether he stank of goat. All his senses seemed to have dimmed. Just as well George had promised to tell him if he did smell. He would do it too, and take pleasure in it. All very well, except that George's faculties seemed to be fading even faster than his own. Nero's frightful musky scent clung to everything and didn't seem to be eliminated by soap and water. Of course, in his youth he could have drowned it out with Old Spice, Brut or something, but then in those days he would have run a mile from a goat. Or a goatherd like himself, come to that! No one who knew him in those days would recognise him now; sans teeth, sans hair, sans eyes and as fat as butter. He no more resembled himself in his prime than he did his photograph, swaddled tight as baby Jesus, on the occasion of his christening.

Carla's shrill bark woke him from his nap and he realised that the phone was ringing.

'Yes,' he said, trying to enunciate clearly, ashamed that he had fallen asleep in the early evening and determined not to betray the fact.

'Callum?'

'Yes,' he repeated, still unable to recognise who was calling and frustrated by his failure to do so. 'To whom am I speaking?' The caller should have introduced himself, it was his call.

'Don't you recognise my voice?' The tone of the other man suggested that he ought to be able to do so. Rattled, he played the man's few words again in his head.

'No,' he replied, 'I'm afraid I don't.'

'It's me. David.'

'David . . .' His voice tailed off as if in wonderment, as he tried to take in the news. No one should have been more recognisable to him. They had, after all, been lovers for over eight years, even though they had not seen each other for three or more decades. It had happened in another life, in another world. And, if such beings existed, he had been The One. But, on a single fateful night, after too much champagne and with too little self-control he had blown everything. A charming nobody had beckoned and he had succumbed. And with David, there had been no second chance.

Shona had known that she was not Callum's first love, but she did not know who was. The mystery of their dry, fruitless union might have been less mysterious to her if she had done. Unwittingly, she had married a man who divided his life into compartments, each sealed, and each locked. She believed his lies, why should she not? Telling them, he did too.

'What do you want, David?'

'To see you.'

Catching sight of his own wrinkled hand, its arthritic fingers twisting over each other like the limbs of a diseased tree, he shook his head. No one, nowadays, could want to see him. Not literally see him. There could be no pleasure in that for anyone, however close a friend they might be.

'Where?' he said wearily.

'In the Western.'

'The Western General? Are you in hospital, David?'

'Yes.'

'Of course I'll come. But what's the matter?'

'Cancer of the oesophagus. That's why my voice has changed. I'm in a room by Ward 14. It's easy to find – on the second floor. I've a room on my own now. A great luxury as you may imagine. I've never been one for daytime TV . . . but I don't need to tell you that. Will you come?'

'Of course. I said I would. I've got a disabled badge, one of those blue ones that lets you park anywhere, double yellow lines, the lot.'

'Your walking's not so good then?'

'Rheumatoid arthritis. Nothing more than that, apart from old age. I use a Zimmer in the house. I'll come tomorrow. Visiting hours, when are they?'

'Yes. Come tomorrow. I'd love that. You can come anytime now that I'm on my own. Every privilege is mine . . .' He paused, before continuing. 'Will you pray with me, Callum?'

'I'll be there. Say, eleven o'clock?' Was he on his deathbed or something?

'Good. Eleven o'clock. Will you pray with me, Callum?'

'Sure you want me to?'

'Yes.'

'Then I'll pray with you.'

He looked in his cupboard and was pleased to see that the ironing woman had done her job. Plucking a creaseless blue-and-white striped shirt from its hanger he added it to the primrose yellow tie and the fawn pullover that he had already selected. If he fed the billy after the visit there could be no possibility of the goat smell clinging to him, as long as it had not contaminated the clothes chair in the bathroom. Even if it had, that could be solved by storing tomorrow's clothes in the spare room. Blue socks. A pair of thick black cords would set everything off nicely and, perhaps, disguised in such style the ravages of time would be less apparent. He made a mental note to trim his eyebrows, nose and ears too, and to polish his shoes.

David, of course, would be in bed. Maybe, just maybe, if he was not too ill, he would be allowed out to come home with him for a little? Then he could look after him, treat him. Look after him for longer, if they agreed, until others required to do so, at least, and that might be a long time away. He could afford professional nurses, a sister, a matron, if the need arose. Cancer of the oesophagus might even be curable for all that he knew. And an uncle taking in his sick nephew sounded plausible enough. Or he could say they were cousins, the neighbours would buy that. They would have to. Whatever happened he must take his chance. He had been given this opportunity to put things right. To make amends. He would surely do so.

Carla's yapping alerted him to someone at the front door. He bundled her and his clean clothes into the bedroom. No one enjoyed a lapdog snuffling about their ankles, tripping them up, snarling if they as much as tried to pat her. Only Shona had been safe from those plaque-coated teeth.

But as he opened the door to find a young stranger facing him, she managed to escape from her incarceration. Tutting, he bent down to pick her up, and found himself being shoved backwards, indoors, away from any prying eyes.

When her master's body was found, over a week later, the little dog was released. By then the carpet by the front door was in shreds, green underlay exposed, and the bichon's tiny front paws were bloody and torn. An army of rats appeared to have been gnawing at the base of the door. The sharp ridges of the dog's spine protruded, and her dehydrated skin hung off her like an ill-fitting coat. Constable Wren picked her up and cuddled her, smoothing the soft fur on her forehead while talking to her in a gentle, singsong tone as if she was a baby. Later, when she inadvertently squeezed the dog she got a nip and almost dropped her. Hidden under Carla's unkempt coat were three broken ribs. They were the only tangible testament to her bravery. Defending her master, she had earned each broken rib in return for a mouthful of the killer's calf, until, screaming in fury, he had kicked her into unconsciousness. Seeing her lying there lifeless, the old man ceased all resistance, accepting everything the stranger did to him as if it was his due.

CHAPTER ELEVEN

'It's my serve,' Father Damian said, reaching out for the squash ball and clicking his fingers impatiently for it.

'Is it? Right,' Vincent replied, handing it to him and bending over, his palms on his knees as he fought to get his breath back. At least when it was his serve he could do things in his own time, hold up play for a minute or so, give his lungs a chance to recover. Still bent double and trying not to gasp too loudly, he glanced at his opponent. Annoyingly, the man was not even red and had hardly broken sweat. He looked healthy, as if a brisk walk in the cool air had put roses into his cheeks. Somehow, despite his victories in the two earlier games, his whites still appeared crease-free, and it had not even occurred to him to remove his pullover, to at least pretend that he was hot. Had he been modelling sportswear, he would not have appeared less flustered.

The thwack of nylon on rubber alerted Vincent to the fact that the game had started again, and he straightened up, trying locate the little black ball. By the time he had, it was already behind him and he spun round, flailing the air with his racquet. The ball, meanwhile, careered off the back wall and was now dribbling along the floor at his feet.

'Seven–nil,' Damian announced, scooping it up with the end of his racquet in a single, smooth movement, oblivious to the farce of his opponent's play.

One point, Vincent thought, one point would be enough, would amount to a victory for him. It had been eleven–nil in both earlier games, but surely not this one. Honour would be saved, in his own eyes at least, if he could retrieve a single point. Perhaps even Damian would feel that? Superhuman effort might be required but, for a second or so, that could be tried without fear of heart failure. Consciously visualising himself as a big cat, muscles twitching and rippling in readiness to pounce on its prey, he watched his opponent serve. Once more, the ball bounced off the front wall and straight onto the back one. This time he kept his eye on it throughout its entire trajectory and managed, somehow, to belt it after the first bounce. Thrillingly, it hit the front left corner and lodged for a second in the angle, which absorbed all speed from the ball. It then flopped to the floor like a dead bat and, despite his last-minute dive, Father Damian was unable to retrieve it.

'That'll be seven–one, eh?' Vincent said, startled by his own success and, unthinkingly, punching the air in his joy.

'No, it's still seven–nil. You've got nothing, but it's your serve.'

Vincent's massive backswing resulted in a miss-hit, the ball shooting off the frame of the racket and fooling his opponent completely. Freakishly, it struck the front wall above the red line and then dropped spinning to the floor only centimetres from the point of impact. This time, dizzy with elation, Vincent jumped in the air, celebrating his triumph, until he was reminded that the game was not yet over. Less than three minutes later it was, and as they left the court Father Damian was amused by his opponent's euphoria. The man was a wreck, his hair matted with sweat, his face the colour of a beetroot, and he was struggling so hard to breathe that he was whooping like a seal. But he wore a radiant smile. In the changing-room, the two priests hardly exchanged a word. One had no breath to spare, the other was engrossed in thought. Father Damian was trying, and failing, to think of a sensitive, or even tactful, way of mentioning the newspaper article. He had been sickened by it, had crumpled it up in disgust and dropped it in the bin. Sport itself might prove a useful route into the subject.

'Who taught you squash, Vincent?'

'Hugh, a friend, an old friend from college. Neither of us were much good, actually. Sport isn't really my thing.'

'You don't say. Hugh?'

'Brightman.'

'No doubt, but what was his surname?'

'Brightman. And he is . . . he's teaching at a college in Trongsa, in Bhutan.'

'Never come across him. So, it's three pots of honey for me, Vincent, as we agreed. Hand them over. To the victor go the spoils.'

'How about double or quits?'

'At squash?' The man could not believe his luck.

'No – you might have a heart attack. How about a quiz on, say . . . I don't know, anything. Social insects? No, that might give me an advantage. Plucking a subject at random . . . from the ether . . . how about the wines of Australia?'

'Do you think I was born yesterday?'

'Did you even bother to bring your homemade marmalade?'

'I did indeed. You might have improved.' Damian replied, opening his sports bag to show three pots in bubble wrap. He buttoned his black jacket and took out a comb. With his hair slicked down and bag in hand, he held open the changing-room door for his erstwhile opponent.

'See you tomorrow then?' he said.

'Will you?' Father Vincent replied, surprised. He was still trying to stuff his shorts and T-shirt into a carrier bag, and a trainer had just ripped a hole in the bottom of it.

'It's Paul Ogilvie's twenty-first. Yvonne said you were coming. She certainly thinks you are. She told me she was looking forward to seeing you. They all are.'

'Right.' Father Vincent nodded his head. He had forgotten all about the party in Kinross and his promise, given months ago, to attend. He could not disappoint his friend, and if, despite his unexplained absence from the parish, she was still counting on him turning up, he would not let her down. But the thought of returning to the parish in such circumstances weighed heavily on him, sucked all the sweetness from his one-point victory.

'It'll be fine,' Damian said, putting an arm around his shoulder. 'Everyone knows it was trash. They'll say anything, they have to sell papers somehow. I expect sometimes you wish you'd been the one with a foam pie handy for Rupert Murdoch at that Commons committee . . .'

'Yes. Except that on today's form, I'd probably have missed!'

The music from the Windlestrae Hotel could be heard on the far side of the grassy expanse known as Market Park, along the western fringe of the golf course and even at the bowling green, despite its thick hedges. The velvet of the night air was being slashed by the sharp chords of an electric guitar, then pounded to dust by a prolonged and merciless drum solo. In the entrance porch of the hotel, a man leaning against the lintel nodded at the priest as he walked in, raising a wine glass at him in a good-natured mock salute.

The McMillan suite was dark, dense with people, and few took much notice of him as he worked his way through the pulsating crowd, his eyes searching for Yvonne Ogilvie. In the warm, humid atmosphere, he could feel a drop of sweat trickling its way down his brow, coming to rest on an eyebrow. But the heat was only the half of it. He felt tense as a cornered cat. Once his reception would have been entirely predictable, but he could no longer count on that.

'What you doing here?' A man he did not know stood in front of him. His eyes were heavy with drink, his tie loose, and one missing shirt button had created a porthole through which the hairy flesh of his white belly could be seen. A girl, his teenage daughter, pulled on one of his arms, trying to move him away, keep him out of trouble.

'Stop it, Stacey!' he shouted, ripping his arm free so violently that he unbalanced himself and careered sideways onto the dance-floor. He collided with a dancer in full flow, her exposed, tanned flesh rippling in time to the music, lost in a world of rum and coke and the Bee Gees.

'Careful, you,' she said, grinning, her body now supporting his, preventing him from falling over but almost losing her own footing in the process.

'That's my pal, Father Vincent, you're speaking to,' she added, using her hip to shove the man out of the way.

'Hiya, Father.'

'Hiya, Lauren.'

Smiling gratefully at her, the priest moved on, elbowed accidentally in the ribs by an over-enthusiastic dancer, and deafened by 'Bohemian Rhapsody', which had started up and was now being belted out by most of the people on the dance-floor.

'Father! Good to see you!'

The voice came from behind him and he spun round, finding himself looking into Janie Walker's reddened features.

'I . . .' she murmured, beckoning him with a crooked finger for him to come closer, 'I . . . I . . . want you to know . . . I didnae believe a word o' it . . . no' a . . . single word o' it!' Then, winking at him affectionately, she allowed herself to be pulled away by her partner, a bald man in a black leather jacket. Vincent continued to burrow through the crush of people, waves of beer, aftershave and sweat fumes washing over him.

'Hi de hi, Father,' chirruped Mamie, catching his eye as he shouldered himself onwards, and swivelling her bulging hips to the music as if inviting him to dance with her. Having tried and failed to make himself heard above Freddie Mercury, he pointed towards one of the buffet tables, miming a drink, letting her know that he had other

144

things on his mind at present. Finding himself beside a table loaded with filled glasses, he took one and downed it quickly, pleased to have chanced upon some red wine. It was as bitter as grape pips and set his teeth on edge, but he took another mouthful. An elderly man, baseball cap low over his eyes, sidled up to him.

'Hello,' the priest said, 'are you looking for a drink? Red or white?'

'Scum like you, Father, are not welcome here – I read all about you,' the man replied, nodding and smiling benignly at the nearest dancers, then catching Vincent's eye and grimacing as if disgusted at the sight. Father Vincent held his gaze but said nothing. This was neither the time nor the place, but the effort of remaining silent was taking its toll and he found that his whole body was now bathed in sweat.

'You could *not* be more wrong there, Grant,' Yvonne Ogilvie said, coming to the priest's rescue and bestowing a kiss on his cheek. 'Father Vincent's very welcome here – at *our* party. I wanted him here. He's here to celebrate Paul's twenty-first. He baptised both my sons and gave them their first Communion. He's almost part of the family – my family.'

'Thanks,' the priest said, watching as Grant helped himself to a handful of crisps and then disappeared into the melee of people, shaking his head at the way he had been treated.

'I meant it,' the woman said, 'and I hope you'll be back here, in the town, with us all, very soon. Grant's only here because he fishes with Jim, ties his own flies and everything.

He's got a freezer full of roadkill, apparently. It's good to see you, Father. Father Roddy's not a bad man, not a bad man at all, but he doesn't know our ways. He's not you. We all miss you. I'll away and tell Paul that you've made it, and he'll be that thrilled too . . .'

A loud clattering noise interrupted her, as an ashet laden with sausage rolls was knocked off the table by a couple of over-energetic dancers. Tutting loudly, Yvonne Ogilvie left the priest, telling all and sundry to let her through before someone broke their neck slipping on the mess.

'Jim, Jim!' she shouted to her husband. 'Leave those sandwiches alone and go and get one of the staff, eh? There'll be one at reception, or the bar, if nowhere else.'

'Aye, aye, doll. I'm onto it the now.'

Looking over the heads of the revellers, Father Vincent steeled himself to work his way through to the seats on the far side, anticipating a crushed foot or two and drink spilled on him. Out of the corner of his eye, he saw Elizabeth Templeton waving at him. She was sitting beside one of the tables and the seat next to hers was vacant. Helping himself to a couple more of the glasses, this time filled with white wine, he clutched them to his chest and edged his way through the heaving mass of humanity towards her. Twice his elbow was jostled, but keeping tight hold he managed to avoid spilling them onto himself or others.

As he reached her, she smiled up at him and patted the seat by her side. Looking at her in her party clothes, a green silk blouse and a knee-length dark blue skirt, he felt a wave of sadness wash over him. Her smile had been as warm as ever, not a trace of reproach in her eyes. If all of this had never happened, had they been meeting outside the church or by chance in the street, she would have greeted him in the same fashion. Sensing that she seemed to be as comfortable as ever with him, for a second, he wondered if she had read the article. As if she had heard him speak the thought, she said in her husky voice: 'Don't worry, I do know – I heard all about it. The Daily Drivel, we get it in the library along with the rest of them. I know the Houstons too, we all do. You're not the first to get caught up in their stupid games – and they are games.'

'I wish I'd known.'

'This'll all blow over. The next scandal will sweep it out of the way and people have surprisingly short memories.'

'I must admit I wasn't looking forward to returning here, not this way. I want to come back, obviously, but to my own job, my own home. Properly. With things just like they used to be.'

'Is that on the cards, then?'

'My return? Yes. Yes, it is. As soon as I can make it happen. Yes.'

He offered her one of the glasses and she took it, glanced at it and then laughed out loud.

'What's the matter?'

'You have this one! It's got a cigarette-end dunked in it. Are you trying to poison me or something?'

'Oh, but you're a fussy woman!' he said, looking inside the glass himself and then adding, without a thought, 'Take mine. It was dark!'

She took it, smiling at him as she did so. The next number was so loud that it was impossible for them to speak.

So, while it lasted, they sat side by side companionably, watching the dancers, admiring the gusto and skill of the uninhibited and trying not to laugh at the elephantine efforts of a trio of children. A dumpy couple, fuelled by neat vodka, appeared deaf to the barbs hurled at them as they collided first with one dancer and then another, bouncing off them like dodgem cars. Neither showed any signs of injury or pain, despite being elbowed by the irate and poked in the back by the aggrieved. Their eyes were locked on one another and the rest of the world remained out of focus.

In a brief interval between songs, Vincent looked at his friend.

'Is Michael here?'

'No. I came with the Cochranes. He's away . . . inside. In Perth Prison, I'm ashamed to say.'

'Elizabeth, I'm so sorry. What happened?'

'He won't take his medication any more, and I can't force him. He was with his friends . . . although they're not really friends at all. Not as you or I would define the word. Anyway, he was with them and they were all coming back from a party in Graham's car. Graham was so drunk he couldn't drive, so the rest of them persuaded Michael to take over. They all know he's got no licence, insurance, that he's only had four driving lessons in his entire life. You know the lights by the community campus, the ones with the pedestrian crossing beside it?'

'Yes.'

'He hit another young lad, right there, on the crossing. I think he'd been on the booze too, though not with them. After he was hit they all panicked, took off. Thank God the boy wasn't killed, but he got a fractured skull and a crushed foot. He's all right, back at college, I gather, but . . .'

'Forgive me, I've been so preoccupied with my own troubles. How long did he get?'

'Three years. If he's lucky he'll be out in one. If you've time, would you visit him, Father? I get the impression that, at last, he's beginning to think about things. You might be able to help. He might talk to you. To be honest, I'm almost glad he's in there.'

'Glad?'

'Not about the accident, obviously, but I'm glad he's safe. He was driving a lot, not just on that night. And he was being driven by some of those half-witted boys. At least he won't be in a car – lose his own life or take someone else's. Could you go and see him, Father? He asked me to ask you.'

'Of course I will. I'd like to. I've known him practically since he was tiny after all. And to tell you the truth, I haven't got a lot to do at the moment.'

'When will you be able to come back, do you think? You're missed, you know.'

'I'm trying, Elizabeth, I'm trying. Believe me, I'm doing my very best.'

Perth Prison is made up of a number of separate buildings. A few of these are grand old edifices, such as the guardrooms which remain from Napoleonic times, and the gatehouse, with its battlemented centrepiece and clock face dating back to the 1840s. But many of the others look more like the campus of a new university, all steel and tinted glass. Other structures, mostly late twentieth century and uneasy with their penal function, disguise it behind the clichéd architectural style of the bus station or DSS office. Close to the entrance and unfurling in the wind, as if at a royal palace, are flags; the Union Jack and the cross of St Andrew. The third and final flag, however, dispels the illusion of majesty, having the letters 'SPS' emblazoned on it, impressing upon all that the Scottish Prison Service are in charge here. A high perimeter wall, part rubble-built and part pre-cast aggregate panels, an unhappy marriage of old and new, screens the complex from the city, dividing it on the north side from the pleasure grounds of the Inch, and on the west from the Edinburgh road.

Father Vincent, his anorak zipped high to the chin to conceal his dog collar, joined the line of visitors preparing to go through the metal detector. Once he had been scanned, he looked around the waiting-room, thinking he would be able to check out the pamphlets as he usually did. But before he had a chance to do so a queue began to form for entry to the screening-room. Passive, like cows in a slaughterhouse, they all shuffled forwards.

'Open your mouth, please,' a man wearing green Marigold gloves ordered him.

The priest obeyed, trying not to breathe on the prison officer, who was now inches away from his face and inspecting his gums. Beside him, a woman was having her tattooed hands swabbed for traces of heroin or cannabis; silently co-operating, familiar with the routine and accepting meekly that she must be subjected to it. Together, they were then escorted upstairs to the visiting hall. He had been told to go to table 13 and saw, across the room, Michael Templeton waiting for him, already seated, his fingers drumming on the top of the circular glass table.

''Lo, Father,' a man said, tapping him on the elbow as he passed by.

He turned to see one of his parishioners grinning at him. He nodded his head but said nothing, knowing any conversation would attract unwanted attention from the warders. No visit had been scheduled between them this time, although it had many times previously. The fellow, he had discovered many years earlier, had an independent mind, idiosyncratic morality and a very good constitution. He did not consider incarceration to be depriving him of anything very valuable, viewing it as a respite from his otherwise overwhelming urges to possess other people's goods.

''Lo, Father,' the man repeated brightly.

'Fancy seeing you here,' the priest whispered.

Michael Templeton kept his eyes downcast when the priest took the seat opposite him. He was pale, but no paler then when living at home, and his upper lip sprouted fine, fair hair like the cobwebby down on a half-fledged squab. He drummed his fingers silently on the table, the nails bitten to the quick, dried blood visible where his nibbling had gone too far. An old Tourette's symptom had returned, and every few seconds he raised his chin and cleared his throat energetically. For a second, the priest caught a glimpse of the little boy he had first met, brow furrowed in concentration, sucking on his paintbrush as he completed his mother's birthday card.

'Is my mum OK?' he asked, peering upwards slightly but not meeting Father Vincent's eyes.

'She's fine, managing well. You've no need to worry about her, Michael. How are you getting on yourself, in here?'

'All right,' he replied, eyes back on the table.

'Are they feeding you OK?'

'I get by.'

'Sleeping all right?'

'No – but I'll get used to it. I miss my own bed.'

'You'll be pleased to hear that the boy's out of hospital, the one you hit. He's got a cast but otherwise he's fine.'

'OK. Good.'

Despite the priest's continued attempts, the conversation, more or less stillborn, died in minutes. Throughout, the boy's fingers continued drumming, their rhythm broken only by extended bouts of throat-clearing. Looking at him, Father Vincent was reminded of a penitent puppy, tail down, glancing up every so often to ensure that no hand was raised against it. Suddenly, a toddler careered into their table, letting out a loud wail on impact. Apologising as she did so, his granny scooped him up into her arms and carried him, wriggling like a worm, back to the play-area.

'Father,' the youth said, finally raising his eyes, 'will you tell me something?'

'Of course, if I can.'

'My mum will be all right, without me, won't she? You'll look after her?'

'I will, I'll do my best.'

'Promise?'

'I promise.'

The boy smiled his gratitude, scratched the back of his head self-consciously, and then asked, with a spark of genuine vitality in his voice for the first time, 'How's Satan, prince of cats? I remember him when you first got him, when he was just a wee kitten.'

As Father Vincent made his way out of the hall, working his way between the tables, he felt someone tug the hem of his anorak. Surprised, he wheeled round and found himself staring into a pair of pale eyes. They protruded from their owner's face like those of a rabbit suffering from myxomatosis. Gazing at the man, he was sure he had encountered him before. A face like his would not be easily forgotten. Holding his gaze, the prisoner mouthed silently, 'Visit me, Vincent.'

On his table, he put both his hands together as if praying for the favour, then moving them upwards in supplication until they were opposite his chin.

Still unsure who the man was, the priest nodded and carried on walking towards the exit. He tried to place the face, put it in its normal context. If he could do that, with luck a name would emerge from the mist. The prisoner was not one of his parishioners, not from Kinross, he was pretty certain of that. Had he met him on holiday, or at a conference somewhere, or on a retreat? Sparse, grey hair crowned a sloping forehead, above eyes as rounded and protruding as a couple of poached eggs and an unexceptional mouth merged into a receding chin. To whom did those features belong? He ought to know, because their owner had recognised him, called him by name.

Standing outside on the pavement by the Edinburgh road, deliberately exhaling the stale air of the prison from his lungs as the traffic whizzed past, he cudgelled his brain for an answer. The information was, undoubtedly, in there somewhere. Frowning hard, he conjured the image of the man's face in his mind's eye again, trying to associate those features with something, anything that would give him a clue to the man's identity. He sighed out loud when it came to him.

'Penny for them,' a beaming lady said in passing, wheeling her tartan shopping bag behind her. He neither saw nor heard her.

Fig rolls, the man is associated with, of all disgusting things. Fig rolls. But with something else too. Something bleary and strangely unsettling, something disturbing. Anxiety, acute anxiety. Deep in thought, he set off northwards, heading along the Inch to his parked car. A chill wind had risen and his fellow pedestrians, muffled in their hats, scarves and gloves, rushed by, sensing that rain was in the air. Dark clouds were gathering in the sky above, preparing to unburden themselves, obscuring the sun and ready to turn day to night.

'Mine's a pint,' Bertie said, clambering up his cage to get closer to the priest's face. Fixing him with his intelligent little yellow eyes, he waited until Vincent had taken a seat and was apparently relaxed, then shrieked at him, as if he had been thwarted, 'I said mine's a bloody pint! Mine's a bloody pint!'

'Bertie!' Sister Monica said, looking up from her copy of the *Times Literary Supplement* and frowning at the bird. Blinking at her, and as if responding to her shocked tone, the parrot closed his beak around one of the bars of his cage and began to twirl himself down it, eventually coming to rest on a perch less than a foot from the ground. From his new vantage point, he looked up at her as if genuinely cowed.

'Anything interesting?' the nun enquired, seeing the priest returning his letter to its envelope. They were seated opposite one another at a table in the communal sitting-room. Sister Clare, her Dyson temporarily parked by the TV, was doing her morning dusting. Two of the oldest members of the community, Sisters Frances and Jane, were sitting together in armchairs, whiling away their time before the first relaxation session of the day by playing a game.

'If this person was a food, what sort would they be?' Sister Jane asked.

'A meringue. No, no, an Arctic Roll.'

'And weather?'

Sister Frances hesitated. 'Mmm. Clear blue sky, and icy.'

'Do you know of someone called Nicholas Rowe?' the priest asked Sister Monica.

'Author of the *She-Tragedies*, friend of Pope and Poet Laureate?

'Doubtful. This one's currently in prison. He saw me there a week ago, when I was looking in on someone else.

He's got permission for me to visit him. Got it all arranged for today, in fact.'

'Are you going to go, then?'

'I'll have to, I think. He used to work for James, before . . .'

'If they were a piece of music?' Sister Jane persevered, looking baffled, sufficiently intrigued to neglect her crossword.

'Elgar – "Pomp and Circumstance".'

'I've got it,' Sister Jane said, rising from her seat, then turning round to smooth its creased loose covers, 'it's Prince Charles, isn't it?'

'No,' Sister Monica interjected, unable to resist, 'it's Margaret Hilda Roberts or Thatcher – obviously.'

As Sister Frances was now bent double with a coughing fit, all Sister Monica got by way of a reply was a fleeting thumbs-up.

'You weren't even supposed to be playing,' said Sister Jane peevishly.

'Mine's a *fuckin'* pint, boyo! A *fuckin'* pint, you drongo!' Bertie squawked, clambering up his bars again to glare at the priest again, as a passing nun flicked an orange duster at his head.

'Where do you go from there, my feathered friend?' Sister Monica enquired pertly of the bird, and added, by way of explanation to Father Vincent, 'He is, fortunately, unacquainted with the C-word – the one derived from coney.'

'C-word, C-word!' the parrot trilled, before getting his revenge on Sister Clare, making her jump by producing a perfect facsimile of the sound of her Dyson roaring into life.

Had Vincent Ross no sense of duty he would not have visited Nicholas Rowe. On the rare occasions they had met he had instinctively disliked him, never understood him. But he could not plead lack of time or even an alternative engagement, because in his new, slow-motion life, he had almost nothing to do. Why the man might want a visit from him, he could not fathom. They hardly knew each other, and apart from the priesthood had little in common. From their few past encounters in the Bishop's office, he was almost sure that his own lack of friendly feeling was reciprocated. In character, Rowe had the reputation of being the administrator's administrator; someone whose eyes lit up at the thought of well-kept files, efficient data storage and information retrieval systems; a mind happy devising new and improved protocols and processes, revelling in the world of audit and regulation and worshipping at the altar of health and safety. Faced, however, with a living, breathing person, he would recoil like a hermit crab from a probing finger.

For decades he had been employed in the diocesan office, and he had become so indispensable that the Bishop's own ability to read a spreadsheet, draw conclusions from a financial report or reconcile accounts had withered away, shrivelled from disuse. In the diocesan office Nicholas Rowe had reigned supreme, was deferred to by all, and, unthinkingly, had intimidated most of the parish priests in the diocese, including Vincent. He had, long ago, classified, and dismissed, the little priest as just another 'people person', a damning epithet in his view.

His own particular strength, in his mind, was his skill at information-gathering, something fundamental to all efficient operations. For that reason, and that reason alone, he knew everything there was to know about everybody. He did not gather the information himself, his lack of charm making him incapable of doing so, but relied instead on his secretary, Miss Boyars. A middle-aged, devout spinster in thrall to her boss, she had a deep interest in people, and was described by him to others as an 'inveterate gossip'. But, ruthlessly, and on a daily basis, like a dairy farmer with an old Friesian cow, he milked her for information.

Routinely they had elevenses together. Beaming at her over the instant coffees and fig rolls, he watched as she blossomed in the warmth of his smile. Sipping from his cup, he would invite her to share any particularly exciting titbits with him. Eager to please, she never failed, handing over her little store of tittle-tattle in exchange for his approval, and considering it a very fair return. Unlike him, the minute the gossip left her mouth she had forgotten it. Later, she would be surprised herself by the extent of his knowledge about Father X or Father Y. How did he do it, she wondered, looking at him with renewed respect. The answer, for a man like him, was of course, simple. He had created a large database he called 'Gold Dust' to which she did not have access. All her offerings had been meticulously tabulated, with details of the original source, the content, the date on which it had been imparted. Then, a single letter had been allocated to each item. 'A' signified 'reliable', 'B' signified 'probably reliable' and 'C' signified 'possibly unreliable'.

The administrator's career had ended, dramatically, with his conviction for paedophilia. The offences for which he had been imprisoned had occurred in the 1980s during a brief period spent as a teacher of maths at a private school. On hearing the charges against him he had immediately responded by admitting his guilt. He had, he knew, no defence.

In prison, he whiled away his waking hours as a librarian, attempting to improve the cataloguing system and compiling, for his own amusement, a chart correlating types of offenders with types of books. The 'beasties', those like him imprisoned for sexual crimes, had an unexpected penchant for Catherine Cookson, he was delighted to discover. The embezzlers tended to go for Jeffrey Archer, and the thieves for Danielle Steel. Everyone inside, without exception, liked Jeremy Clarkson. Most of the time he was either bored or afraid but, to date, he had managed to avoid assault by the simple expedient of allying himself to the biggest bruiser that he could find. His letter-reading and letter-writing skills functioned as a currency in the prison, and after one of his letters resulted in a lawyer reconsidering the prospects of an appeal, he was looked upon with awe by his fellow inmates. That feat had earned him the nickname 'Judge Rowe'.

'I saw you, Vincent,' he said, sounding excited, eyes round as golf balls, 'and I couldn't resist, just couldn't resist, getting you back. I can't tell you how dull it is in here.'

'Yes, I expect it is a bit lonely,' Father Vincent began, already unsure where this conversation was going.

'Don't be ridiculous. I'm bored, not lonely! Why would I be lonely?'

'I imagine it takes time to find friends . . .'

'I don't need friends, Vincent. I never have. I need inter-est, stimulation, neuronal activity – *news*. Have you any news for me?' Rowe fingered his ear lobe intently as if to check that it had not disappeared.

'Mmm . . .' Father Vincent Ross said. Then, remember-ing Dennis May's murder and considering it likely that Rowe might know him too, he added, 'Dennis May's dead – murdered. It was in the *Scotsman*.'

'My, my,' Rowe replied. 'Him too. I'd heard about Cal-lum Taylor, Lizzie Boyars told me in her last letter, but not him. Of course, the bad boys are all in the book. Mind, so am I by now, I expect. You too, probably, come to think of it. We might be next to each other, back to back, with "R" for Ross and "R" for Rowe.'

'What are you talking about?' Father Vincent asked, not following this thread at all.

'In the book, the Secret Archive,' he replied. 'May was in it for . . . let me think . . . no, easy. Same as me, but he was compulsive. He'd had psychotherapy, been coun-selled, in treatment with the Servants of the Paraclete, the works, but . . . he was, as I say, unstoppable. As he was never laicised they kept tabs on him forever. They had to, of course. Callum Taylor was different – he "fell in love" with a sixth-year pupil and they moved him on, obvi-ously, but it didn't work. Eventually the pair of them lived together for a bit – not in Bo'ness, I think, but somewhere up north.'

'You're in this book too?

'Certainly. I expect so. Not that I made the entry this time, another hand will have attended to that.'

'And I'll be in it too?'

'Well, after your misdemeanours . . . we get the papers in here – well, all the tabloids, anyway. Frankly, Vincent, the way you have been behaving! I don't know how you managed to keep it all under wraps for so long. Word usually gets out, doesn't it? Almost always! But I had no idea, no idea at all, and Lizzie was as good as useless.'

'Lizzie?'

'Busy Lizzie, my secretary. You *goat*! Come to think of it, you'll not be in that book. Another one, maybe, but not the green leather-bound tome I'll be in with May, Taylor and the rest of them.'

'Why will I be in a different one?'

'Because it was taken, stolen from the office, from James's office when he was attacked. Your misdemeanours came after that, didn't they? Well, the exposure of them, anyway. So you'll be in a brand-new volume, I expect. A red one, instead of the old green one, perhaps? You might be the first entry on the otherwise white pages.'

'I hope not.'

'Now, I'd like some chocolate, please.' He held out both hands, cupping them like a beggar. 'From the vending machine. You'll have money on you, eh?'

'Not a bean. Cocoa or otherwise,' Vincent replied, rising, getting ready to leave.

That evening, in his room at the Retreat, Father Vincent dragged the cardboard box out from under his bed. The first bottle which came to hand was a Chilean Merlot with a screw-top. He filled the glass to the brim, feeling he had earned it after his meeting with Nicholas Rowe. The man was corrupt, unclean and completely unrepentant. No spoon was long enough to sup with him, and he felt tainted by the meeting, having to listen to his excited words, seeing his unconcealed glee at Vincent's own fall. But, perhaps, thanks to him, the puzzle had been solved. The man in the confessional, whoever he was, had crowed about two things. His first boast had been of killing the Bishop. But his second, at the time, had gone quickly from the priest's mind, because it had not appeared to make any sense.

'I got it. I got it – and that's what really matters.'

Now, it did. But only if Rowe's tale could be relied upon, and that sick imp enjoyed power, gloried in his ability to manipulate others and would cackle with laughter at the very thought of sending a blind man into a labyrinth to stumble, trip and circle about for all eternity. Vincent would be that blind man. Hard facts alone could be counted on. There were three facts in this case. The Bishop had been attacked. Whoever had attacked him remained free and had boasted about getting, taking, something. Two men, both former priests and, allegedly, listed in the Secret Archive as paedophiles, had recently been murdered. But were those three facts connected?

Looking out of his window, he took another swig. Briefly, his attention was caught by the sound of geese flying overhead, their liquid cries faint against the noise of the wind. A fraying skein was travelling northwards, a couple of stragglers hundreds of feet behind the main flock. Thinking about things, it was inconceivable that the Church would not have such a record. All that then needed to be confirmed was whether anything had been stolen from the Bishop's office. Rowe's word was not enough. Allan was the man to talk to; he would know, or, if not, he would find out.

CHAPTER TWELVE

Allan Ross was a sociable individual, extrovert and easy-going. He had many and varied allegiances and enthusiasms and, despite his hectic life, was rarely conscious of any conflict between them. In any event, living in the moment as he invariably did precluded any deep consideration of such matters. A good goal by Ryan Gauld or Gary Mackay-Steven at Tannadice Park could draw the sting from any marital argument, however heated it might have been. Returning home, exhilarated, belly replete with five cans of Tennent's Special and a Chinese carry-out, his memories of the game kept him warm, oblivious to his wife's habitual post-match frostiness.

Beside him in bed that night, their flesh touching, she might fume over his thoughtlessness for never repairing the weak flush in the toilet or letting the lawn turn into a jungle. But he bore no grudges against anyone, meeting her annoyance with genuine sweetness, and long ago having forgotten that they had had an argument, never mind what lay behind it. Although he was in his late forties, his plump, cherubic face remained doughy and unlined, and he looked what he was, a middle-aged, overgrown boy. Peter Pan made a conscious decision not to grow up. Allan Ross had not been so deliberate about it, but fate had decreed that, like an axotl, he would remain in a permanent state of immaturity.

The faith of his birth, Catholicism, with its inescapable emphasis on sin, had never suited him. Consequently on marriage to Audrey he had taken the opportunity presented to him, abandoned his religion and adopted a new allegiance, one more in keeping with his own tastes. The Episcopal Church, into which he had been received, appeared to lack passionate attachment to anything very much, was neither dogmatic nor bombastic and required very little from its followers: token appearances in church at Christmas and Easter, the provision of regular donations in little brown envelopes and Audrey's participation in the occasional Bring and Buy sale. Membership of it was less tribal, less demanding, he had concluded, than that of Alyth Anglers or the local tennis club. It brought with it no clubhouse cleaning, no open days with compulsory attendance, no quiz nights or committee meetings. Loyalty was desirable, but not required.

That morning, Police Sergeant Ross was relaxing, his coffee mug clamped between his hands, and his feet up on his desk, when a head appeared around his door.

'Vincent!' he said, pleased to see his younger brother. They had arranged a meeting, but not for another ten minutes.

'I'm early, I know. Does now suit?'

'Yes. Derek's out, looking into a report of a stolen car on Reform Street. Take a pew. He'll not be back for a bit.'

The priest sat down, feeling slightly uneasy at occupying someone else's desk and finding himself faced with a screensaver showing an unfamiliar woman in an eye-poppingly low-cut dress. In front of the screen, a crushed Coke can rested on a plate with an abandoned, half-eaten sausage roll. A pile of thick blue folders was balanced precariously on the edge of the usual occupant's metal in-tray, half the contents of one of them spilling onto the desk.

'Did you ask about . . .' Vincent began, realising how tense he was when the phone on his brother's desk began to ring and in response his shoulder muscles went into spasm.

'It'll go onto voicemail in a second,' Allan said, ignoring the call and finishing off the contents of his mug, placing it, carefully and centrally, on his favourite coaster. It was a memento from an unusually protracted post-match session in the Braes and had been given in honour of the number of pints of lager he had managed to down.

'Yep. I did ask about . . .' he continued, catching his brother's eye, 'and nobody knows anything about it. No theft was reported. It was a green book, you said, a book of names, eh?'

'Yes. Big. Leather. It contained names and addresses, and, I suspect, more. It may have had other details about the people listed in it. I don't know, I've never seen it myself.'

'After your call I went and spoke to the DCI, Donny Keegan, about you. Donny said . . .'

'About me, Al? But why on earth? I specifically asked you on the phone just to see what you could find out, behind the scenes . . . casually. To leave me out of it. That was the whole point. I don't know what's going on, I told you that, and I didn't enjoy my last visit from your colleague, Mr Spearman. I was hoping to keep myself out of the picture this time, as far as possible. I'm in a difficult enough situation as it is, Allan, a very difficult situation. I wish I could explain . . .'

'Yes, but . . . I know Donny, you see. We were at Tullieallan together and it seemed the quickest way, the best way. You know, to go to the top and everything. He's the main man, he was in charge of the whole investigation. He won that bottle of your mead I put in the raffle, by the way. I could have farted around for ages asking people about it and never found out anything. I just took my chance when it came and, when I saw him, I asked outright.'

'What did you say?'

'To him?'

'Yes. To him.'

'Nothing much. I said that you were convinced that a book had been stolen from the office when the Bishop was assaulted.'

'Shit! Allan, I never said that!' Vincent interrupted, shaking his head. 'I just wanted you to find out *if* anything had been taken. I never said that anything had been stolen. You've stuck a stick into a hornet's nest.'

'Come on, Vincent,' Allan replied, looking crestfallen. 'You're talking to me, remember. I know you. I knew you must have been pretty convinced, otherwise you wouldn't have asked me. That's right, isn't it? I went to the very top to find out for you, and I have. I've done it. Nothing was taken.'

'OK. Yes, yes, you have, Al. And thanks very much. Thanks for looking into it for me. I'll give you a ring tonight, OK?' Vincent rose from the chair, hardly aware he was doing so, but obeying some sixth sense which was telling him to get out of the place as quickly as possible.

'One second, Vincent,' Allan said, rising with him and crossing the room to stand opposite him. 'Donny wants to see you. He's in the station today. But don't you call him Donny, mind. Chief Inspector to you. I told him that you were coming here. He thought that a little chat might be in order.'

'A little chat?' the priest replied, feeling his stomach lurch at the words. His brother's open, anxious, childlike eyes, now fixed upon him in concern, told him everything that he needed to know about his own folly. None of this was Allan's fault. The man, despite a career in the police force spanning over twenty-five years, possessed no guile. Entrusting him with such a delicate task had been like asking a hen to polka or a goldfish to croon. Subtlety formed no part of his vocabulary and his only experience of calculation, abandoned with pleasure decades ago, involved blackboards and chalk. He had, as Vincent had anticipated, shown little curiosity as to why his brother might be interested in the assault on the Bishop. A fleeting reference to 'my employer' had sufficed to quell any scruples. Then, artlessly and characteristically, he had moved on to matters of real interest to himself and therefore, surely, to the whole world: Gloria's likely results in her nationals, and the escape of Martin's pet rat. Allan Ross's life centred around his family, plus football, and from one day to the next he did not think about his brother. It was not that he did not care about him. Reminded of his existence, he cared deeply. But in contrast to the vivid primary colours in which he viewed his own life and that of his immediate circle, the pastel shades of priestly life passed him by.

'Yes, Donny said he'd like a wee chat with you. Don't worry, Vincent, he's one of the good guys. One of his sisters-in-law, Susie Drysdale, lives in Kinross, you know at the farm, the one at the far end of the loch? You'll get on just fine together; he goes to Our Lady of Succour in Dudhope Crescent.'

'I certainly do – feels as if I'm never out of the place! Would now be all right for our chat?' a cheery voice said, as a large man in plainclothes advanced into the room. The sleeves of his pink shirt were rolled up, revealing golden-haired, fleshy forearms, and he looked hot. There were dark stains in his armpits and his brow glistened under the strip lighting.

'Yes, now's fine,' Allan Ross replied, as if the remark had been addressed to him. Knowing that there were only two chairs in the room, he added, 'I'll get us another one, eh. It'll just take a tick.'

'No need,' Detective Chief Inspector Keegan replied. 'This'll only take a second. You could go and help out at the charge bar, Allan. I'll speak to Vincent – if I may call you Vincent? – on my own, for now.'

'Of course, sir,' Allan Ross replied, retreating through the door, coffee mug in hand.

Seated once more before the image of the busty woman, Father Vincent dragged his eyes away from her cleavage and forced himself to concentrate on his surroundings. He tried to shrug off his anxiety, remind himself that he had once viewed the police as no more than adversaries in a game. 'Plods' they had called them in the solicitors' office and gown room. But the old professional insouciance that he had worn like armour and which had served him so well had gone, and suddenly he knew how his clients of old felt, naked and afraid, in the lion's den. However innocent they might be. In here, canon law would come second to the criminal law.

'Vincent,' the man began, addressing him almost matily, as if they were colleagues or friends, 'Allan told me about the book. Can you tell me how you came to first hear anything about this theft?'

'No, Chief Inspector Keegan, I'm afraid I can't.'

'No?'

'No.' Now, he thought, the informality would be ditched. But he was wrong.

'Of course, silly of me,' the policeman exclaimed, smiling and leaning forward. 'I'm very sorry. My fault entirely, Vincent. I should have made something quite plain from the outset. I spoke to Sergeant Spearman after he saw you the last time and I understood what you were trying to get across to him. He didn't, he's a bluenose, you see. A black Protestant – practically a Wee Free in some of his attitudes. No knitting on Sundays and so on. But, as one of the faithful, I understood . . . correction, understand, completely. Com-plete-ly. How you'd first heard, I mean. So you need have no worries on that score. No worries at all.'

'Thank you.'

'Now that we've got that little issue out of the way,' the Inspector continued, keeping his eyes unswervingly on the priest as he spoke, 'and we know that the Bishop's attacker is dead . . .' He paused momentarily, as if waiting for the priest to say something, interrupt him, before continuing. 'Meehan, the man who attacked the Bishop is dead.'

'You're sure he was the Bishop's attacker?'

'Means, opportunity, motive, confession in the note. What more could you ask for? We've no doubts. Why, have you?'

'I know Raymond's voice.'

'And? I have to have something to work on, Father. The Monsignor found it entirely plausible, and he knew the man too. Have you nothing else to add?'

'I know Raymond's voice, that's all I can say.'

'Right, well, if that's it we'll turn to the book for the moment, shall we? The book that Allan told me you're concerned about and which was, supposedly, taken from the Bishop's office. The one with the addresses and so on in it. Can you tell me anything else about it?'

'Just to clarify things in my own mind, Chief Inspector, are you telling me then that a book *was* reported stolen? I thought from what Allan said that nothing had gone missing.'

The policeman leaned back in his chair, hands behind his head, cogitating, and inadvertently displaying his oval-shaped sweat stains in their entirety. Less than two minutes had passed but, already, he had learned one thing. Allan and Vincent Ross might be brothers but they required very different handling.

'No,' he began, 'no, I'm not saying that at all. In fact, I can confirm that no report of any theft was made when the

Bishop was found. Allan was entirely correct. No church property was found in Meehan's house either. But I'm interested in you, Father, very interested. I'd likely be – after all, you knew about the attack before anyone else . . .'

'I told your sergeant, I wasn't involved in any way,' Father Vincent retorted, frowning unconsciously, unnerved by the note of accusation that he was sure he could hear creeping into the man's tone. Before he knew it, he might fall foul of criminal law or canon law, or both.

'Relax, Father. Relax. I told you, I understand completely how you knew. I'm not suggesting for a second that you were involved. All I want to know is what you think is in the book.'

'I'm getting muddled. Are you talking about the book that hasn't been stolen?'

'Yes.'

'The not-stolen books, plural, no doubt. I imagine the Bishop has a fair collection of them, of books that haven't been stolen. Anyway, I still don't understand, if there is no stolen book then there can be, surely, nothing in it? Have I misunderstood something – was a book stolen then?'

'No. Focusing purely on the book you're interested in.'

'I've never seen it, or its contents. It's an employment record of sorts, I think. Full of black marks.'

A frown crossed the policeman's face. Seeing it, it occurred once more to the priest that Nicholas Rowe might have been playing games with him. Manipulating him and disturbing him, just for the fun of it. It would be in character. He had a reputation for deriving pleasure from the grilling that he subjected priests to when their accounts did not balance, befuddling them with his talk of fixed assets, double-entry bookkeeping and contingent liabilities.

But, more likely, the book had indeed been stolen and he – no, Monsignor Drew – had failed to draw the police's attention to their embarrassing, their compromising loss. Perhaps they had only discovered that it was missing days later. But without a report to the police there would be no search for it, and it might never be found. Crucially, its contents would not be exposed. If they were, the police would be desperate to get their hands on it, and for their own reasons, not just to solve the reported crime. In amongst the few drunks, lechers and embezzlers within the Secret Archive, would be a fair number of paedophiles.

'We'd be interested in that.'

'But if it hasn't been reported as stolen?'

Sighing good-naturedly, the Inspector nodded his head at the priest's words, and, as if he followed and accepted his logic, he answered, 'You're right, of course, Father. Incidentally, Allan told me about your present little difficulty, your present troubles and travails. I hope you can return to Kinross soon. Hell has no fury and all that. Take it from me, one who knows all too well what they can be like once they've got you by the short . . . well, once they've got you. Women, eh? We can't live with them, but we can't live without them. Well, most of us. One other thing. A very important thing. A favour, if I may.'

'Yes?'

'If a book – your book – stolen from the Bishop's office, ever came to light, came to your attention, would you let me know? At present, as you'll appreciate, we can do nothing. Devote neither time, money nor sweat to the matter. With no theft reported, I can devote no resources to it – however much I might like to. But I would like to help – to see it, whatever it may contain.'

'Yes, I'd let you know immediately,' Father Vincent replied, without a moment's hesitation. If the Church's attitude to paedophilia had genuinely changed, as was asserted on an almost daily basis by the hierarchy from the Pope downwards, there could be no reason to withhold the thing from the police. Not that there ever had been one, in his view, whatever those who covered up such things in the past might say. It would contain evidence, be evidence, just as much as fingerprints, DNA or fibres of fabric. Anyway, if Rome had, not before time, decided that the Augean stables were to be cleaned out, he would wield a dung-shovel eagerly, along with the rest of them, whether they wore cassocks, uniforms or plainclothes. In fact he would do it, even if Rome had not changed.

Abruptly, the policeman stood up, walked towards him and, to Vincent's surprise, extended a large ham of a hand towards him. 'Good luck, Father,' he said. 'You're a good man. If you need my help, just ask.'

Pleased that Keegan seemed to have understood his predicament, and appeared to trust him, he took his hand and shook it gladly. At last, he thought to himself, he was not on his own. He had found an ally, and a powerful one at that.

In the garden of the Bishop's office in Dundee, Monsignor Drew was seated at one end of the white cast-iron bench and Father McBride sat at the other. Both men were enjoying the warmth of the spring sunshine, their eyes shut, arms folded over their bellies and legs crossed. The sun glinted off their highly polished black leather brogues, as if they were made of jet. Neither was actually asleep but both were uncomfortably full, weighed down by a steak and kidney pudding, courtesy of Sister Celia. Like a mother blackbird, all of her maternal urges were channelled into feeding them, attending to their gaping beaks. And happily, unlike any other fledglings, they would never leave the nest.

The petals of the snowdrops in the garden had withered, leaving behind green seed heads on spindly stalks. A single daffodil had forced its way through the hard earth and stood erect, head tight, still furled, like a lone bather unwilling to remove her towel and expose her body to the cold air.

Just as the Monsignor was about to drop off, his mobile rang and, rubbing his eyes, he answered it. 'I see, Alison. Yes. He's got no appointment? Then send him away. Insistent, was he, indeed! Oh, he'll wait, will he – till Kingdom come if need be. Aha. No, no, not to worry. If you've got to go, you've got to go. Send him out. Yes, now. I've a few minutes to spare before I set off for St Andrews.'

'Botheration!' he said to himself as he stuffed his mobile back into his pocket.

'What is it?' Father McBride asked, his eyes still closed, basking in the unseasonal warmth.

'Vincent Ross is on the rampage again. Honest to God, you'd think *I* was the one who'd done wrong, the way he's taken to hounding me.'

'That's the one that had a woman on the side, eh? Will I leave the pair of you alone?'

'If you please, Kevin.'

The young priest rose, stretched his arms skywards, yawned noisily like a dog and wandered off in the direction of the Bishop's office. Vincent nodded at him as they passed one another, aware that the other priest offered no greeting in return.

'Vincent!' the Monsignor said, patting the space on the bench beside him in an avuncular fashion, but not leaning back as before. 'Lovely day, eh,' he added affably, 'and rare enough for this time of year.'

'Lovely, Dominic. It is a lovely day,' Vincent began, 'and thanks for seeing me. You'll be in a rush, Alison told me. I just came to let you know that I saw the police again, earlier today.'

'Mother of God! What have you done now?' Monsignor Drew exclaimed, blinking hard and looking at the man beside him with horror.

'Nothing. I've done nothing,' Vincent replied, antagonised, catching a glimpse of his superior's real opinion of him. 'I went there of my own accord. I went because Nicholas Rowe told me that when the Bishop was assaulted, a book was taken by his attacker.'

'You went to the police about that! How did you come to be seeing Nick in the first place?'

'It's a long story. Too long, trust me; you'll not have the time. I know you're due to leave for St Andrews, Alison made a point of telling me. Suffice it to say, I visited him, at his request, in Perth Prison.'

'He's a blessed troublemaker, that one,' the Monsignor said, shaking his head. 'A bad apple – ready to infect the whole barrel with his horrible brown mould.'

'He told me about the book, the record which detailed the misdeeds of the priests of the diocese. He said that it had been stolen.'

'Rubbish. It's all complete rubbish, Vincent. You should know better. He's a troublemaker. I told you he simply wants to blacken the Church, besmirch it.'

'So it hasn't been stolen?'

'He's a bad one, him. He'll say anything . . .'

'The book wasn't stolen?'

'There is,' the Monsignor snapped, rising to his feet and looking down at his colleague, '*no* such book!'

'But,' Vincent said, genuinely taken aback by the response, 'there's bound to be, surely? You employ these people, us . . . apart from anything else, you'd need a record of such things. You decide where they go, when they go, whether they go . . .'

'Vincent!' Monsignor Drew retorted, 'I've heard enough, really, *enough*! You misbehave – do wrong, in short, and then harry me, and there's no other word for it – demanding, yes, you did, you demanded to be reinstated. I'm finding this intolerable, quite intolerable . . .'

'Monsignor Drew,' Vincent replied hotly, rising to his feet and facing his colleague, 'I didn't come here to "harry" you about anything. I never even mentioned my own case.'

'Your case, your case,' the Monsignor muttered, 'all you can think about is your case. You're obsessed. You did wrong and you simply have to accept the consequences.'

'As I said,' Father Vincent continued, 'I haven't come about my case. I've come about the theft of the book. The police say . . .'

'There is,' Monsignor Drew said, his face now flushed with temper, 'no such book. No such record. How dare you, you of all people, set yourself up in this way? Out of good manners, I agreed to see you. You have made no appointment but, nonetheless, I see you. I'm supposed to be somewhere else already, but for you I made an exception And here you are harrying me about yourself, about some non-existent book . . .'

'You have no record of the misdemeanours of any priests in the diocese then? Let's see, shall we? Suppose in 2006 Father . . . Father Christmas, a known alcoholic, abuses a child in his parish of Gateside, a complaint is received and dealt with. The man goes to prison. When he comes out, after counselling and whatever else you give them, he applies to you for another job in the diocese. Are you telling me that you, his employers, have kept no records about him?'

'How dare you attempt to cross-examine me!'

'No,' Vincent retorted, 'how dare you hide things, after all that has happened . . .'

In his cold fury, he could not bring himself to finish his sentence, or even look at the other priest.

The Monsignor suddenly sat back down on the bench, eyes closed and head bowed. He put his hands together as if in prayer, but hooked his thumbs under his chin, breathing slowly in and out between his fingers, as if to calm himself.

'Vincent,' he said quietly, the sound of his voice muffled by his hands, 'sit down.'

'No.'

'Who did you see at the police station?'

'A Detective Chief Inspector Keegan.'

'Fine. Good. I repeat – no such book was stolen. It was not removed.'

'That,' Father Vincent replied, turning his back and walking away in disgust, 'is not what you said.'

Sister Monica, giving way to Vincent's pressure, and taking his sorry state into account, had finally relented and accepted a glass of his best South African Cabernet Sauvignon. They were sitting, side by side, in the communal lounge with only Bertie for company. The bird was scuttling up and down its cage continuously, patrolling it as if annoyed that nobody was paying any attention to it and intent upon remedying the situation.

'What d'you taste?' Father Vincent asked, swirling the wine around his glass, putting his nose to the rim to catch its full bouquet. He would make a connoisseur of her yet.

'Sweetness, earthiness, fruitiness, nothing very unexpected.'

'No hint of cherries – no undertone of violets? No breath of damp grass?'

'Have you had anything to eat tonight, Vincent?'

'No. No trace of vanilla oak spice? Not a smidgeon of tobacco?'

The parrot came to a halt at the level of the nun's ear and bellowed, '*Not a smidgeon of tobacco?*'

'Sssh, Bertie!'

'It's full-bodied like a . . . medieval kitchen maid, or an aged . . .'

'Scottish nun? I thought I'd better get it in first!'

'*Get it in first, get it in first, get it . . .*'

'Sssh, Bertie.'

'*Sssh, Bertie!*' the bird repeated, his head cocked to one side, fixing the woman with his unblinking stare, his pupils like pinpricks, his beak opening and closing silently as if struck dumb.

'Bertie,' she said returning his gaze, 'I'll only say this to you once, only once, mind. Any more of your antics and I'll get the cloth cover. The *cloth cover*, OK?'

Father Vincent's phone chimed, letting him know he had a text. As he read it, he laughed out loud.

'Well, well,' he said, putting the phone back in his pocket, 'there's a thing. That's Fergus McClaverty, the solicitor, the one investigating me, the whole mess. He's arrived here now. He'd like to see me this very minute.'

'Good luck,' Sister Monica said, finishing her wine and adding, 'take the Sophie Barrat room. It's not been used today because the reiki session was cancelled, but it was cleaned this morning in readiness for it. We'll put your supper in the oven.'

In his traineeship with Elliott & Elliott, Vincent had taken hundreds of precognitions. The skill in taking them, he had learned over time, was to know as much as possible about the subject matter before the first question was asked, but to keep an open mind. With even a little knowledge, conflicting versions of events could more quickly be recognised and, sometimes, even reconciled. Differing perceptions could be properly explained, inconsistencies checked out and illogicality exposed. It was a sifting process. Sometimes there genuinely was more than one version of the truth. Fergus McClaverty, a bluff young fellow with a fashionably large-knotted tie and hair brushed flat over one side of his forehead, did an adequate job. But he did not attempt to hide his own complete ignorance of the facts, and asked, 'The woman, was she married?'

'Yes.'

Surprised that he had not known at least this, Father Vincent enquired quite mildly whether he had been given any information from on high about the situation he was supposed to be investigating. No, he replied artlessly, there had been a letter of instruction but in the afternoon rush he had not had a chance to go back to the office and re-read it. Hector Alexander, his senior partner, had waylaid him on his way back from an employment tribunal and redirected him here.

'So, this morning, you had no idea that we'd be speaking together?'

'This morning,' the young man smiled, patting his smooth hair to check that it was still in place, 'I thought I'd be taking my girlfriend to Nando's in Perth tonight. So someone on high must have fairly yanked old Hector's tail. Suddenly, this report has become *quam primum*!'

Three of the nuns were watching the television. Curled up like a dormouse, Sister Agnes had fallen asleep in a large armchair, her spindly legs in their oversized slippers dangling an inch or two above the fawn-coloured carpet. Gentle snores emanated from her open mouth.

'It's the news,' Sister Monica said, as he took the chair beside her, 'it's nearly over. We're on the regional bit. Have you had a bite to eat yet?'

'Yes, and I've washed up my plate . . .'

'Murder, murder and more murder – in Glasgow,' Sister Frances chipped in, 'or murder, football, more murder and more football – in Glasgow.'

'The police were called today . . .' the newsreader began, batting her long eyelashes at her viewers, 'to a house in the village of Cleish, Kinross-shire . . .'

'My! An east coast murder?' Sister Frances murmured. 'By a Glaswegian, no doubt.'

'Sssh!' Sister Monica hissed, determined for once to hear the whole report.

'. . . where an elderly gentleman, Mr Patrick Yule, aged eighty-two . . .'

'Patrick Yule!'

'Sssh!'

'. . . was found dead. His death is being treated by the police as suspicious. And now to the football . . .'

'Patrick Yule! Of all people – how dreadful! I thought he was already dead,' Sister Monica said, switching the sound down and turning to her colleague in amazement.

'Yes, Patrick! Murdered. It's hard to take in.'

'Who's Patrick Yule?' Father Vincent asked, picking up his half bottle of wine and recorking it. He put it under his arm and switched off the standard lamp next to him.

From under his cover the parrot drawled sleepily 'Hail Mary, full of . . . rum 'n' Coke.'

'It was when the convent was still going. That would be in the seventies, I suppose?' Sister Monica asked.

'Yes,' Sister Frances replied, nodding her head, 'the early seventies, I'd say. The girls were clumping about in those ridiculous platforms.'

'In the early seventies Father Patrick was with us for, I don't know, about five months or something like that. He left unceremoniously. We learned years later that he'd become "too fond", as the powers that be put it, of Joseph, one of the local altar boys. Before he left he asked me to say a prayer for a special intention of his. I never heard what happened to him.'

'You didn't hear,' Sister Frances interrupted, 'in those days. It was all different then, it was all swept under the carpet then. Whoosh! All we knew was that one day he was there to celebrate the Mass and the next he wasn't. He was replaced by Father . . . Father . . . it's no use, it's gone. That great big, freckly redhead. Anyway, he was replaced tout suite.'

'MacLeod. Father Robert MacLeod. You should take your Vitamin B6, Sister, it would help your memory. I got you a bottle only a couple of months ago.'

'I forgot to take it. Anyway you are my B6, dear,' Sister Frances replied. Adjusting the cover over the parrot's cage to make sure he got enough air, she added, 'And a little nicer than a pill. So, as long as you're around, I'll know who I am.'

No one in the village of Cleish was aware that the elderly resident of Crabtree Cottage had ever worn a dog-collar. He kept himself to himself. They knew that he had once owned a garage, regularly enjoyed a game of bowls and was more than partial to Bell's whisky. At the Kinross Show, he regularly won the Fisher Bowl for his dahlias. The police questioned many of his neighbours and discovered those few fragments of biography. But no connection between the three murders was made by the different forces investigating them in Edinburgh, Bo'ness and Kinross-shire respectively.

This was not surprising. Neither fingerprints nor DNA were found in Colinton. Carla had, inadvertently, destroyed any traces left by her master's attacker, and the forensic evidence from Crabtree Cottage had not yet reached the lab. But, with the report of Yule's death, Father Vincent was almost certain what bound them together. Their offences would be detailed in the same leather-bound volume. One, he mused as he climbed into his bed that night, which did not exist; and which had not been reported as stolen. Or so his masters maintained. And if his suspicion was correct, in the confessional he had been inches away from the murderer.

CHAPTER THIRTEEN

The first call came at 7 a.m. Hurriedly, wiping away the shaving foam from his cheek with a towel, he put his mobile to his ear. It was Barbara Duncan and she was apologetic for ringing so early, explaining in a breathless gabble that she was booked on the nine o'clock London train but thought that she ought to speak to him before leaving.

'I got the impression,' she continued, 'from our last conversation that you were interested in Father Bell's parish work for some reason or other. Of course, with him in hospital at that point you couldn't talk to him, could you?'

'No, that's right. He was in I.C.U.'

'Well, if you are still interested, I think I can help. He's back, apparently. I haven't seen him myself, but Flora said that Ashley said that she'd seen lights on in the presbytery. So, he must be back, mustn't he? Unless, of course, you know differently. Incidentally, I wondered if you'd heard anything about Christopher Avery? Or about his partner, for that matter? Sonia thinks they're arranging a petition about you. Someone who arranges the models for the art club told her.'

'Is it for or against?'

'For, silly.'

'No, I've never heard of him or his partner. But thanks for the tip, Barbara.'

'I just thought I'd let you know. In case . . . you know, it helps.'

'Are you seeing family in London, or is it a little holiday or what?'

'Joan's been summoned there, back to the Department. I'll stay in the Royal Overseas League with her. We're planning to go to the Hockney and the Freud exhibitions, although I gather tickets are like hen's teeth. But I have my ways, as you know. I'll arrange it through a "Friend", they can get into everything. Any news on when you'll be getting back to Kinross?'

'No, not yet.'

'There was something else I wanted to tell you,' she hesitated, trying to remember what it had been, 'but . . . it can't have been important. Never mind. Father Roderick's been complaining, he says that he had never expected to be in the parish for such a long haul. He's over seventy-five, Mamie says, did you know that?'

'I didn't either. Is he . . .'

'He started life as a naval officer, attended Dartmouth and everything. Anyway, must dash. The parking's diabolical in Inverkeithing nowadays and I've still to lock up the house.'

He finished shaving but, now preoccupied with the thought that a paedophile might be back in circulation, made a poor fist of it. Blood poured from a nick on his lip and another by his ear. Looking in the mirror as he was applying pressure with a twist of tissue, he noticed that he had missed a clump of bristles to one side of his Adam's apple. Just as he had the skin taut and the blade of the razor against them, his mobile rang again. It would be Barbara, having suddenly remembered the bit of gossip that had escaped her, and desperate to impart it before she headed south. With his left hand he fished his mobile from his trouser pocket.

'Hello, Barbara.'

'Is that you, Father Vincent?'

'Yes.'

'It's not Barbara. Do you know who I am?'

He had no idea. On balance, he reckoned that the voice was probably female, but it was hard to tell. It had a low, gravelly quality, as if its owner's vocal cords were as rough as sandpaper, and chafed against each other as she spoke.

'No, I'm afraid not. I'm sorry, but should I?'

'I'm just another Mary Magdalene – another loving woman who fell for a priest.'

'Right . . .' he began guardedly, unsure what to expect next but bracing himself in case she suddenly turned on him, began spitting a froth of abuse into his ear.

'Like women, do you?'

He said nothing, conscious that for him there could be no right answer. Yes, and he would be a sex maniac. No, and he would be a misogynist.

'Don't be shy now. Any idea what I think you are?'

Now, whatever he replied, however emollient he tried to be, he knew that she was going to tell him. And that it would not be pleasant. In the silence between them he could sense the tension in the woman rising, her breathing becoming faster as she prepared herself to let rip.

'No?' she said, unable to contain herself any longer, her voice loud with suppressed excitement.

'No,' he replied, aware that his answer would be the cue for her to release her spume of bile, all her misdirected rage. But, until she started her diatribe, he could not put the phone down on her. Not while there was a chance, however remote, that he might be wrong. She might be phoning him, needing him, hoping for help from him in some way.

'I don't know how to love him . . .' she sang, every slurred word extended unnaturally, the extra syllables caressed by her tremulous vibrato. 'He's a man, he's just a man . . .'

'I'm not sure what you want from me,' Vincent said.

'Yeah, you do, pal. You're a fucking, molesting . . .'

He dropped his phone onto the hard, tiled floor, careless whether it broke or not. In the mirror in front of him, he saw reflected a gaunt, pale face with a haunted expression. He hardly recognised himself.

His head hurt. A pulse seemed to have started up at the base of his skull, pounding it, beating him, hammering his skull, as if his own flesh had turned against him and wanted to batter him, punish him.

Making a deliberate effort to relax, to breathe, he looked out of the window, a pair of buzzards catching his eye. They were no more than dots in the sky, circling slowly together, ascending into the pale blue nothingness, moving clockwise above the dark crowns of some Scots pines. In the silence, he watched them, hypnotised, calming himself, as they revolved, moving ever upwards in the cold morning air. Eventually, they disappeared altogether and he looked again at the pine trees. Those trees, he thought, although battered and misshapen by the elements, had somehow managed to keep their shallow roots anchored in that hard and stony soil. Generations of birds had flown above them or roosted in their branches and, after he had gone, more would do so. World wars must have been declared, and fought, as they added ring to ring. Man's footsteps on the moon had not altered the rhythm of the seasons for them. In the face of everything, they remained utterly and monumentally impassive, oblivious to mankind and all its petty concerns. Contemplation of them restored a proper sense of proportion.

Glancing again at himself in the mirror, he breathed out slowly and noisily. Breakfast would be ready. He had places to go, things to do, crucial things, and this morning's caller and her venom would be forgotten. Connor Bell must be seen and then St John's inspected. But first he must speak to Donald Keegan.

After less than seven rings, the answerphone in the man's empty office clicked into action, prompting him to leave a message. 'Donald,' he began, 'I really need to talk to you. I think they're connected, these murders: May, Taylor and Yule. They were all priests, you see, eons ago. All child-abusers too, or so I've heard. Suppose they were all listed in that book, the one that wasn't stolen? Ring me back as soon as you can, please. It's Vincent, Father Vincent Ross, and I need your help.'

The disordered state of Connor Bell's sitting-room in Scotlandwell took Vincent by surprise. The walls were painted scarlet as he had been told, but the emulsion on the ceiling

189

was faded and powdery, peeling in parts, and the skirting boards looked in sore need of a coat of gloss. Only three pieces of furniture remained in the room: a couch, a table and an old-fashioned armchair. Half a dozen cardboard boxes had been deposited around the unlit gas-effect fire, and in one of them could be seen the ship picture that the boy, Kyle, had described. Its glass was smashed, a star-shaped fracture radiating from the centre. Old copies of *The Times* were stacked on the stained cushions of the couch, and on a tray beside them were packages, each wrapped in a single sheet of newspaper. The brown carpet on the floor was pocked by the imprints where chairs had stood, and in the middle of it was a perfect, fawn-coloured rectangle where a rug had once been. The rug itself had been rolled up and laid across the arms of the one remaining armchair. The air was cold and damp, and condensation ran down the inside of the picture windows to collect on their ledges.

'Would you like a coffee? Or something to eat?' Connor Bell asked, taking a forkful of cold baked beans from a tin on top of the pile of newspapers. One of his arms was in a sling, and on his left cheek, above the edge of his black beard, he had a red scar. It looked as if someone had slashed a knife across his skin.

'No thanks. Are you moving or something?'

'Yes.'

Still holding the forkful of beans, the man did not look up to meet his eyes.

'When did you get out of hospital?'

'Yesterday. They let me out yesterday. Well, I asked to go, actually. I discharged myself. Having had a double fracture, pins, plates and everything in my leg, they said I should wait for the consultant but I walked away – hobbled, really.'

Father Vincent said nothing, watching the man as he ate and then attempted, with one arm, to wrap a glass ornament in a sheet of newspaper.

'Need a hand? Sorry, tactless of me, but could I help?'

'No thanks, I'd rather do it myself. I've got a system, you see. I needed out,' Bell continued, head down, biting his lip with concentration. 'I'm out of here, I said. No time to spare. Need to get home and go. Vamoose, eh? One of the nurses, she can only have been seventeen, twenty at the most, she said to me, "Father, be responsible." But I didn't listen.'

'Are you in a hurry, off to a new parish, then?'

'No. Nope. Not me. I'm done . . . giving up, setting off on a new life, a different life. No one can talk me out of it. I've had enough of this – life. In someone else's crappy house. No life. No life at all, actually. Always at everyone else's beck and call. No time to yourself, no time for yourself. Unappreciated . . .'

Father Vincent stood by the window, looking out onto the garden. Concrete slabs covered the small area and a couple of frost-chipped ceramic pots were dotted about its dismal expanse, weeds and moss growing in them. The front of a newly cleaned VW Golf peeped out of a wooden garage that was parallel to the main road. Looking at it, suddenly something struck him.

'Is that your car?' he asked idly, keeping his back to the other man. 'The one in the garage?'

'Yup. That's her, Lydia, my pride and joy, a gift from my dad,' Bell replied, stowing his most recently wrapped parcel into one of the boxes and turning his attention back to his visitor.

'Do you know,' Vincent asked, turning round to face the man, 'a boy called Kyle?'

'Why?'

It was the answer that a guilty man would choose, the response of the defensive or the afraid. A simple yes or no would not, in themselves, have betrayed him as much as that question had. He was hiding something.

'You weren't in a car crash, were you?'

'What d'you mean? What are you talking about, Vincent? I was . . . I was going along on the back road to Stirling, you know, the one by Vicar's Bridge. I was going on the downhill stretch and, from nowhere, a car came out of the junction on my right and went straight slap-bang into my car! Then he drove off, just drove off, leaving me there. I told them in the hospital, you know. I said that often quiet country roads are much more deadly than motorways with a seventy miles an hour limit and so on. Because, well, because . . .'

'So,' Vincent interrupted 'while you were in hospital someone else attended to your car, the paperwork and so on, dealt with the insurance company, got the car repaired, had had it returned here in its present as-new state.'

Connor Bell did not answer immediately. Unconsciously, he began to stroke the elbow of his damaged arm with his good hand.

'Yes.'

'Sure about that?'

'Sure! How could I not be sure?'

'Who did all of that for you?'

'My mother. Well, no, not her, actually. No, she was going to, but, for various reasons, she couldn't, so, instead, my brother ...'

'That's what the insurance company would say, is it? He's the man they dealt with, is he? Who are they by the way? And the police, were they called? Or an ambulance, maybe? It'll all be in their records, of course. Or, perhaps, despite your broken right arm, you managed to drive yourself from Vicar's Bridge to hospital?'

'No. No police, no ambulance. My brother, he took me to hospital ... honestly, he did.'

'He may well have done. In fact, I expect that he did. But not because of any car crash. He probably took you from here, eh? From this house. You were beaten up, weren't you? That's why you're leaving. You abused Kyle and he, or his pals, took the law into their own hands and assaulted you, beat you black and blue. Broke your bones. There was no car crash, no car repairs – they beat you up.'

'I'm saying nothing more,' Bell retorted. 'Dominic knows everything. No one's complained, including the so-called victim. It was all rubbish anyway. You say one word, Vincent, just one word ... to anyone. Do you actually want the Church to be further disgraced? I've no worries about you, anyway, because you're tainted goods yourself, aren't you?'

'No,' Vincent replied. Now simply looking at the man sickened him.

'Oh yes, you are. No one would listen to you, or to anything you have to say any more, and I'm out of here. Out of here! No, no one will listen to you – they'll think you're just trying to get your own back on the Bishop or whoever. You've a grudge of your own now, haven't you? That's why you've turned on poor old Mother Church. No one, inside the Church or, probably, outside it, would listen to you, Vincent. Not after that newspaper report. After all, you've had it away with hundreds of women, haven't you? Donkeys, for all I know. I'm not taking lessons in morality, or anything else, from the likes of you. There's nothing to pick between us – except that everyone knows about you.'

Twenty minutes later, Vincent entered the church, his church, and it brought tears to his eyes. The place seemed so tranquil, so calm after all the storms that had been buffeting him for so long in the outside world. Its silence enveloped him, embraced him, and in the half-light he felt at peace. The only illumination in it, apart from the muted daylight which filtered through the stained glass, came from the flickering sanctuary light. The very air was familiar, scented with the usual mix of damp carpet and stale incense. Deliberately breathing it in, he felt, immediately, that he had come home, felt like a small child returning to the bosom of its mother. Nowhere else could one find oneself alone and yet not alone, an invisible presence watching over and giving love from afar. As he walked towards the nave he slid his hand along the edges of each of the wooden pews, feeling the warmth of the wood and its smooth solidity. Taking a seat opposite the altar, he looked up at the stone sculpture of the crucified Christ and tried to lose himself in the place, abandon all his thoughts and anxieties, and just be. In here he would be bathed and cleansed. In here he could rid himself of the distrust, anger and hostility that now clung to him like a second skin, went with him wherever he went. In here he could be his old self, drop this heavy burden.

Maria de Thuy, a harp teacher at a nearby private school, crept past him on her pigeon toes and then, realising belatedly who he was, she turned back to give him one of her widest smiles. Along with a clarinettist and a guitar player, she was a founder member of the church music group. Her head was covered by a black mantilla and, genuflecting and crossing herself at the same time, she edged into a nearby pew. Immediately, she knelt down and began praying, whispering excitedly through her thick lips, transported to find herself in the presence of her Lord. Having made the sign of the cross again, she began passing her rosary beads between her extraordinarily muscular thumb and forefinger, focusing her entire body and soul on her prayer.

Looking at the kneeling figure, the priest felt envious of her; envious of her certainty, her simple faith and the joy she found in it. She, he felt sure, experienced no shame in being a Catholic or admitting that she was one. All the child abuse scandals in the world would not dent her admiration for the papacy. Il Papa could do no wrong in her eyes and nor could his minions: the cardinals, archbishops or bishops. Always it would be someone else's fault. She had an innocent, childlike faith, and however bright the light which was shone into the Church, she would never see the snakes writhing in its darkest corners or hear the scratchings of the rats. Her faith was, truly, blind; deaf and dumb too.

The confessional box had, in his absence, undergone a transformation. It no longer functioned as an extra broom cupboard, and in a nice touch someone had placed a vase of flowers on the shelf which had been cleared. He sat inside the box, trying to recreate in his mind the circumstances of that fateful confession. The CD which had been playing that night had come to an end, so there had been no background noise. All that he had heard had been the man's voice, a rumbling baritone, with an accent suggestive of Tyneside or Northumberland; the singsong sounds that he associated with fishing boats, cold winds and the North East of England. With his spine resting against the back of the box, he had seen almost nothing, partly because the penitent's head had been bent down, and partly because the grille had obscured the man's features.

Unforgettably, of course, there had been that strange odour, and breathing in he tried to smell it again, analyse all the constituent parts that made up the full aroma. The scent of the freesias in their vase proved a distraction. That night the dominant strand had been the warm, fruity tang of raspberries. That was the part which had surprised him the most. Running through it had been something else; a sharp note, possibly Dettol, and then an undertone of something industrial, paraffin or some kind of oil or petrol fumes. The scent of raspberries suggested that it was some kind of household product, designed to appeal to the noses of domestic consumers. He sniffed the air delicately, filtering out the perfume of the freesias, analysing what remained, concluding that the box had recently been occupied by an illicit smoker, one keen to camouflage the scent of tobacco on his breath with minty polo fumes. So, almost certainly, a teenager, and that narrowed it down to three.

As he was stepping out of the box, he almost bumped into Father Roderick. A look of annoyance flashed across the old fellow's face, as if he had caught someone snooping or playing in forbidden territory, but it evaporated as he recognised Father Vincent. In his outstretched hands he held a tray with the chalice, the water and wine vessels and the Tupperware box with the unconsecrated hosts in it.

'I'm sorry, I'm just setting up for Mass,' he said, as if he was the one required to explain himself, 'and I'm on the late side as usual. I fell asleep after confession, in my chair . . . or rather, your chair . . .'

'Right,' Vincent replied, 'I was just . . .'

He stopped, unable to finish his sentence. No truthful explanation was possible even if it would have been believed, so he carried on walking, adding lamely, 'Since you're late, Roderick, I'll not hold you up any more.'

Someone had flung a couple of raw eggs at his windscreen. One had slid all the way down the glass, some of it now trapped by the windscreen wipers. The other, which had caught the edge of the roof of the car on impact, was still dribbling down, dragging its eggshell with it and leaving a smear of orange yolk in its wake. He looked around, searching for the culprit, and saw, stationary on the other side of the road, a male figure watching him. The man was silhouetted against the dim, late afternoon light but the priest recognised him without difficulty. The giveaway was his hair which looked unnatural, all over to one side and with a fixed, solid look. Pausing to allow the Perth bus to pass, he crossed the road and approached Mark Houston.

'Did you do that?' he asked, his anger banishing his fear despite Houston's bulk and proven aggression.

'Aha.'

'Why? Haven't you done enough already?'

'No,' the man replied, matter-of-factly, patting his toupee absent-mindedly, smoothing it down over his own thin locks with his pudgy fingers.

'I never touched your wife!'

'I know that.'

'What?'

'I said "I know that."'

'You know? Then what's all this about? What the hell's going on?'

'I didn't always know. I thought you had when I came after you with Norm, but one night, a couple of weeks ago, she told me. She'd had a few too many. Vodka and Coke, that's her tipple, or Bacardi and Coke. Said she'd been after you, I mean, not the other way round. She threw it in my face. 'Course you're not the first – not by a long chalk – but that's worse for me, like, isn't it?'

'Is it?'

'Obviously it is. You're not very savvy are you? It doesn't reflect well on me – as a man. Her putting it about, or at least trying to. How do you think it makes me look? I'd rather everyone thinks you came after her. We moved from the last parish because she'd picked someone up there. I'm not having that again. But I can't tell Norman and the rest that, can I?'

'If you know I didn't do it – touch your wife – why are you throwing eggs at my car, for God's sake?'

'You not listen? People here have got to think you were after her. It's better for me . . .'

'It's not better for me.'

'Yeah,' the man replied, unmoved. 'I can see that, pal. But what can I do? She's my wife, isn't she? If she tells the truth to anyone else, hopefully they'll just think she's trying to protect you now anyway. You lot are into suffering, aren't you? Nails through hands and spears into ribcages – crowns of barbed wire and that. You papes think it does you good, don't you? Well, add it, add all of this to your total. Every little bit helps on the way to Heaven, doesn't it? Think of it like air miles or something.'

To his mind, Elizabeth's kitchen in Curate's Wynd was perfect. It was painted a bright yellow and felt light and airy as a summerhouse. It was neat, but not too neat, warm, but not too warm; felt alive, occupied by someone intent upon living their life to the full. A mouth-organ rested on top of a music tutorial booklet and everywhere paperbacks were piled high, ranging from a book of recipes for chocolate to the autobiography of the aviator Beryl Markham. Stacks of cookery books had taken over an entire kitchen unit and a small table, and on the top of the fridge perched two pots of red geraniums. In one corner of the room there was a dog bed occupied by a pair of elderly Labradors, Humphrey and Lauren, the dog's head resting on the bitch's flank. Vincent loved the orderly chaos of the house, saw in it only the outward manifestations of a lively mind. He was blind to its cobwebs and its crumbs.

Elizabeth gave him a cup of tea and then, explaining that she had a meeting to go to in less than half an hour, she continued with her housework. Her voice sounded thick, dulled with a cold.

'It'll all be over soon,' she said, pulling a couple of chairs to one side, intent upon sweeping the wooden floor underneath the kitchen table.

'Not if Mark Houston has his way. It suits him to keep it all going. He actually told me that.' Neurotically, as he was talking to her, he checked his phone for missed calls. Still nothing from Keegan, not even a text.

'Would you mind moving your feet, please. Maybe it does. But he's shot his bolt and so has she. According to them there isn't a woman in Kinross who's been safe from you – except me, of course.'

'No offence taken, I hope, as I'm obviously not very choosy. Anyway, at least things seem to be moving in the diocesan office. I saw their lawyer yesterday, and the only other person he really needs to see is Sarah Houston.'

'And he'll see straight through her,' she interjected, her head now in the cupboard below the sink as she searched in it for a duster and a jar of furniture polish. Upright once more and standing beside him, she sneezed twice, then tried to unscrew the lid, using first her strong right hand and then, having failed, trying her left.

'Maybe, but the lawyer, McClaverty, is not much more than a boy.'

'It's no good. Could you give it a go?' she asked, passing the jar of polish to him.

'If you failed with this there's not much hope for me,' he replied. He applied all the torque that he could muster, his face reddening with the effort. Unable to budge it, he went to the sink and ran water from the hot tap over the lid. Taking a deep breath, he tried again, and failed to move it even a millimetre. Flexing his hand to ease the pain in his fingers, he shook his head.

'Shall I try it in the door hinge?' he said.

'Weak as I am, I'll have another go first. You'll just chip the paint,' she said, raising her arms and flexing her biceps like a Victorian muscle man.

As she wrestled with it, bending double and groaning with the effort, a man entered the kitchen as if it was his own. He was dark-haired and dark-skinned, with a sleek, overfed look about him. But his red nose and rheumy eyes, and the paper hankie in his hand, signalled his heavy cold. Seeing him she blushed slightly, straightened up and handed the jar to him.

'You've caught it too? Have a go, see if you can unscrew this,' she ordered.

'OK,' he answered, in a hoarse, high-pitched squeak, clearing his throat noisily as if the sound he had made embarrassed him. Then, smiling at her as if pleased to have been asked, he unscrewed the lid in a second and handed the jar back to her. Shrugging his shoulders as if to say what was the problem, he grinned and swung himself onto a tall stool.

'I must have loosened it for you,' Father Vincent said, and grinned.

Looking at him, amused by his cheek, Elizabeth dabbed some of the contents of the jar onto a duster. As she did so, a distinctive smell spread through the room. It was one Vincent had encountered only once before, a strange mix of raspberry, Dettol and paraffin.

'Where did you get that stuff from?' he asked her sharply.

'You saw where – from the cupboard.'

'No, no, that's not what I meant. What sort of polish is it? What's it for? Did you get it at the supermarket, or the hardware place, or where?'

'Let me see . . .' She held out her hand for the jar, and then, addressing the newcomer, she added, 'Hello, Hal. I wasn't expecting you. You're early.'

Having her full attention at last, the man rose and unselfconsciously kissed her on the cheek.

'Father Vincent, Hal. Hal, Father Vincent,' Elizabeth said, putting the jar down on the table and bringing another mug over. Always, the priest noticed, her eyes returned to the stranger.

'Hal's just moved to Milnathort. Like some tea, Hal? Heavens, I forgot all about Mike. He'll want some too.'

'Mike?' the priest said. Hal was already one other man too many.

'He works for Millers, the plumbers. He's outside in the cold. He's been clearing the gutters for me. He'll want tea, if it's being made. Would you see if he wants some for me, love?'

At her words, both the priest and the newcomer began to move towards the door until Vincent, realising his error, halted.

On Hal's return, she handed a steaming mug to each of the men.

'Where are we going for dinner?' Hal croaked, cradling his drink in his hands before taking a sip.

'Is that your meeting?' Vincent asked, deliberately catching the woman's eye, trying to smile but, feeling as heavy as lead, unable to do so. It was none of his business. She was none of his business. The question had left his mouth before he could stop it, and it sounded rude and intrusive.

'Yes.'

'Fine.'

A prolonged silence followed, a deep, uneasy one which chilled them all like a cold bath. Eventually, the plumber broke it, putting his empty mug on the kitchen table and murmuring as he left, 'No rest for the wicked, eh?'

Hal resumed his place on the stool, crossed his arms and looked at the priest, raising his eyebrows as if waiting for him to say something. His ploy worked.

'I'll not hold you up then,' Vincent said, rising from his chair, 'but going back to the polish for a second, Elizabeth, can you tell me anything about it?'

Before she could reply, Hal ostentatiously lifted up his wrist to look at his watch, wordlessly indicating that there was no time for any further conversation.

'Hal!'

Meekly accepting her rebuke, he blew her a kiss and mouthed 'Sorry' to her. Vincent glanced at him, incapable of masking his instinctive dislike.

'It's furniture polish. Dougie gave it to me. He got it from his work,' she said.

'Dougie?' Hal enquired sharply, before beginning to cough uncontrollably with the effort of speaking.

'Douglas Templeton, my ex-husband,' she said, blushing. 'I told you about him. He lives in Kinnesswood, on the other side of the loch. It was a sample or something, Vincent. You'd have to ask him about it.'

'I will,' the priest said, watching ruefully as the man, holding his gaze, slid a proprietary arm around her shoulder.

CHAPTER FOURTEEN

The next morning, stopping in mid-stride, Vincent looked at the sky around him and drank in its beauty. It was black, heavy with rain, except for a band of light along the horizon as if the sun had risen late that day and its weak early rays had not yet the strength to penetrate any higher. A flock of seagulls passed overhead, the lazy rhythm of their wing beats making him feel as if time itself had slowed down, and the world come to a standstill. To the west, a single shaft of light, as if from the heavens themselves, emerged through the otherwise impenetrable cloud, illuminating three of the nearest peaks and turning them to molten gold.

He had been walking for over an hour, trudging onwards with his head down, his mind full to bursting and blind to everything around him. All that he had seen had been the tarmac below his feet. The noise made by his boots provided a sort of comfort, rhythmical and regular, reminding him that he was still on the move. Now, standing motionless for the first time since he'd left the retreat, he allowed his eyes to wander over the landscape spread out in front of him. Its early spring colours were as muted as the wools spun into a Harris tweed; an expanse of yellowish-grey marking out the rain-soaked stubble, burnt umber where the plough had been and a haze of fresh green where the spring barley had broken through the hard earth to greet the new year. Roundels of dark conifers, standing in rust-brown patches of dead bracken, were joined one to the other by hedgerows of hawthorn, beech and elder. The loveliness of the scene suddenly hit him, acted as balm for his troubled soul.

Throughout the night, twin anxieties had plagued him, eating into his sleep and making him glad to hear the shrill ringing of the alarm clock. Why hadn't that bloody policeman phoned him? A madman was on the loose. Perhaps their investigations had already uncovered the connection between the victims, knew even of their vile predilections? Fingerprints might have linked the killings, have alerted them to some common thread. If so, the sod could at least have told him. But whatever they had found out, he agonised, they had not listened to that confession, heard the drunkard confess to a murder and boast about the theft of the book. And he could not help them there. If it was a matter of excommunication for himself, that could be borne; but in the wider context, how could any penitent disburden himself of his sins and find absolution, without the sure and certain knowledge that whatever he said would go no further?

Thoughts of Elizabeth Templeton had been eating away at him too. In her kitchen he had noted Hal's ease, his assurance, and had experienced the hot scald of jealousy for the first time in years, in decades more likely. It might have been Hal's bloody kitchen, the way the creep had behaved in it. His house! He knew where the sugar was kept, where to find the biscuit tin. How long did that take, how many visits?

Of course, he told himself, she would have friends, male friends, of which he was unaware. A woman like her was bound to. A lover, quite possibly, quite probably. But saying the word, even silently in his head, pained him. Intellectually, he had long ago acknowledged such a theoretical probability, but actually meeting it, meeting him, for the first time in the flesh, had almost floored him, proved harder to bear than he had imagined. And she, usually so wonderfully straightforward, had been coy, describing what was clearly a date as a 'meeting'. Not that she had anything to hide, or of which to be ashamed. Why should she be lonely? He had made a vow of celibacy, not her. And what had he to offer? The occasional visit, small, insignificant and largely communal outings, interspersed with warm chats. No more than the illusion of intimacy. It was pitiful. They were no substitute for a proper flesh and blood relationship. If ever he had imagined that they could be, he must have been living on Mars. Unworldly did not begin to describe him.

And now, on top of everything else, she seemed to be connected in some, please God, peripheral way to that awful night. But hunting out Dougie Templeton might well be a complete waste of time for all concerned. Households all over the country likely used that polish; factories too, for all he knew. It could be a top-selling brand. He was no policeman, had no forensic tools, no laboratories or white-coated assistants at his disposal. Had he a proper job, had he been as busy as usual, celebrating Masses, visiting the sick, baptising squalling infants, performing all the multifarious duties of a parish priest, then he would have had no truck with this . . . this nonsense, this preposterous adventure. But, but . . . the missing book, three dead priests, all with a hideous past, and the Bishop's assailant still at liberty? Somehow he had blundered into hell. Where was Donald Keegan when he was needed most?

In the distance, a single shot rang out, disturbing a gaggle of Canada geese in a nearby stubble field, and they rose as one, honking their indignation as they took to the air. In amongst their deafening cries his phone went, and he knew before a word had been spoken who his caller was.

'Donald,' he said, pressing his mobile to his ear, trying to block out the sound of the birds.

'Vincent, did you say Donald?' the Monsignor's disembodied voice replied, sounding taken aback. 'It's Dominic. Perhaps that's what you said? Haven't you one of those phones that tell you the number that's calling – doesn't yours give you the number?'

'No, it's an old cheap phone,' Vincent said, watching as the skein took shape, the stragglers at the ends of the V-shape weaving from side to side as they endeavoured to keep formation. He did not feel like talking to the Monsignor.

'You should get one, they're very useful – oh, the wonders of modern technology! I thought I should let you know that James is back on his feet, at last. I've been dealing with things in his absence as you know. Our lawyer, that McClaverty fellow, spoke to Mrs Houston last night, after he'd seen you. I said it was now urgent, you see, and he's quite convinced that there's nothing in the woman's allegations.'

'Is he now?' Father Vincent said evenly.

'He is. Apparently, she's quite changed her story – only now, after the damage is done, I'm afraid. With her husband still in the room with her she said . . . well, that she'd been the chaser not the chased. Not the chaste! Women are indeed clothed serpents, Vincent, as they used to tell us in the college. They're graveyards – tended and flowery above and corrupt below. But that's not the modern way of thinking, is it? Of course, times have changed. We all know that, don't we? But human nature doesn't change, it can't, and that's not taken into account unfortunately. The point is, you're in the clear whatever that woman said to the papers. I've spoken to Father Roderick and he's happy, more than happy in fact, to vacate the parish today.'

'I can go back?'

'You can go back.'

'Today?'

'This actual and glorious morning. But Vincent . . .'

'Yes?'

'Go cannily, eh? Go cannily. You've already been burnt once.'

'Do me a favour, Dominic?'

'What?'

'Tell Mamie Bryce about the result of the investigation, would you? You could dress it up – make it something to do with sorting out the cleaning for the handover between me and Roderick. I don't mind how – just let her know that I've been cleared.'

'Why?'

'In the Beginning was the Word – and Twitter's got nothing on Mamie.'

The presbytery, Father Vincent discovered as he walked through his own front door, no longer smelled like home. Its appearance was the same in every respect; Father Roderick had moved no furniture, added no pictures and he, or someone on his behalf, had dutifully waved a duster about the place. The walls had not been repainted, and the carpets were of the same muted hue. To the eye it was unchanged. But an odour of age seemed, now, to permeate it; a dank, fungal smell, redolent of basements, incontinent tomcats and damp bath towels. The unfamiliar smell, disconcertingly, made the whole place feel alien.

An old-fashioned, misshapen canvas grip was in the middle of the sitting-room floor, secured with twine, and on top of it was a teddy bear-shaped hot-water bottle with a flat cap resting on it. The old man was seated in an armchair nearby, sipping tea from a cup, and his ebony walking stick rested across his shrunken thighs.

'This'll be my last,' he said mournfully, looking up at Vincent, dunking a digestive biscuit in his tea and then explaining. 'My days as a parish priest are over – even as a locum. I can't manage your stairs, you know. No pensioner could. They're lethal. I didn't dare take a bath the whole time I was here. You've got no rubber mat, no handle on the wall. Who'd get me out? At home I have a shower with a wee plastic seat in it. Social services provided me with the seat . . . Glad you're in the clear, by the way.'

'You've looked after everything wonderfully well – in the parish, I mean. Everyone says so. After you've had a rest you'll feel quite different. It's an arduous business running a place like this.'

'It is. And I'm well over seventy, you know. Nearer to eighty since January.'

Like an aged tortoise, the old man blinked slowly, and with a trembling hand lowered his empty cup, rattling noisily against its saucer, to the carpet.

'Look at these,' he added, rolling up one of the legs of his black trousers to reveal a pale, hairless shank terminating in an elephantine ankle. The top of his grey sock had an uneven slit in it as if it had recently been hacked with scissors to accommodate the ankle's unnatural girth.

'It's blown up again. The other one's just the same,' he explained, looking up, an unexpected note of pride in his voice, 'if anything, worse.'

'Can't they do anything about it – reduce the swelling or whatever? It looks sore, maybe jaundiced.'

'It is sore,' he replied, rolling down his trouser leg, 'but I'm old. When you're old they expect things to fail – limbs, eyes, ears and so on. The lot, actually. Conventional medicine, doctors and nurses, NHS people, they've quite given up on me. I'm like an old vessel, a hulk, consigned to the scrapheap. Returning the compliment, I've given up on them. Chinese medicine, that's the thing nowadays, that's the way ahead. They're capitalists too, like us. In all their thousands of years they've learned a thing or two about circulation. About the tides, ebbs and flows, currents and so on. Meanwhile we were running around naked, painted blue and clad in furs.'

'What do they recommend?'

'Apparently, my kidney, spleen and lung yang isn't working properly. So then the yin accumulates and that's why there's all that water under my skin, waterlogging it. That's my problem.'

'I see.'

'I'm taking something, some herby pills that Joe from the Chinese takeaway got for me over the internet. A type of water pill, he says. But I've found bathing the ankle helps too. You're supposed to use herbs, onion-skins and the like, boil them up and let them cool down and then stick your feet in it. I just go on using the same old infusion, time after time, it's easier. I've dyed my legs in the process – yellow, like a Chinaman's. That's the stuff, over there,' he said, pointing at a basin in the corner of the sitting-room.

Vincent wandered over to look at it, realising as he drew close to it why it was that the house now smelled so odd. A dead moth floated on top of the cold dark fluid.

'You made it yourself?'

'I did. You have to be open-minded nowadays, Vincent,' the old man said, getting to his feet. 'Other cultures, other civilisations, other religions even. But for the aborigines, you know, we'd not have the wheel. Now, parish matters. Tomorrow, you'll need to take Jean Fleming's funeral service.'

'She's died, has she?' Vincent said, saddened on hearing the news although he had been expecting it. The only surprise was that she had lasted so long.

'Well, put it this way, it'll not be a pet hamster in the coffin, Vincent,' the old man chuckled, shaking his head at the stupidity of the question. 'She's to be interred in the Kirkgate. The service is scheduled for two-thirty tomorrow. I'll be glad not to have to be the one standing at the grave in this weather. My balance is so bad I'd be in danger of falling in.'

Kinnesswood is a small village clinging on to the very skirts of the Lomond Hills, perched precariously on the high ground, with the flat, turf-bearing fields of the plain below and the calm waters of the loch less than a mile away. The main road to Leslie snakes its narrow way between the jumble of stone cottages, crow-stepped and pantiled houses scattered along and overshadowing it. Wherever one looks the hills loom large, simplifying everything, dwarfing the cottages and making them seem like the abodes of hobbits.

Having waited patiently for the red fish van from Pittenweem to move on and unblock the street, the priest turned left opposite Drummond Place and found himself in a narrow yard which terminated in the premises of the Barr Chemical Company. This business was housed in a run-down brick building with dusty, opaque windows and an elm seedling growing out of its cracked, leaf-filled guttering. Its asbestos roof had large cracks in places, and one corner appeared to have been chipped off.

Inside, the space was partitioned, and in the part of it which functioned as an office, Douglas Templeton was enjoying his elevenses of a jam doughnut and milky coffee. His feet rested on a small, rusty filing cabinet and he was absorbed in his newspaper, reading about the runners in the two o'clock at Hamilton. It had been a quiet morning. Since ten o'clock, the office phones appeared to have gone dead and some kind of maintenance on the line had now cut off the internet connection too. When the priest came through the door, absent-mindedly forgetting to knock, Templeton rose instantly, surprised and thinking for a moment that it was his boss. He was the only other person who came into the office without knocking, most others obeying the sign on the door. Doughnut in hand, he scrutinised his visitor, spotting his dog-collar and realising that he was a clergyman of some sort. He wondered anxiously if he was about to be given some bad news.

'Can I help you?' he asked warily.

'Are you Dougie – Douglas Templeton?'

'I am.'

'I'm Father Vincent, from St John's in Kinross and I know your wife.' The priest hesitated, still working out in his head the best way to introduce the topic in which he was interested.

'Charmaine – is she all right, has something happened to her?'

'No, no,' the priest said hastily. 'I'm sorry, I mean your ex-wife, Elizabeth.'

'Oh, OK, her. What about her? Would you like a seat?' Templeton returned to his own revolving chair, spinning on its base and gesturing to his visitor to sit down. He put the remains of his doughnut back into its paper bag and licked each of his fingers in turn.

'Thanks. I'd like to talk to you about something a little odd, some furniture polish that you gave her. It was pink. I know it might sound a bit peculiar, very peculiar in fact, but you'd be doing me a great favour if you could tell me a bit about it.'

'Polish? That's what we manufacture, that's our business. What do you want to know?' the man asked, relieved it was nothing more serious and happy to talk about anything else. The rain outside suddenly began to fall more heavily, pounding the roof and almost drowning out the end of his question.

'Anything you can tell me, really. Where it's sold, what it's supposed to be used on.'

'The pink stuff . . . was it in a screw-top jam jar?'

'That's right.'

'No problem. We only made a tiny batch. It was experimental, you see. It worked as a polish all right, buffed up everything nicely – beeswax is always good for a shine – but nobody liked the smell. It was a bit sickly, that's what the feedback was. And it's too expensive, too expensive for the domestic market at any rate. Why do you want to know about it?'

'So who got it – to try out or whatever?'

'That's what I'm saying. Nobody. Nobody got it.'

'Well,' the priest said tentatively, conscious that he was trespassing on the man's time and goodwill, 'you got it, and Elizabeth got it. I don't mean bought it. So, apart from you, what other employees . . .'

'Oh, OK. Sorry. I got some and Colin got some, that's it,' he said. Then, catching the eye of an employee who had popped his head around the open door, he added, 'Now, if you don't mind, we're a bit busy this morning.'

'Another leak – it's dripping through the main seam again, boss,' the man said, shaking his head in disgust.

'Colin? Colin who? Where does he live? Is he at work

today?' the priest asked, rising from his seat, nodding at the newcomer, eager to get across that he understood the crisis and did not intend to waste any more of Templeton's precious time.

'Data protection, I'm afraid – I can't tell you these things.'

'I just need to know where he lives.'

'Hang on a sec. Father Vincent you said, eh?' the man asked, swinging round in his chair, smiling. He smiled, said 'Bucket!' to his colleague and waved him away dismissively.

'Yes,' the priest answered, still standing in front of the desk.

'Oh, you're the one who visited my boy, eh? In the jail . . . in Perth Prison. I know who you are now. Thanks for that. He appreciated it. I appreciate it. Colin Gifford, that's your man, but he's not in today or tomorrow. He stays at Caple Cottage in Crook of Devon, but to be honest it's little more than a bed and breakfast for him. He's never there. On his days off you'll likely find him at the Green, drinking or curling or, more likely, drinking and curling.'

'I think I've met him – played against him.'

Driving back home on the northern side of the loch the priest found himself in a queue of cars which had formed behind a tractor. Blue-grey smoke was belching from its exhaust as it chugged along, straining to pull its load of round bales. On impulse, he drew in to the car park at Burleigh Sands, intending to sit in his car among the Scots pines to think, have a smoke too, while waiting for the line of traffic to get out of the way.

Crossing his arms over the steering wheel, he rested his forehead against them. So, now he had met Elizabeth's former husband. And he was an unexceptional man, and, thank God, not the murderer. From his accent, he must have been brought up in Kinross-shire, or Fife at the furthest, and he had a high, light voice, quite unlike the deep, sonorous tones that had resonated in the confessional box. What, he wondered, had been the draw for her? His boyish looks, possibly, but what else? There must have been more than that. Maybe they had been at school together, first loves, familiar and safe with each other. But how could a woman as . . . as original, as unique, as beautiful as Elizabeth have fallen for him? He raised his head from the wheel, looked at his watch and lit a cigarette. It was twelve-thirty already. He was busy, had a funeral to prepare for and the accounts to do as well. It was all pointless, anyway, none of his business, and, plainly, she now had a new man in her life. Hal, the slimy Lothario. Whoever the hell he was.

The grave had been dug at the eastern end of the old parish churchyard at the Kirkgate, within a few yards of the Bruce Mausoleum. On three sides the land fell away, merging, finally, into the tussocky marshland that bordered the loch. As he intoned, 'I am the resurrection and the life,' his words were lost; the rustling sound made by the wings of a dozen swans as they came in to land on the loch drowning him out and, momentarily, distracting the mourners from their thoughts. There could not be, he thought to himself, a finer place in all the wide world to be buried, to rest while waiting for the last trump.

A cordon of hills ringed the graveyard. Beyond the shimmering body of water, with its pale reed-fringed shores, lay, far to the east, the Lomonds. To the south, the soft contours of the sleeping giant merged into the low mounds of the Cleish hills. Even from the north and the west, it was sheltered, the undulating slopes of the Ochils forming the third side of the triangle which protected it. Coming to from his reverie, he moved away from the graveside to leave room for the cords men to lower the coffin into the dark earth. As, working wordlessly together, they manoeuvred it in, veins bulging on a couple of the older men's red foreheads, a new sound broke the silence. A clinker-built dinghy, its outboard motor phut-phutting its way doggedly onwards, was heading towards Castle Island, leaving a white trail behind it. The coffin now lowered, the priest threw a handful of sandy earth onto it, trying to make sure that he was downwind of everyone. As the soil clattered onto the wood, a loud sobbing to his right started up. Instinctively, he put his arm around the dead woman's daughter, Helen Compton, causing her to sob louder yet.

'You'll be coming to the wake, won't you Father? Father Roderick said he would,' she whispered, dabbing her eyes with a hankie and trying to regain her usual self-control. 'We're having it at home, just as Mum would have wanted. She wasn't one for hotels.'

By the time he had changed out of his robes, the rest of the mourners had arrived at Swansacre and wasted no time in finding the drink. Most of them had glasses of wine clasped in their cold fingers. A few men had, somehow, found the whisky, and determined to warm themselves up, uncorked it and helped themselves, hoping it would be taken for a dark white wine. Tiny triangular sandwiches were doing the rounds and Jean's old Dachshund, Tizer, wandered between the guests' legs as if searching for his late mistress. A couple of young children, dragooned into assisting as waiters, bumped into people, giggled, and spilled their bowls of crisps. Giggling yet more, the pair crawled on the floor to retrieve them, competing with the dog to get to them first. The crisps they gathered up went back into their bowls, fluff and all, until their mother, scarlet-cheeked and unamused, snatched the bowls from them, reminding them in a hissed whisper that this was a wake, not a party.

Helen Compton, catching sight of the priest as he came in, rushed over to him with a glass that she had filled in advance with him in mind. Handing it over, she murmured her thanks and, then, seeing how chilled he looked, tried to create a path for him towards the open fire.

As he went towards the warmth, he felt a couple of hands pat him on the shoulder, enough to reassure him and let him know that his return was welcome and that the life of the parish might continue as it had done before. Standing with his legs apart, allowing the crackling flames to warm his back, he viewed the people in the room. A teenager, one of the Morrisons, was slumped against the wall with a bored expression on her perfect features. As she stood there her little sister was using one of her legs as a climbing frame to raise herself from the floor. Once upright, the toddler began to wail loudly until the girl swung her upwards, plumping her onto her shoulders. From this lofty perch, the child watched everything going on, now calm, letting out an occasional sniffle and licking her Ribena-stained lips. It was, the priest realised, one of the things that he had missed most in the Retreat; the bustle of lives, young, untidy and colourful lives. The noisy, fruitful chaos of it all. In the nuns' orderly household there had been quiet, calm, peace even, leaving aside the occasional short-lived spat between the sisters, but a tomb would offer much the same. He wanted the sights and sounds, the smells, the clashing colours, the messiness, in a word, of family living. Such a life demanded energy from all, but it gave far more than it took, and already he felt revived, more alive than he had for a long while.

'Father Vincent!'

He turned to see Donald Keegan standing, smiling, beside him. As before, the man looked too hot, but this time he was encased in an over-tight charcoal-grey suit, its black buttons straining to contain his rounded belly; a striped tie, loosely knotted, protruding below the hem of his jacket.

'Donald!'

'I thought I might see you here. Allan, or somebody or other, told me that they'd allowed you back.'

For a second the priest bristled at the policeman's choice of words. But, reflecting that he was being too prickly, he raised his glass as if in a toast and said, 'They have. I'm home at last. Didn't you get my messages?'

'No, I'm just back from a couple of days' leave. Don't look so surprised. I'm off-duty. What did you need to tell me?'

'Later – after the wake or in private. It may be nothing, nothing at all. I don't know. It's a small world, isn't it? I didn't realise that you knew the Comptons.'

'I don't really, well, not very well, but Kate, my wife does. Kate . . . Kate!' he said, touching a woman with a page-boy haircut on the shoulder and interrupting her conversation with her neighbour. In response, she glared at him.

'This is Father Vincent – remember I told you about him? His brother works with me at the station in Dundee.'

'Aha,' she replied, looking underwhelmed by the news. As if he had done his duty by making the introduction, the policeman then whispered, 'Now, I'm needing a top-up, if you don't mind,' and began to make his way between the other guests in the direction of the buffet table.

'Get me one and all, Donny boy,' his wife called to the retreating figure.

'You've a sister who lives in Kinross, I understand?' Father Vincent began, suddenly feeling hungry and wishing he could follow her husband to the buffet.

The woman laughed uncertainly. 'Sisters, Father, plural!'

'Oh,' he said, feeling more relaxed after managing to snatch a couple of sausages on sticks from a passing plate, 'I knew you had one, living at the farm by the loch – Mossbank, isn't it? But you've another one here too, have you? I'd no idea. How can I have missed her?'

221

'That's easy,' Mrs Keegan said, downing the last of her red wine and scanning the room for her husband and her refill. 'She's a pagan, doesn't come to church or anything. She's unmarried, very definitely unmarried, if you know what I mean. Rather despises those of us who have tied the knot, I suspect, like her sisters, Susie and me. She's an old-fashioned radical feminist of the crop-haired and dungareed school. No children for her, just her bloody . . . sorry, just her job. That particular Miss Mann is loaded, the cow. Sorry, Father, sorry, her important, well-paid job as . . . as . . .' She began to laugh uncontrollably, tears forming in her eyes. 'As a tax inspector! Or, as I prefer to call it, a professional leech!'

'This should be your last one, my angel,' Keegan said, passing a full glass of wine to his wife and then watching nonplussed as she handed her empty glass to the priest, muttered 'toilet' and made a bee-line for the door.

'She's emotional, she was very fond of Jean. We came back specially for the funeral,' Keegan said, apparently feeling the need to explain his wife's conduct. 'We could follow her, talk outside?'

'Right.'

Standing in the hall, the hum of conversation from the front-room barely audible, Donald Keegan sampled his whisky. A woman edged past him, looked at his glass and murmured, 'You're the lucky one, aren't you?'

He winked at her and then, as she moved away, asked the priest, 'Is this about your quest for the missing book?'

'Yes and no. Those three recent murders may be connected . . .'

'Hold on, you'll need to remind me. There's a lot of it about.'

'Dennis May, Callum Taylor and Patrick Yule. They were all priests once – and paedophiles, apparently, too.'

'How on earth do you come to know that?'

'A priest, also a paedophile, told me about May and Taylor. He's in Perth Prison. Someone else told me about Patrick Yule.'

'Is the Perth man reliable?'

'To the best of my knowledge.'

'The other source?'

'Utterly.'

'Christ, Vincent, that sounds like dynamite to me. Bloody dynamite. I'm not involved with any of those cases, so I don't know what they know. But I can easily find out who is. May will be dealt with by someone in Lothian and Borders. Taylor . . . don't know who again, but I'll find out. They'll call you in, they're bound to with that stuff. Do you think this is connected in some way to the book? Because that one is my bag.'

'Possibly. Did Dominic Drew really say nothing to you on the night? About its disappearance?'

'Who?'

'Monsignor Drew. He handled things while the Bishop was in hospital.'

'Never heard of him. Father Tony Cross was our contact. Vincent, I'll pass your information on to whoever is in charge ASAP, and well done by the way. And I meant what I said, if you need any help, any help at all, just give me a ring. Don't forget, I understand your little difficulty,

you know I do, but, if we are talking about stolen property, then I can use *all* the resources available to me. I'll
give you my home number and you could put it in your
phone. I meant to give it to you the last time I saw you.
Call me any time, eh?'

By way of response Vincent simply nodded his head.
But, gazing into his burly ally's kindly face, he could have
kissed him.

Walking through the doors into the curling rink, Father
Vincent shivered, regretting immediately that he did not
have more layers on. There were only four figures on the
ice, grouped together in the distance, and two of them
appeared to be male. The man he was looking for might
be among them. One, apparently recognising him, waved,
and though he was not sure who he was, he immediately
and automatically waved back. In the raw cold, his glasses
had begun to steam up.

'Is Colin Gifford with you?' he called to the unknown
man, surprised when he put a hand to his ear to indicate
that he had not caught what he had said. The echoes
in the vast open space had distorted his words, turning
them into gibberish. Determined to find his quarry, he
decided to join the group on the ice. A pair of blue slippers was lying, as if discarded, by the edge of the rink,
and he pulled them over his black brogues and set off
towards the four curlers. As, he drew closer, he realised
that the quartet was composed entirely of females. The
bulkiest of them pointed at his shoes and said hoarsely,
'You shouldn't be in those slippers, Father. They're mine,

I left them there for a friend – I thought you were him.'

'I'm sorry, I assumed they were finished with,' he replied.

As the woman glared at his feet, she suddenly sneezed, slipped and began to fall over. Arms flailing, she grabbed at his jacket, yanking him forwards so that he almost fell onto the ice himself. Meantime the woman saved herself from falling by grabbing at the handle of the broom in her neighbour's hand. The other woman, who had been enjoying the little drama of the shoes, all but toppled herself on finding her broom suddenly yanked like the rope of a church bell.

'Christ Almighty, Virginia!' she expostulated, still reeling.

'I had to, Fiona,' Virginia replied, righting herself, 'needs must.'

'So, Father, you'll not have come onto the sheet for a game, I'm thinking,' the third woman said.

'Quite right,' he replied, 'and I'd better get off here before I cause another accident. I was looking for Colin Gifford. Someone told me that he'd probably be here today.'

'He's here all right,' the woman's nearest neighbour chipped in, slip-sliding in his direction and catching Fiona's elbow, briefly, to steady her again.

'He's in the bar preparing himself for the next competition – working out the strategy for next week's match,' Virginia said. Her eyes were watery and her nose tinged red with constant blowing.

'With the aid of a little tipple as usual,' the third woman added, laughing, picking up the granite curling stone beside her as if it weighed no more than a bag of crisps.

'Which bar? The one in here, or do you mean Jock's Bar in the Hotel?'

'No, the one in here. You'll find him upstairs annoying Betty as usual. You'd think he had no home to go to.'

The atmosphere in the bar was lively, chatty, scented with sausage rolls and alcohol, and warmer in every sense than the rink. A middle-aged barmaid stood behind the bar, her chin propped up on her elbow, watching the players through the open expanse of glass overlooking the ice. One of the curlers, sliding on one knee, was just about to release a stone.

The second it began its leisurely journey towards the house at the opposite end, the barmaid murmured, 'On you go, on you go, you beauty!'

'Sweep, Enid, sweep!' another spectator shouted a few moments later, standing up in his frustration, convinced the woman's stone was going to stop short, unconsciously miming a frenzied sweeping action himself.

Spectators occupied many of the seats, their glasses on the tables in front of them and their attention divided between their drinking companions and the action going on below them on the ice. As the priest approached the bar, a ruddy-faced farmer who knew him said cheerily, 'I seen you sliding all over the shop. Can you no' walk on water then, Father?'

'No, he cannae,' his drinking partner butted in, 'but he can drive out demons, so you'd better watch yourself, Davie boy. Is that not right, Father?'

'Haven't had much practice lately – but I'd happily give it a go.'

'Wish he'd turn that water to wine . . .' Davie replied lugubriously, peering into the little water jug on the bar, an empty whisky glass beside it.

'That's Jesus. Father just does wine to blood, you numpty,' the man's wife said, shaking her head at the display of ignorance.

'Have you seen Colin Gifford about, Sue?' the priest asked her.

'Good to see you back here, Father.' she replied. 'He's over there, behind the newspaper.'

The man in question was slumped on a bar-stool, an empty pint glass in front of him, pen hovering above his crossword. Defeated by the clue, he had turned to the barmaid for help.

'Four down, Betty. Six blanks and four blanks, OK? "Party food for a donkey"?'

'Mmm . . . got any letters?' she asked, nodding at Vincent by way of acknowledgement and adding 'Father'.

'Father? That's an "F". Both words begin with "C".'

'I know, I know. Crème caramel . . . cream crackers . . . chipolatas . . .'

'Donkeys are vegetarians, woman, for Christ's sake!'

'Maybe not by choice, Colin?' the barmaid replied testily. 'This is party food, remember!'

'What about . . .' the priest said, coming and standing beside the man, 'carrot cake? Would that fit?'

'Mmm, it would,' Gifford replied, already writing it in, 'and it goes with "corncrake" and "arrow", so it's bound to be right. Well done – give that man a drink, Betty. Make it a double. No, a treble. What'll you have, Father?'

'I'll not have anything at the moment, thanks, but I wondered if I could ask you a question about your work? I saw Dougie yesterday, and he told me you'd be here. I just need to know something about the trial polish that the factory produced, the bright pink stuff?'

'Rightio, fire away, I'm with you there,' Gifford replied, slightly blearily, the pen back in his mouth and all his concentration ostensibly on the crossword once more.

'Did you get any of the stuff?'

'Aye, three jars, but I chucked them all out. I tried it on a wooden chair in the kitchen, but I couldn't stand the smell. Poofy, if you know what I mean. Tell me, does a dromedary have one hump or two?'

'One,' Vincent said.

'Right. That'll be "got the hump", then.'

'Babs'll get the hump if you don't get home for your tea, Colin.'

'I'm off, Betty. Tell the old camel that, if she phones,' the man replied, slipping off his stool and jamming his rolled-up newspaper into his jacket pocket.

'Before you go,' the priest asked, 'did anyone else get the stuff apart from you and Dougie?'

'No. We only made a wee batch. None of them liked it right from the start. The boss said we may as well give it a try but, like I said, I couldn't hack the smell.'

'Do you know if your boss gave it a try too?'

'He may well have done, aye. Jackie Shand doesn't do waste. He's a mean bastard. Counts a' the pennies. That's why he's the boss.'

The telephone in the bar rang. 'That'll be Babs now,' Betty said, 'she's like bloody clockwork that one.'

CHAPTER FIFTEEN

Running back to his car, his jacket tented over his head to protect himself from a shower of hail, the priest's mind was buzzing with Colin Gifford's words. He knew the manager, and had long pitied the man. Not because he had a marked squint and suffered from psoriasis, although he did. Not even because money was his real god, although it was, but because he was a cuckold, had been cuckolded many times. His wife, Jemima, a woman who perfumed the air of the confessional box with the stifling scent of Opium, availed herself of the sacrament only in certain circumstances. Usually when her latest affair had come to an end, but once when she had shocked herself with a one-night stand involving several Bacardi Breezers and a sales rep. The apparent sincerity of her contrition was, however, undermined by her habit of immediately seeking solace, a fresh distraction, in other arms. He had lost count of the number of times it had happened.

Putting on his safety belt, he speculated on the identity of her current lover. A Protestant, he hoped, as he jammed the clip into the socket. It seemed no time since she and a recently cast-off lover had met outside the confessional, eyeing each other like hostile dogs, both seeking absolution for their shenanigans together. Only he, in his privileged position as confessor, knew that; and neither of the pair witnessed his wry smile as they confessed all. As always, Barbara Duncan had been ahead of the pack, observing acidly that Jemima seemed to have a very fast turnover amongst her male acquaintances. With effort, he had managed to look suitably uninterested, conscious that every movement of his facial muscles was being watched. No doubt Jemima Shand's affairs would continue. Unfortunately, she was more likely to understand Einstein's theory of relativity than to appreciate the necessity for a firm purpose of amendment when making her confession. To her way of thinking, the sacrament was there to be used like a laundrette; only one that cleansed her conscience rather than her dirty clothes.

Maybe the current lover had received the polish from her? It was not so far-fetched. Jackie Shand was certainly not the sort of man to pick up a dustpan. If he had brought home samples of new lines, it would be his wife who would either use them in the house or dispose of them. Add to that the fact that the stuff had ended up in the possession of a man with a Geordie accent and a deep rumbling voice. How had that happened? The most straightforward answer would be because she had given it to him.

Now deeply absorbed in this train of thought, he took the wrong turning out of Green Road and, minutes later, found himself on the edge of Kinross, going past the AlphaVet's surgery and near the turn-off leading to the road around the loch. On impulse, he decided not to retrace his steps to go to the supermarket as he had originally planned, but rather to continue on to Scotlandwell and talk to Barbara Duncan. While he had been away from there, distracted and obsessed by his own troubles, she would not have lifted her ear from the ground. It was more likely that a swift would cease to fly. Listening was in her nature. If anyone knew the identity of Mrs Shand's latest lover, it would be her. Both women played bridge, sometimes in the same four, and, crucially, they shared the same hairdresser. Long ago, Barbara Duncan had explained to him, not disguising her amazement at his ignorance, how much could be learned from an intelligent, personable hairdresser. If Eva Braun had tiptoed out of the bunker for a sneaky perm, she had said, World War II would have been over months earlier. Warming to her theme, she had gone on to explain that while trainees dealt in little more than holiday destination chitchat, the stylists and colourers were in an entirely different category. They, like priests, routinely heard confessions. But, not being bound by the seal of the confessional gave them a significant advantage over their clerical competitors. They usually had ample opportunity to double-check their choice snippets of gossip, testing and refining them as they smiled, reassuringly, in the mirror. That process ensured quality information.

When Barbara Duncan came to the door she looked frazzled. A stray lock of white hair had fallen over her forehead and her face was flushed. She was wearing her late husband's blue and white striped pinny, its hem mid-shin on her. At her feet, was a brass coal scuttle, filled to the brim with coal.

'Vincent . . .' she exhaled, patting him on the shoulder, 'thank goodness it's only you. I thought it was Mr Goodenough, my next B&B person. He's coming up from

Lancashire and isn't supposed to be arriving for another hour, but I thought for one horrible moment that he'd arrived early. Come in, come in.'

'If it's not a good time, I could easily come back later?'

'It's always a good time to see you,' she said, picking up the scuttle and turning towards the kitchen. 'Come on, I'm dying for a sit-down and a cup of tea. Mamie said you were back.'

'I'll take that.'

'No, no. I'll pick it up on my way back,' she replied, dropping it to the floor again with a thud.

Humming to herself, she put the warmed silver teapot on to the table and sat down in front of it, waiting for the tea to infuse. Three minutes later, unable to resist inspecting it again, she opened the lid, only to drop it in fright when the doorbell rang.

'Bugger!' she whispered to herself, getting up, pushing the strand of hair off her forehead and inadvertently smudging herself with coal dust.

'Hang on, Barbara! You've got a black streak!' Vincent said, touching his own forehead to show her where the mark was. Glancing at her distorted reflection in the side of the teapot, she muttered 'Bugger' again and wiped the smut off with a hankie from her sleeve.

'Don't go away. Help yourself to everything, you know where it is. I want to hear all your news, Vincent, now that you're back – at last!'

Fifteen minutes later she returned and sat heavily down on a chair. Pouring herself a cup of tea she said wearily, 'It was him this time. I've left him upstairs in his room.

I'm going to suggest that he goes out tonight, either to the Green or the Grouse and Claret. He's only got one leg, you know. The other's artificial. I know, because his suitcase clanked against it – it sounded hollow. The leg, I mean. Perhaps he's a drug-smuggler?'

'Hoping to recruit you as his mule?'

'I'm nobody's mule, thank you. So, just tell me what's been happening, Vincent.'

In between mouthfuls of scone, the priest regaled her with stories about the Retreat, his battle with the Monsignor and the results of the enquiry. For her part, consuming a single finger of shortbread only, somehow managing to make it last a good twenty minutes, she said little but listened intently.

'I wonder what the Monsignor was playing at,' she said finally.

'How do you mean?'

'Dragging his feet like that, then suddenly treating it as so urgent?'

'Well, when pushed I can be quite forceful . . .'

'Quite, dear, quite.'

A head appeared round the kitchen door and a man with too many teeth in his mouth said, 'So sorry to interrupt, but I can't find the TV in the room.'

'There isn't one,' Barbara Duncan replied, 'but you're welcome to watch the set in the sitting-room until you go out.'

'Thank you so much. I'm desperate to catch the news – see if the poor old PM can extricate himself,' her guest said, waving a hand at them before disappearing.

'Perhaps I will offer him supper here. He's a widower, on his own. I've a loin of pork I could do. What would go with it, d'you think? You could become my wine consultant, unpaid, of course. Neville used to insist on Chianti but, frankly, I don't think he had much of a palate, nose or whatever.'

'Why do you say that?'

'After he retired he took up cookery. Not from recipe books, obviously, nothing so mundane. Every dish was created by him, including haddock in cranberry sauce and eggs Neville, like eggs Benedict except instead of spinach, he substituted cabbage, and sprinkled the whole lot with ginger.'

'Maybe no nose but a cast-iron stomach by the sound of things. I'd have the pork with one of the new Australian Viogniers, they're difficult to better . . .'

'Where on earth would I get those?'

'You could try my favourite shop on earth, the Markinch Wine Gallery. Now, there is something, Barbara, that I particularly wanted to ask you.' He came to an unexpected stop, catching her eye, and adding, 'It's a bit delicate.'

The woman grinned and said brightly to him: 'Snap!'

'How do you mean?'

'Me too. I need to ask you something . . . a bit delicate.'

'If it's about Sarah Houston,' he began, disappointed in her, 'I told you. There's nothing more to tell.'

'Goodness, no. There's nothing I don't know about her,' she said dismissively. 'What do you take me for? A rank amateur? Of course it's not about that odd, odd woman.'

'I hadn't realised she was so odd.'

'I know that, but, frankly, I'm amazed you were taken in by her. I saw it immediately. No, I'm interested in something else. I'm interested in Father Bell.'

'What do you want to know?' he enquired as evenly as he was able, pouring another cup of tea for himself and then for her. Her words had both stung and annoyed him, inferring he was naïve, overly susceptible to women.

'It'll be cold,' she said, wrinkling her nose as she lifted the teapot lid and looked inside. Then picking the pot up she went towards the sink, saying, 'Why don't I make us some more?'

'Don't worry,' the priest said, his cup to his lip, 'I like it as it is. Now, Father Bell?'

'We hear nothing – nothing whatsoever from on high, you'll appreciate. All everyone knows is that the presbytery's empty again. Is he coming back or is he off for good or what? Has he gone somewhere else? It's all very sudden.'

'He's away for good.'

'Has he gone somewhere else then, within the diocese?' she asked, emptying the contents of her cup into the sink. 'Posted elsewhere?'

'No,' the priest said 'he hasn't been shuttled about the diocese. He, like so many others, has decided to leave the priesthood. So he'll not be back here – or in any parish – as a priest.'

'Would the words "struck off" be appropriate in this context?'

'I don't know about that.'

She said nothing, looking at him quizzically.

'Really, I don't. What I am sure of is that he won't be anyone's priest ever again. It's in the diocese's hands. In this climate, if anybody's complained about anything, they're bound to have alerted . . . well, the appropriate authorities. They'd have to.'

'I see. Not as much as I'd like to, but I see. Will we get someone new?'

'I suppose so, but I've no idea who.'

'OK. Now what can I do for you?' she asked, curiosity lighting up her small grey eyes.

'Jemima Shand, as we both know, has close male friendships . . .'

'"Close male friendships?"'

'She seems to know men other than her husband – she seems to have men, other than her husband . . .'

'Oh, spit it out, Vincent, for Heaven's sake! On second thoughts, I'll do it, it'll be quicker. Really, at your age, why can't you just call a spade a spade? Jemima Shand has affairs – is that it? If so, it's hardly news.'

'Fine, thank you for that. Has she got a new one?'

'She certainly has one at the moment,' she replied, finding herself on the defensive purely out of habit, then remembering their agreed bargain she added, 'So what do you want to know about her?'

'Do you know anything about the present incumbent?'

'I do. Tinker, tailor, shopkeeper, policeman, farmer, rich man, poor man, bank manager, thief – I could go on. Take your pick.'

'Well?'

'You'd like to know?'

'Of course, I'd like to know. You know I'd like to know!'

'The latest one is a bit younger than her. That much is obvious. I've been told that he's some kind of specialist in antiques – and that's not a cruel dig about her, so save your breath. He "does", sorry, restores Regency furniture. The real stuff, apparently, not your usual jumble. What else? Imogen reckons he comes from Newcastle way, she said he's got a lovely, deep voice.'

'Do you know his name?'

'No – well, not his full name at least. He's got a nick-name of some sort, but I can't remember it. Henry's his Christian name.'

'Where's his shop?'

'In Milnathort, just along from Robertsons. He moved in, or rather set up shop there, when you were away. He's got a boy, or is it two? They were in Cove, Helensburgh, somewhere like that, somewhere over on the west. He's got shops all over, I gather.'

'Our house, I have to say, is much duller without you,' Sister Monica confided, leading him into the sitting-room where the rest of the community had already gathered. The TV was on but the sound was down.

'Bugger off, bugger off, bugger off!' Bertie squawked on seeing him enter, then shook himself violently and spat out a couple of sunflower seeds. A stray grey feather drifted to the bottom of his cage.

'And the same to you!' the priest said, taking a seat beside the bird.

'Off the park with him! Off the park with him!'

'That's not a very welcoming thing to say to Father,' Sister Claire said, approaching the cage, staring into the parrot's unblinking eyes and then relenting sufficiently to poke a quarter of peeled apple through the bars.

'And that's not a reward, mind,' she said, 'for your vile language!'

'Really, Claire! Apple is *not* good for him,' Sister Jane said sharply. 'They don't eat apples in the jungle.'

'He,' Sister Claire replied, rolling her eyes heavenwards, 'has never been near the jungle, dear. He was hatched in Plymouth or Tavistock, somewhere down there. That's what the brewery man told me. So you need have no fears on that front. Alopecia, maybe . . . psittacosis, possibly, but apple poisoning, no.'

Woken by the burst of animated chatter, Sister Agnes, slumped in the depths of her over-large chair, opened a single rheumy eye and fixed it on the newcomer.

'Have you done the milking yet?' she enquired of Vincent.

Seeing Sister Monica looking hard at him and nodding vigorously, he replied, 'I have, yes. My fingers are sore with it.'

But by the time he had reached the end of his sentence, the single eyelid had closed and the old lady appeared, once more, to be deeply asleep.

'It's better,' Sister Monica whispered, looking down fondly at the slumbering figure, 'to go along with it. Otherwise she gets worried, frets that . . . well, that she's not altogether with it. This way she doesn't worry.'

'I've been "Nanny" twice today,' Sister Jane piped up, dropping her knitting-needle accidentally on to the floor and stooping to recover it, 'though whether as a person or a goat I've no idea.'

'A goat, dear,' Sister Monica said sweetly.

'She's not eating properly,' Sister Frances murmured, going over towards Sister Agnes and covering her spindly legs with a tartan rug. Looking at her as she slept, she continued, 'She's disappearing before our very eyes.'

'*I am not!*' came a high-pitched rejoinder from the chair.

Startled, the nuns exchanged glances with each other, unsure whether to be pleased or not at this unexpected bout of lucidity.

'It just comes and goes,' Sister Monica murmured to Father Vincent, and the other women nodded. Nonetheless, they were rather chastened, each wondering what else untoward they might have said in this apparently not so oblivious presence.

'Are you *still* here?' Sister Agnes said wearily, looking up at the priest with her single, open eye.

'Stay for supper with us? Go on,' Sister Claire said, touching his elbow in an attempt to make up for the old lady's rudeness.

'No, I'm afraid not. But I've got presents for you all,' Father Vincent said, shaking a half-eaten sunflower seed off his sleeve. 'I've got a cherry tree for the garden. It's a double-white, so it should be covered in blossoms one day. It's in the car, I'll go and get it. And . . . I've a box set of DVDs for you too. Guess what they are?'

'I know, I know! Is it . . . is it . . .' Sister Frances

exclaimed, 'the lady in the knitted jersey? How wonderful, how clever you are, Father.'

'I think you'll like it. It's very popular – stylish, dramatic,' he replied.

'Oh, it's series three of *The Killing*, isn't it?' Sister Claire squeaked in delight.

As one, the nuns looked at him, smiling broadly, all of them thrilled at the prospect of hours of pleasurable viewing.

'But,' he said, sounding disappointed, 'I thought you all preferred . . . *Downton Abbey*!'

'Oh, how . . . terrific!' Sister Monica said, looking round at the dejected faces of the other nuns and willing them to smile. '*Downton Abbey*, that'll be terrific, won't it, everyone?'

'It certainly will, m'lady,' Sister Claire replied glumly, bowing her head and curtseying simultaneously.

'Relax. I know your bloodthirsty tastes,' he laughed, holding out the box set to them. 'It's *The Bridge*, as dark a Scandinavian thriller as anyone could want – including you, Brides of Franken . . . of Christ.'

Orwell Antiques looked out onto New Road, Milnathort, a broad thoroughfare running east to west with trees on either side of it, and untidily parked cars narrowing it and slowing the traffic to a sluggish crawl. Most of its business depended, certainly during the summer months, upon drivers stopping to buy Italian ice creams from Giacopazzi's bulging freezer, or plants or sacks of hen-food from Willie Robertson's Agricultural Store. Opposite it,

The Zen Zone attracted those in search of a bikini wax but these clients tended to be blind to the antique shop's charms. For them it was a repository of old-fashioned, second-hand junk with laughable price tickets attached to it. A blank sandwich-board stood outside the shop, waiting forlornly for someone to place a snappy advertisement on it or at least a boast about the treasures within.

The priest looked in the window, admiring a pedestal writing-table with tarnished brass handles which stood next to a pair of library steps. Peering into the dimly lit interior, it was obvious from the selection on display that the owner of the shop had a weakness for mahogany, marquetry and gilt finials.

He tried the door-handle but it did not turn. Seeing a bell with the name 'Blackwell' taped above it, he pressed it. After about thirty seconds, he heard movements inside, footsteps on stairs, and then the main light in the shop was turned on. A man appeared on the other side of the glass door. He was preoccupied and angry-looking and had a phone clamped to his ear. Engrossed in his conversation, he hardly looked at his potential customer as he opened the door. Turning round, he went back into his shop, apparently assuming that his visitor would follow him. Still ranting down the phone, he waved his arm as if to invite the newcomer to inspect his wares. Under the harsh strip light, Vincent recognised the man's dark features, and felt suddenly alarmed.

'You're to be in by eleven at the latest, Kyle, I'm telling you – otherwise you can sleep on the bloody street for all I care!' the man bellowed, in his anger oblivious to the fact that he had company.

'I say so. Got it? No, because I say so!'

Still shaking his head in fury, he put his phone back into his pocket and for the first time began to take in the presence of his visitor.

'Can I help you? Are you browsing, or was there anything you were particularly interested in?'

'You're Hal!' Father Vincent said, amazed. It was not just the face he recognised. In the last few minutes he had heard enough of the man's voice and accent to know where he had heard it before.

'I am indeed and, if I am not mistaken, you'll be . . .' The man played for time, scrutinising him and eying his dog-collar, half-covered by the collar of his jacket. '. . . that man I met with Elizabeth, in her house. The local priest?'

'Yes,' Father Vincent said, nodding, 'but you said almost nothing then. Remember, you had a cold?'

'Did I now?' the man answered, his tone and expression implying that this seemed a rather odd or trivial observation. 'Well, it's gone now. So, my friend, what are you after?'

'However,' the priest continued slowly, 'I know your voice. I recognise it. I heard it long before today – in the confessional. On the night that you attacked James, the Bishop.'

'Eh?'

'It was you. I know it was you.'

'Look, pal, I'm sorry, but I've no idea what you're going on about.'

'I'd know your voice anywhere.'

'I've really no idea what you're going on about.'

'Cut the crap. Don't waste my time,' Father Vincent snapped, suddenly enraged by the man and his absurd denials. All he could think about was Elizabeth. Her face had appeared, unbidden, in his mind, her innocent hazel eyes smiling, amused at something. The idea that this scum had, somehow, wormed his way into her heart made him feel physically sick. This man was not worthy to touch the hem of her dress.

At that moment another customer, an elegant blonde woman with a pashmina around her shoulders and a Chihuahua clasped to her breast, came in and began to inspect the stock.

'I don't know what you mean,' the man hissed, 'but come inside – away from the showroom. We can't talk here.'

He turned on his heel. Detaching a brass-handled poker from a fire-set as he passed it, Vincent followed him through his untidy, furniture-strewn workshop and into his living-room. It was chaotic. Piles of dirty dishes rested on a chintz-covered sofa, and newspapers and greasy plastic cartons littered the floor. A couple of golf clubs, propped against a grandfather clock, clattered to the ground as the man walked by. Muttering angrily to himself he pushed an ironing board out of his way, snatching off a sleeping-bag which was laid across the top of it.

'Welcome to my lovely home,' he said, tossing the sleeping-bag onto a nearby chair and facing his visitor. A black-and-white CCTV screen, showing the interior of the shop, was placed incongruously on a three-legged plant stand, and flanked on one side by an empty tomato-ketchup bottle. A large volume bound in green leather lay, unopened, on an embroidered footstool. A gluepot with a broken glue brush rested on top of it. The book looked like some kind of ledger, and had no title or author's name either on its cover or on its battered spine.

'So, what exactly do you want, Father?'

'You're the man that came into my confessional, half-drunk, and shouting about killing the Bishop.'

'I've no idea what you're talking about.'

'You know exactly what I'm talking about.'

'No!'

While the priest twirled the poker in his hands, another image of Elizabeth, this time with her head turning away from him, blushing, pleased to see Hal, came from nowhere and enraged him anew. Bastards like him depended on, traded on, innocents like her. 'Love' she'd called him.

'Don't give me that crap. In fact, don't say another word. I can smell the polish that Jemima Shand gave you, here and now. I smelled it in your workshop. I can smell it on you – just like I could on the night that you made your boast. That's what it was, really – more of a boast than a confession. I know exactly who you are, Hal or Henry or whatever you call yourself. I know what you've done too. I know all about Jemima Shand, I know about Elizabeth – you complete shit!'

'What the hell's any of this to do with you? You're a priest, aren't you?'

'Everything. Elizabeth's . . . Elizabeth is . . . one of my oldest friends.'

'Oh, I get it. You fancy her too, eh? So, are you going to tell her about me and Jemima?'

'What do you think?'

'It'll only hurt her. She won't like you for it, you know. Be grateful, or anything. And Jemima, are you going to tell her?'

'I hardly know the woman. No doubt she'll find out soon enough anyway. You'll mean nothing to her for sure. It'll be easy come, easy go, with someone like you. How did you get into the Bishop's office?'

'Have you spoken to the police?'

'How did you get in?'

'Don't tell Elizabeth, eh? About Jemima? She'd not understand, like I said. It'd only hurt her and she's . . . nice, too nice for her own good, really. I'll not see her again, if you like, but I don't want her to know. Promise me that, OK? Getting in was simple – Ray Meehan gave me the key. Before I moved here, he used to clean one of my other shops for me, the one I had in Dundee. He did it for years. I knew about his other jobs. By the way, are you planning to buy that poker?'

'No.'

'You might as well put it down, then. You're giving me the creeps.'

'Tough. Carry on, please.'

'Put it down, eh? Ray had a key and I knew he'd lend it to me. He was soft, you know, a bit soft in the head. A bit of a village idiot, really, although you're not allowed to call them that nowadays, are you? Not PC. Even if they are, and he certainly was. He didn't even ask why I'd wanted it.'

'And thanks to you, that "village idiot" killed himself – for handing over that key to you. That's all that he'd done, given it to you.'

'It wasn't my fault.'

'It was. Why did you want it?'

'That's my business.'

'No. Not any more. Now it's my business. Tell me why you wanted it. Do you think I'd let everyone go on believing that poor Raymond is guilty?'

'You can't tell anyone what I said to you in the confessional . . .'

'No, that's right. But we're not in the confessional now, are we? You've already told me how you got into the diocesan office. The police would be round in a flash to take a DNA sample from you if I told them nothing more than that. I doubt you cleaned up after yourself in the Bishop's office. They'd easily match the two samples, I reckon. In fact, I'd put money on it.'

'OK, OK. I wanted in, into the office, to get the record. The one that lists the priests who've been interfering with children.'

'How did you know about it?'

'Ray told me about it once, he'd seen it. I daresay they hardly thought he could read. They got careless.'

'But why did you want it? So you could punish them?'

'Eh? What on earth are you going on about?' the man asked, sounding appalled, looking for the first time

247

frightened, as if he had a lunatic standing opposite him. A lunatic armed with a poker.

'Dennis May was a priest, Callum Taylor was a priest. Patrick Yule was a priest. Each one's listed in that record, the book, and they're all dead. Dead within the last few months.'

'Hold on! I've no idea who any of them are. I've done nothing, I haven't hurt anybody except your bloody bishop, and that was an accident. Really it was. He came in when I was searching for the file – for the book – and when I tried to leave he tried to stop me. I shoved him out of the way, no more than that, and he fell over and hit his head. I thought I'd killed him, but it was just a dunt. He's fine, no harm done. I haven't hurt anybody. I don't know what you're going on about.'

'Really? Have you forgotten Raymond so soon? What did you want the file for, then? Why were you trying to steal it in the first place?'

'Because,' Hal said, his tone becoming defiant and angry, 'I needed it. Father Bell touched up my son, Kyle. A paedophile priest, need I say more? Kyle's only sixteen, always in trouble. He . . . after my wife left, I couldn't control him. I still can't. He changed then. He puts anything he can find up his nose, down his throat – into his veins, for all I know. I discovered that Kyle, with a friend, I think, had beaten up the pervert, so-called "Father" Bell. I'd no idea that Bell had abused him. I found out at the same time I heard about Kyle attacking him. I knew that if Bell reported it, it would be Kyle's word against his, and they really, really did the pervert over. A friend who works at the hospital told me how serious it was. I needed to be able to back up what my boy had told me.'

'In this day and age?'

'Have you met Kyle? If you had you wouldn't be asking that question. Who'd believe a wee, unemployed, drunken yob like him? He'd probably giggle, be abusive to the police. They know him, know his baby face. Bell would deny everything, be able to cover up everything. I couldn't leave that to chance. There was no proof. I knew the Church would have a record of those kind of things. Ray told me as much. I thought if I had it I could shut the man up, or stop him going to the police, or at worst prove that what Kyle had said was true. If he had a past record . . .'

'So why haven't you handed the book to the police?'

'Because Bell never went to them about Kyle. Jemima told me that he'd said to everyone he'd been involved in a car crash – the lying shite. So, no one's come after Kyle, and Bell's been punished. Anyway, I didn't dare go to the police after what had happened in the Bishop's office. I thought, for a while, that I'd killed the man, remember? Raymond . . . well, that wasn't my fault. I'm surprised he managed to work out his part in the whole thing. It's a pity, him topping himself and everything, but . . . it's happened. Anyway, the book will have my fingerprints all over it. My DNA probably, and so would the wrapping paper, the stamps, if I'd posted it. They haven't found me so far, and I'm not doing anything to help them further. Why should I? They're not looking anyway. Raymond's dead, the Bishop's all right and Bell never reported anything.'

'So, just you and Kyle have looked at the book?'

'How do you mean?'

'Just the pair of you?'

A telephone began to ring in another room and Hal exclaimed, 'I'll be back in a minute – but I've just got to answer this. I have to. I'm selling a Regency commode to someone in New York. It's worth a fortune. I'll have to answer that.'

Alone in the room, the priest went over to the foot-stool, removed the glue-pot and inspected the green leather-bound book. On the first page he read, 'Diocese of Inchkeld'.

Without a qualm, or even a thought, he put it under his arm and headed for the showroom. As he left Orwell Antiques, he glanced at the blonde woman and gave her a friendly smile. Hal, low-life that he was, was not the killer of the priests. Kyle had had his chance. Finally, the book could speak for itself.

CHAPTER SIXTEEN

The woman with the pashmina gravitated, Hal noticed, back to the carved mahogany washstand several times. Each time she felt the wood with the tips of her fingers, trailing them lovingly along its highly polished surface. On the third occasion, she picked up its price-label. As she did so he watched her, surreptitiously scanning her face to see her reaction to the inflated price-tag. Her expression gave nothing away. Her curiosity apparently satisfied, she wandered over to a glass case with a dusty stuffed capercailzie in it and then threw a casual glance at a reproduction breakfast table. Hal didn't take his eyes off her.

'How much for the stand?' she asked him, bending over, her back turned as if she was interested in the knife case on top of the table.

'Fifteen hundred, as the label says,' he replied, coming towards her, 'but it's a lovely piece, isn't it? A real gem. It's late eighteenth-century English.'

'It's such a shame there's no basin, no ewer with it,' she replied, turning and eyeing him with a slightly disappointed air. 'You don't have them somewhere else, do you, through the back or whatever? Without them I'm just not sure . . . not for that kind of money.'

'No,' he said, 'they'll have been broken long ago. But you don't see many of the stands about nowadays, do you? You used to be able to pick them up all over the place, particularly at the big country house sales, but not nowadays. A lot have been shipped off to America.'

Clutching the Chihuahua more tightly, she looked at him and suddenly flashed a broad, artificial smile, her carmine lips in an unnaturally wide arc.

'Well, Choo Choo and I like it. And it's her birthday. What'll you take for it?'

'Oh, on Choo Choo's birthday? In that case, twelve-fifty with my good wishes and many happy returns. How old is she?'

'How old are you, baby?' the woman asked, looking into her pet's bulbous black eyes and pouting at it. 'She's thirteen, she says. In doggy years that's thirteen, but in human years more like ninety-one. An old, old ladykins. This . . .' she added, looking first at the little dog and then at the shopkeeper, 'could well be her last birthday. So, surely, an extra-special present would be in order?'

'Fine. Twelve hundred, but that's my last offer. I have to say Choo Choo has impeccable taste. She's homed in on the jewel in my collection.'

.'Yes,' the woman agreed, kissing the tiny dog's head, 'she has a nose for quality, doesn't she? You see that oak commode over there – the one with the japanned decoration?'

A tall young man wandered through the door marked 'Private' at the back of the shop, a bacon roll in one hand and a mug of tea in the other. His long auburn hair had been scraped back into an untidy ponytail, emphasising his perfect cheekbones and heavy-lidded eyes. The crotch of his low-slung black trousers reached mid-thigh level, and he moved his hips like a dancer, avoiding the pieces of furniture effortlessly, never spilling his tea. As he came closer to the pair, the Chihuahua opened her eyes wide, curled her freckled lips to reveal a set of minute dagger-like teeth and growled. By way of reply, the youth widened his own large eyes and bared his perfect teeth, terrifying the dog so that she released a volley of high-pitched yaps.

'Choo Choo!' said the woman, giving the animal a sharp tap across its muzzle, 'manners! This isn't your shop.'

'Or yours,' Hal said, looking hard at the smirking boy.

'Dad,' the young man said, 'I need to speak to you.'

'In a minute, Rick, in a minute,' the man replied, stroking the pet's dome-shaped head with his forefinger in an attempt to pacify it. 'I'm busy with a customer.'

'I don't really like commodes – other people's . . . it's just the thought, isn't it?' The woman wrinkled her nose. 'But that wee card table near the window. I'd give you five hundred for that . . .'

'The label,' Hal said, beginning to get annoyed at her assumption, true though it was, that he would haggle over everything, 'says a thousand.'

'Label says "no", then?' she replied, putting on a glum face like a clown's, and sweeping her pashmina back over her shoulder as if readying herself to leave.

'No, label says a thousand, and I say eight hundred. Since it's Choo Choo's birthday.'

'Mmm. Eight hundred. Do you know, it's my birthday too?'

'Ninety-one-year-old twins are you, then?' Hal remarked drily.

'No, we are not. Seven-fifty, that's my last offer.'

'Done.'

After the woman's credit card had been lightened and she had departed with a spring in her step, Hal finally turned his attention to his son. 'God bless Choo Choo. Long may she live . . . to shop,' he said, writing 'Sold' on the two labels with a marker pen.

'Where's the book?' Rick asked, lowering himself on to the embroidered seat of a bow-legged armchair, mug still in his hand.

'Don't sit on that!' his father shouted.

'OK, OK! Take it easy!' Rick said, leaping up as if stung and splashing tea across his shirt.

'It's got woodworm, Rick. I've treated it, but with your weight it'll come crashing to the ground. That's why I'm describing it as "an ornamental chair".'

'Junk would be nearer the mark. Right. I'm needing to go now. So, where's that book gone?'

'What book?'

'The big green one – the one that was in the living-room, the one you said you picked up in a job lot in Edinburgh.'

'I don't know. In the living-room, I expect. That's where it was.'

'It's not there,' Rick said crossly, swallowing the last of his roll and putting his mug down on a sideboard.

'Don't do that, it's wet. Pick it up. It'll leave a ring. The book must be there. I haven't touched it. What about Kyle, have you checked with him?'

'No, he's not in. He wouldn't touch it anyway, he

doesn't know what a book's for. You must have shifted it, Dad. Think.'

'Me, dust anything? Christ, Rick, I don't need to think. I haven't touched the bloody book, OK? If it's not there someone else must have shifted it.'

'Who would have? You threw that cow Ellen out, remember?'

'I don't *know* who and I haven't got time for this. It'll be there, OK?'

'Who else has been in there recently?'

'Nobody! What do you want with it anyway? It's not yours. Now, push off, I've got work to do.' Hal suddenly put his hands to his head. 'Christ! I know who was in there.'

'Who?'

'That bloody priest – that crazy, sodding priest from Kinross. I don't believe it, the wee bastard's taken my book!'

Sitting in his armchair, a chilled glass of Sancerre in his hand, Father Vincent opened the book on his knee. There, in Stevenson's unsightly scrawl, was the first entry. It had been added to and amended in different coloured inks.

ADAM, ALLAN.
Address – 13 Old Deane Way, Scone
1973 – Scone. Star of the Sea.
Complaint dated 13th May 1972 – Father Adam was intoxicated while celebrating Mass. Father Adam denied the allegation. He explained that he was suffering from flu.
14th July – Stopped by the police, breathalysed and charged with drunken driving.

16th July – Admitted to Monsignor Rose that he had a drink problem. Seen by J. Devlin, Psychiatrist. Report discloses that Father Adam is lonely and depressed and is self-medicating with drink. Six sessions arranged, to be paid for by the Diocese.

1st February 1973 – Father Adam injured in a fall while in his own home. Broken femur. Admitted to Monsignor Rose that he's back on the drink and fell downstairs while intoxicated.

Action: Agreed to attend Alcoholics Anonymous and Bishop informed. Moved to fill vacancy at St Mary and St Joseph's, Blairgowrie.

11th September 1974 – Deceased.

Immediately, he turned to the entries for 'M' and found:

MAY, DENNIS.

Address – 'Broxbank', South Street, Perth

1975 – Perth, Curate, at St Francis of Assisi. Complaint by Mrs Susan Dando that her daughter, Anne (age 11) had been encouraged to sit on Father May's knee at a youth group picnic. Father May said any apparent sexual contact was purely accidental. Mrs Dando was reassured by Monsignor Giuliani.

1983 – Complaint by parents of two girls (both aged 11 years) to Bishop McSweeney that in the changing cubicles of the swimming pool, while 'helping them dress', Father May involved in inappropriate touching. Youth Group Outing. Investigated by Monsignor Donnelly, a former Chancellor, and both lots of parents found to be credible. Father Ranaghan, Parish Priest of nearby St John Bosco, accepted the allegation and observed that it confirmed his suspicions of his colleague. Bishop concluded that a Crimen Pessimum committed.

Action – Father May to retire from the Parish but not for six months in order to protect his reputation. Thereafter, he is to go to Granada Institute for assessment. The assessment concluded: 'Diagnosis is mild paedophiliac urges, but Father May was very responsive to counselling . . . unlikely to reoffend. He should still be able to serve as valuable priest.'

1987

Address – "Wood End", High Street, Alyth

Alyth – Mater Admirabilis

A complaint made by parent that after early morning Mass Father May touched 10-year-old serving girl inappropriately. Complaint investigated by Monsignor Carron. Parents found credible and Bishop apologised to them.

Action: Father May granted leave of absence due to his growing spiritual and vocational crisis. He has indicated that he may apply for laicisation.

It was evident that he had not done so. The entries relating to him continued for another two pages, covering a spell in Rome, teaching at the Scotch College, and then ministering to a further four towns within the diocese. In the margin, opposite his current address, was an 'X' in red biro and the figure £1,000 written in pencil. Father Vincent turned over several blank pages, searching for the entry for Callum Taylor, his nose aware of a strange, dry peppery smell. The notes on him were much shorter.

TAYLOR, CALLUM.

1962 – Bridge of Earn – Curate at the Blessed St John Ogilvie School.

Address – 5 Sorrel Bank, Bridge of Earn.

Complaint made by parents of sixth form boy (18) that Father Taylor had 'corrupted' him and turned him into a homosexual. Father Taylor admitted a 'relationship' with the boy. Ordered to go on compassionate leave. Grounds given as 'mother sick'. Petition for laicisation sent to Rome in October 1963. Granted 1964.

Address – The Cottage, Forge Street, Bo'ness.

Opposite that entry there was another 'X' in red biro and 'Try £500?' written in pencil. After a Yarrow and a Youngson he came across the entry for Patrick Yule.

1963 – Dunning – Stella Maris – Curate.

Address – The Auld Byre, Dunning, Perthshire

April 1964: two separate complaints by mothers that Father Yule had been taking photographs of their sons and others when naked in the showers after a football match. Separate occasions. Investigated by Father Hennessey. Father Yule denied the allegation and said he was taking pictures of the showers to show a plumber as new showers were needed and he wanted advice on what types would be suitable. Each of the parents unaware of the other's complaint.

Action: Reassurance to parents and warning to Father Yule to call plumber in personally.

1968 – Gateside – St Joseph's.

Complaint of inappropriate 'washing' of twelve-year-old boy in showers after football match. Mother complained. Monsignor McDonald investigated. Father Yule denies the allegation and his denial was accepted. Parent counselled.

Action: Canonical Precept put in place prohibiting Father Yule from having any contact with children on his own. Moved to replace Father McBride as chaplain at Our Lady's Hospital.

1969 – Chaplain at Our Lady of Fatima's Hospital, Perth.

Address: 10 Learside Street, Perth

1st August 1970: Bishop informed by security officer at a photographic company that some of the transparencies of a colour film sent for developing showed the private parts of young boys. Father Yule admitted and explained that the photographs caused no physical disturbance in himself and that the photos are 'art studies'. Fr Yule advised to depart on sick leave. Referred for psychological counselling to the Servants of the Paraclete.

Conclusion: Offence out of character and resulted from naivety about the ways of the world. Not an objective or subjective crime within the meaning of Canon Law.

1972 – Address – Convent of the Blessed Wound, Forgandenny

Chaplain at Convent of the Blessed Wound, Forgandenny.

Complaint of touching genitals of servitor. Complaint investigated by Monsignor Barratt.

Father Vincent read on, appalled, flicking through the further catalogue of crimes and excuses contained in the next two pages. In Ireland the man had been moved on several times as he had in New Mexico. By 1975 the police had, finally, become involved and he had been imprisoned for five years. Thereafter, a formal process of compulsory laicisation had been instituted, but the decision of the tribunal, that Yule be dismissed from the clerical state, had been overturned on appeal to the Roman Rota Tribunal. It had substituted for the dismissal only a seven-year period of suspension. Opposite the man's final address in the village of Cleish was, once more, a red 'X' and an entry stating '£3,000+'.

Sickened by what he was reading, Vincent closed the book with a bang, picked up his telephone and dialled.

'Hello?'

'Is that Detective Chief Inspector Keegan?'

'It is. Who am I speaking to, please?'

'Father Vincent Ross.'

'Vincent, good to hear from you. Are you all right? You sound different. Have you any news?'

'Yes, and I'm sorry to disturb you because I know it's late. But you are the only . . . the obvious person to call. I need to speak to you. That missing property, the stolen property, which you and I talked about, it's come to light,. It's come into my hands, and I think it should be in yours, Donald. For lots and lots of reasons.'

'Where are you now?'

'At home in Kinross, in the presbytery.'

'Fine. Perfect. Have you told Dominic yet?'

'I want to get rid of it, get shot of it. Shall I bring it to you?'

'No, no. Just stay where you are, Vincent, OK? It'll take me twenty minutes at most. I'm getting in my car now, but put it somewhere safe for the moment, eh? I'll be round as quick as I can.'

He did as the policeman told him, and then poured himself another large glass of white wine and sat in his armchair, with Satan purring on his lap. He felt numb. Touching the book, turning its pages had made him feel dirty, soiled, as if he had touched sewage and would never again be clean. It was a chronicle of evil. Judging by the book, everywhere, all the time and all around him, close by, this evil had been going on and, somehow, he had failed to see it. In Ireland, in America, yes, but elsewhere in Scotland, even here, right here in Inchkeld? Once, a few years ago, he'd heard a rumour about someone he knew, someone that he had been on retreat with in Edinburgh, but he had chosen to ignore it, had given the man the benefit of the doubt. After all, he knew the man, and he was a priest like him. And he had continued as the chaplain at a school. So there could have been no foundation, no truth in the rumours. If there had been, he would have been got rid of, removed from the Church by the Church. He would have been reported to the police. That was what happened nowadays. Well, so in his naïvety, he had thought. But he had been blind.

Because the book told a completely different story. In it was recorded, revealed, the true concerns, the continuing concerns, of the Church. His church. What had been done had been done by them, first and foremost, to prevent scandal and, secondly, to protect their own. The concerns of the victims were incidental, were accorded minimal importance. The names of most of them had not even been thought worth writing down. In all the entries he had seen, the 'Action' had not once included reporting the allegations to the police, counselling the children or compensating them. And the book was not simply a historical document recording sins committed in the distant, dusty past. The last entry he had seen had been for a year ago. Connor Bell and his like could still keep their secrets. The book might be thin on recording previous convictions, but it bulged with previous complaints. It was crammed with a series of narratives establishing patterns of behaviour over many years. Armed with its contents a complainant might not be a lone voice calling in the wilderness. Hal, whatever he might think of him, had been right in that respect. Kyle's story more than likely would have been believed, if it had been supported by the rest of the complaints recorded against Father Connor Bell.

The town clock chimed eleven and he took another sip of wine, keen to dull the turmoil of his emotions. How could they have done it? The Church, his church, had protected its own rather than the innocent, the children. And right here in Inchkeld. It had no heart, and there could be no excuse. The whole host of Heaven must have wept, be weeping still.

When the doorbell rang he went to answer it eagerly, keen to rid himself of the repulsive volume, to hand it over to the police, to his ally. But he did not immediately recognise the man who confronted him on his doorstep.

'Hello,' he said, taken aback.

Without a word, the pony-tailed stranger pushed past him and walked right through into his sitting-room. Father Vincent followed, alarmed by the forced intrusion into his territory. As he stood and watched, the young man paced about the room, pulled a drawer out of his desk, briefly inspected his bookcase and then yanked a couple of leather-bound volumes out of it, letting them crash on to the floor.

'What on earth d'you think you're doing?' Father Vincent said angrily, coming over to the stranger and, as he appeared to be about to continue to ransack the room, grabbing hold of his arm to restrain him.

'Where's the book?' the young man asked, seizing Vincent's wrist and banging his hand hard on the bookcase, making him yell in pain. Getting no other answer he glared at Father Vincent and then, not shifting his gaze, he aimed a kick at the television. The screen shattered into hundreds of pieces of glass, flying into the air, hitting a nearby table and showering the carpet.

'Where's the holy book?' the man shouted, staring the priest in the eye. Getting no response, in a single, swift movement, he swept all the papers off the nearby desk. A second later, he picked up a china table lamp and threw it against the wall, smashing it to pieces and gouging a hole in the plasterwork.

'The book?' he repeated.

'The police are on their way here . . .'

'Sure they are.'

'Who are you?' Father Vincent asked, knowing already, trying desperately to make him pause, distract him, delay him. His heart was throwing itself against his ribcage, his breath hard to come by. The door was closed, shards of jagged glass were within easy reach, and in front of him, his pale face contorted with anger, was a killer. Trying not to make it obvious, Vincent scanned the room with his eyes, frantically searching for a suitable weapon with which to defend himself. If this man did not get what he had come for, perhaps even if he did, he would turn on him. Murder him, as he had others. His best hope seemed to be the half-empty bottle of wine that was on the floor by his armchair. Unconsciously cradling his damaged hand against his chest, he began to edge towards the bottle, but the flow of adrenaline in his bloodstream was hampering him. Everything was too bright, too fast, too colourful, too loud, confusing him so that he couldn't think straight. As he made a lunge for the bottle, a sickening blow hit the side of his head. At the weight and the shock of it he fell forwards on top of a low stool and landed heavily on the floor. Something warm and wet began to pour down his forehead and into his right eye, pooling in the eye itself, blinding him.

'Get me the fucking book!'

Dazed, and before he could say anything, he felt another blow from the man's heel. This time it struck his nose, causing instantaneous agony and a gush of blood which spouted and streamed down the back of his throat and made him gag. Gasping for breath, trying to concentrate, he saw the man pick up the bottle that he had been trying to reach. Utterly defenceless, he looked up into his face, hoping to find some trace of humanity, believing, despite the blows he had already received, that he would, and that the assault would stop. Surely nobody, no human being, could kill another while looking into their eyes. Some meeting of souls would take place. Breathing in loudly, uncertain any more where he was, he gazed into the man's deep brown eyes, searching desperately to make the bond that he believed must save him. But only a cold, pitiless stare met his. Glorying in his absolute power, the man slowly raised his weapon.

In the distance, in another world, a shadow seemed to be travelling across the room. A large figure, as solid as a house, suddenly loomed up behind the attacker, grabbed his raised arm and yanked it behind his back, wrenching upwards until he yelped in pain. A swift kick to the back of his knee collapsed his long legs and he crumpled to the floor. In a moment, Donald Keegan was on top of him, astride his back, pulling both his arms behind his back and handcuffing him. The youth squealed, making a high-pitched, breathless noise, sounding more like a wounded animal than a human being.

'I can make my own stew,' Father Vincent said queru-lously, sinking back on his pillow and watching as Sister Monica, with difficulty, picked up the newspaper that he had inadvertently kicked off his bed onto the floor.

'You couldn't before – what's changed now?' she said briskly, gathering up the sheets, scrunching them into a ball and stuffing them into the waste-paper bin. Tutting to herself, she picked up an empty wine glass from the bedside table and tapped it.

'A head injury means no drink, you were told that.'

'You wouldn't know about my stew. You've never had it.'

'No,' she conceded, looking at him, 'but Sister Frances has. She says your talents lie elsewhere. Now, no more drink.'

'I don't know where, then . . .' he said, feeling cantankerous and unwilling to please anyone. He was determined to regain control of his life, and more importantly his home, as soon as possible. Pampering, which he had regarded as bliss in the first few days after the assault, had soon became tiresome.

'I'm sure I don't either,' she said. 'No doubt you keep them well hidden. Now, would you like peas or cabbage with your stew?'

As if she was a waitress, she licked an imaginary pencil and held it poised above an imaginary pad.

'Cabbage, please. When's he due?'

'And for dessert, sir?'

'What's on the sweet trolley today?'

'Mmm. Much the same as yesterday. Ice cream.'

'And? Or?'

'And or ice cream.'

'Are you trying to kill my palate? When's he due?'

'Any time now,' she said, looking at her watch. 'Are you sure you want to see him – couldn't it wait?'

Before he had opened his mouth to answer, they both heard the doorbell ring, and by way of reply he simply nodded his head. At the sound, Satan, who had been snoozing near the foot of the bed, leapt off it and slunk below into the dark cave made by the trailing bed cover.

'I'll be off then,' she said, 'to get your order, sir.'

Donald Keegan clumped up the stairs, hauling himself up the last few steps with the banisters, puffing loudly like a steam engine. As he came into the bedroom he looked round, saw only a chair laden with clothes and, shaking

266

his head, still breathing deeply, came and sat on the end of the bed.

'I gather you're on the mend,' he said jovially, loosening his tie and looking at the priest expectantly.

'I am. I'm allowed to get up tomorrow. Sister Monica's finally given me permission.'

'Women, eh! Give them half the chance and they'll take over your life!'

'It's all thanks to you that they've a life to take over, Donald.'

'Aye, he was a nasty piece of work, that one.'

'Mamie told me that he's Kyle's older brother. A junkie too. Apparently, he went off the rails when his mother walked out on them. She's a Catholic, couldn't take any more of Hal's womanising. He couldn't cope with the boys, gave up long ago. Let them run wild.'

'Mamie's mighty well informed,' the policeman said, taking out a handkerchief and wiping his glistening brow with it.

'Better than the BBC.'

'Incidentally, I hope that no one from the force's been bothering you yet? Since the assault, I mean? You'll have needed rest.'

'No. Sister Monica's been standing guard over me. No one's been allowed in or out. So you're the first.'

'No one would get past her, literally. I'm glad you've been allowed a little time to recover. That doesn't always happen, you know. Have you any idea why the lad picked on you?'

'Didn't he tell you?'

'Yes, but I want to know he said to you.'

'He wanted to get the book back. Looking at the entries in it, I think he'd been using it for blackmail – blackmailing the priests listed in it.'

'What exactly was in the book?'

'It was a record of crimes, misdemeanours . . . horrors. Child abuse, alcoholism, dishonesty – all committed by priests employed, or once employed, within the diocese. What began as blackmail for Rick turned into something else, I reckon. Maybe some of them refused to pay or threatened to go to the police. Maybe he'd bled them dry and demanded more when there was no more. Maybe he just hated them. I looked at Connor Bell's entry and Kyle wasn't his first. Maybe Rick suffered too. They'd moved from Helensburgh and so had he.'

'Father Bell! Christ almighty, I had no idea that he was involved. And you think he abused the pair of them?'

'I don't know. It's only a guess on my part. All I know for certain is that he abused Kyle, and that he was in the book. But not for abusing Kyle.'

'Of course,' Keegan said, shifting his position on the bed and dabbing at the sweat under his eyes. 'The good news is that we don't need the book for the purposes of the murder inquiry. So at least you needn't worry yourself about that.'

'Worry myself?'

'Well, they've already got their man, haven't they? He'll not be harming anyone else, thank heavens. They'll have his DNA, witnesses too, quite possibly. He may even have confessed by now. And you can tell them about the existence of the book, a little about its contents even, if necessary . . .'

'How do you mean?'

'You know, the entries for Dennis May, Callum Taylor and so on. You saw them, didn't you? If Rick doesn't plead guilty, if there's a trial, you could say that you saw their entries about child abuse and so on, so you don't need to worry.'

'Sorry, Donald, worry about what?'

'About the loss of the book.'

'But I've still got the book.'

'You've still got it?'

'That's what I said.'

'I thought it had disappeared,' Keegan said, moving up the bed to get closer to the priest.

'No, it's here.'

'Well, I never! Thank goodness for that. After you'd been taken away in the ambulance I couldn't find it anywhere. I searched this place high and low, ransacked the whole house. Where on earth did you hide it?'

'Like you said, somewhere "safe". I put it somewhere safe.'

'I can't tell you what a relief that is,' the policeman said, beaming widely and standing up as if he was ready to go.

'I'd better take it with me now. Where is it? That strapping nun'll get it for me, no doubt.'

'It's somewhere safe.'

'Good. Can I have it now?'

'No.'

'Sorry, Vincent, what did you say?'

'I said,' the priest replied, looking up into the man's red face and speaking more slowly, 'no. You can't have it.'

'But . . . but I need it for the investigation. If you've still got it, I need it. There's a murder inquiry under way. Three men have been killed, three priests, and that book will be very important evidence against the murderer. It'll form part of the evidence in the trial '

'I know that, but you're not involved in the murder investigation, are you?'

'No, no, I'm not. It's purely a Lothian and Borders police investigation now, because the Colinton killing was the first. They're heading it, taking the lead. But I'll take it to them. That's why I came – I'm to take it to them.'

'Do you think I'm a complete fool, Donald?' the priest asked, elbowing himself up on his pillows in order to increase his height slightly.

'No. I know you're not. I learned that early on.'

'I'm glad to hear it. It took me a while, lying here . . . but everything, eventually, fitted together. All the little pieces of the jigsaw added up to make a complete picture, but not a very pretty one, sadly.'

'And?'

'And I realised, long ago, that the Church didn't want the book to be found, least of all by the police. Having seen its contents, I'm not surprised. If the press were to get hold of it, well, it would be a complete sensation, wouldn't it? It would blow everything wide open again. The embers of the scandal would be re-ignited yet again, only this time, tenfold, a hundredfold, and in the heart of Scotland. Dominic seemed relieved when he realised it was you that I'd been talking to, and I know why now.'

'He would be. It's natural. We know each other. Mostly socially, and through some sports schemes, youth schemes, we're both involved in.'

'But to me, Donald, you denied knowing him at first. Then, on the night of the attack, you called him "Dominic", even though I hadn't mentioned his first name. You're on first-name terms, nickname terms, with the man. Why hide it? That started me thinking. More importantly, James Mann's your brother-in-law, isn't he? I was slow, shamefully slow, in figuring that out . . . but when I remembered what your wife said it led me there. About Miss Mann, the tax inspector. What I don't know is whether you're trying to protect him because of your wife or because of yourself. I imagine it's him at the bottom of all of this. I know she's got you by "the short and curlies", as you almost put it, and I know why. I spoke to a pal of mine in Kinnesswood; she told me the nature of your woman trouble. I understand she's called Jemima. So, maybe you've been doing these things for your wife . . . or yourself, I'll probably never know.'

'You've quite lost me.'

'You lost yourself. You're part of the cover-up.'

'I'm trying to protect the Church.'

'Don't make me laugh.'

'Vincent, think what will happen if that book ever gets into the wrong hands. I told you, it's not even necessary to convict the killer. It could just disappear – there could be a fire, a theft, a flood, God knows. But if it's gone, it's gone. Think of the *damage* it will do. I saved you from that maniac. He would have killed you too – he had three under his belt already, remember? I saved you. Now, I'm just trying to save my . . . everything. She said she'd leave me . . . I've got children, too.'

'Damage? Don't talk to me about damage! The damage, the real damage, has already been done – and to children. Other people's children. I'm going to hand the book over to the Lothian and Borders Police, after I've made a copy of it, and once it is in their hands they will do what they must with it – act on the information that it contains. If, mysteriously, nothing happens, I'll go to the press myself.'

'Vincent,' Keegan said pleadingly, 'James wants it back – he really wants it. A great deal hangs on the safe recovery of that book. Rome is adamant that it must not get into the wrong hands. Things could change for you, radically, dramatically; things could get so much better. Gratitude can be shown in a million different ways. Like I said, it's not even necessary for the man's conviction, if that's what's worrying you. The deeds have been done. You can't undo them, any more than I can. What happened, happened. But it's in the past. Just give it to me – you could even say you'd done that, tell everyone that. I'll lose it. You wouldn't even have to explain. All you'd know, all you'd be responsible for, would be for handing it over to me. You wouldn't be criticised, not for handing it over to the police.'

'Go now, just go!'

'Vincent, Dominic will ensure . . .'

'Get out of here.'

'If you'd told me,' Sister Monica said, bringing in his supper tray, 'that your "little printing job" amounted to a hundred and fifty pages, I would have declined it. Thanks to you we've run out of paper – ink too, and it costs a fortune. We should never have bought a Dell.'

'But you've done it?' he replied, taking the tray from her and looking anxiously into her face.

'Yes, of course I have. And I feel two hundred years older now,' she said quietly. 'I read the odd pages of it while I was doing it. It sickened me. It made me feel so ashamed . . .'

'You've done nothing of which to be ashamed,' Vincent said.

'But didn't you feel that? Reading it? How could they do that?'

'You had no part in it, I had no part in it, and we will have no part in it. We will make sure that the truth gets out.'

'Do you ever wonder why you stay . . . ?'

'Yes, often. It's not easy. I can't get excited about the knuckle-bones of saints any more, or any of that kind of thing. And I'm out of step too. Birth control, gay rights and women priests – bring them on, I say. I don't think the sky will fall in when they finally come. The only reason, the *only* reason, I stay is because I'm needed. I know I am. And for as long as I'm inside, still hanging on, I'll do my bit. What about you?'

'I don't fancy being a bag lady.'

'Fine. Now, tomorrow, if you'll let me, I intend to take the book to the police headquarters at Fettes and hand it over myself.'

'I'll drive you there, happily. What will we do with the copy?'

'We'll keep it secure, in my safe under the stairs. Just in case through any mischance of any kind something happens to the original. You've still got the copy on disc, I assume?'

'Yes.'

'It's even more important. Can you keep it somewhere safe, where no one will ever find it, in the Retreat? No one would ever expect it to be there.'

'No problem. I'll toss out that *Sound of Music* DVD – no-one ever watches it. Not with all that "A flibberty-gibbet, a will-of-the-wisp, a clown", nonsense.'

'Nonsense, is it? Remember, you removed the Nazis' carburettor. Nuns played their part in defeating the forces of evil . . . apparently.'

'Apparently.'

'Now, my wine glass? There seems to be no wine glass on my tray. What's that supposed to be?' he asked, pointing at a striped mug by his bowl of ice cream.

'Tea – remember tea? A drink with jam and bread? Doh? My dear. You can fetch your own poison.'

Satan, satisfied that the coast was clear, sprang back onto the bed and padded towards his master, his back arched in greeting and his tail held high.

'Shoo! Be off with you,' Sister Monica said, flapping her

huge hands at the creature. 'That beast should not be on the bed.'

'Talking of Nazis . . .'

A couple of days later, Father Vincent was sitting having tea with Barbara Duncan in her kitchen. By the butter-dish was a vase of roses, some of their heads blowsy, their loosening petals edged with brown; others were no more than dark-red buds, the blooms still tightly furled. Self-conscious about his appearance, he fingered first the bruise on his forehead and then the sticking plaster that covered one side of his nose.

'Another DIY mistake with a hammer, you say.'

'Yes.'

'I see.' Her sceptical tone left him in no doubt that she did not.

'Where did those come from?' he asked, keen to distract her and gesturing at the vase.

'That's the least of it. He's a pest, a complete pest. He "refreshes" them daily,' she replied curtly, stabbing the fruit-cake in front of her with the bread knife and starting to cut a slice from it.

'Who?'

'Mr Goodenough.'

'Is he not then?'

'Not what?' she said, through pursed lips, intent on the cake.

'Good enough?'

'Don't be flippant, please. It's serious. He's trying to bat-ter me with blooms – court me with carnations, woo me with weigelas, seduce me with salvias. Such horrid flowers too, the lot of them. Now he's riling me with roses – if he but knew it.'

'When did this happen?' he asked, putting out his plate for the slice of cake she was offering him.

'Hard to say, really. I gave him dinner myself that first night he came to stay, and I think he got quite the wrong idea. I thought he seemed all right then. He's in dog food, so to speak. Actually, he could bore for Britain about canine nutrition, dentition . . . perdition for me, of course. His hobby, I discovered, if you can believe it, is plotting all the radio masts in the country, and he's trying to persuade me to go out on "reccies" with him. He's just odd, very, very odd.'

'Frankly,' he said, parroting her words about Sarah Houston back to her, 'I'm amazed you were taken in by him. I saw it immediately.'

'You never even spoke to him!'

'I didn't need to . . .'

'Vincent,' she replied, giggling out loud, 'I am so glad that you are back. Now, tell me what happened to your face, and don't give me any of that nonsense about a hammer, eh?'